TRACER

BOOKS BY BRENDAN DENEEN

NOVELS

The Ninth Circle

The Chrysalis

Morbius: Blood Ties

Guardians of the Galaxy: Annihilation—Conquest

Alien: Uncivil War

Tracer

GRAPHIC NOVELS

Scatterbrain

Flash Gordon: The Mercy Wars

Flash Gordon: Invasion of the Red Sword

Flash Gordon: The Vengeance of Ming

The Island of Misfit Toys

Green Arrow: Stranded

PICTURE BOOKS

Night Night, Groot

First Day of Groot!

Snow Day for Groot!

Summer Adventure for Groot!

PRAISE FOR *TRACER*

"In a city where plastic is the new gold, *Tracer* blends gritty postapocalyptic action with heart-pounding romance as one woman's lethal skills are tested against the darkest secrets of humanity's desperate new civilization."

—NICHOLAS SANSBURY SMITH,

New York Times bestselling author of *Hell Divers*

"Brendan Deneen's *Tracer*...sends you on a frenetic, action-packed ride through a trash-filled, dystopic wasteland with a badass femme fatale at the wheel. Hold on!"

—A. G. RODRIGUEZ, author of *Space Brooms!*

"*Tracer* is an action-packed adventure that asks us to imagine rising from the trash to create a better world. Full of memorable characters and a tension-fueled plot of deceit and danger, this is a story worth reading for any fan of near-future dystopias."

—CHRIS KLUWE, author, activist, and former NFL player

"The lifeblood of the world of Deneen's *Tracer* is recycled waste, but this story is anything but a regurgitation. Smart characters, top-notch world-building, and ferocious action scenes combine to take us on a wild ride through a thrilling, noir-tinged, rubbish-strewn future."

—DAVID MOODY, author of *Hater* and *Autumn*

TRACER

BRENDAN DENEEN

BLACK
STONE
PUBLISHING

Published in 2025 by Blackstone Publishing
Cover and book design by Sarah Riedlinger

Printed in the United States of America
Originally published in hardcover by Blackstone Publishing in 2025

First paperback edition: 2025
ISBN 979-8-212-63821-0
Fiction / Science Fiction / Apocalyptic & Post-Apocalyptic

Version 1

Blackstone Publishing
31 Mistletoe Rd.
Ashland, OR 97520

www.BlackstonePublishing.com

This novel is dedicated to all teachers everywhere.

But in particular—

To Angela Morganthaler, my fourth-grade teacher, for being an early supporter of my imagination. As she told us, she had cold hands and a warm heart—and truer words were never spoken.

To Bruce Murphree, my senior year AP English teacher, who was as close to a real-life John Keating as I've ever met, and who lit the literary fire inside me.

And to the teacher's aide who worked in my fifth-grade classroom. When I made a continuing story out of the weekly vocabulary words (instead of just writing random sentences), you told me I was a good writer and encouraged me to keep going. I desperately wish I could remember your name. But whoever you are, wherever you are, *thank you.*

You better make sure you're looking closely
Before you fall into your swoon.

—"There's No Secrets This Year,"
Silversun Pickups

PART 1

PH CITY

1

Tracer wiped the blood from the corner of her mouth and watched as her opponent tensed to throw another punch.

She'd been told by President Bell that this job would be an easy one: pay a little visit to Jonny Nix, a strung-out junkie hiding in a tiny apartment down in the ground-level slums—just outside of PH City, situated between the massive building and the garbage heaps that ringed it.

Nix was in debt to the president. It was Trace's mission to track the punk down, have a little talk with him, and then extract the proverbial pound of flesh if the drug addict couldn't—or wouldn't—pay. But Trace hadn't been warned about Jonny's jacked-up younger brother, who now circled Trace, gloating, having landed a fairly impressive right cross to Tracer's jaw. Her SIG Pro, the same gun she'd been using for a decade, lay nearby on the floor.

Easy, my ass.

Ignoring the pain, Trace crouched slightly and then shot out her own fist, catching Jonny's brother under the chin with a perfectly placed uppercut—just like she'd been trained to do—causing spit and at least one tooth to go flying. He took a step back, then shook off the punch and beckoned for Trace to try again, grinning like some sadistic clown. He hadn't said a single word since he'd come charging out of the shadows a minute earlier.

"Kick the *shit* out of her, Jevon!" Jonny screamed from the corner, cracking his knuckles and giggling with drug-enhanced excitement.

The brother—*Jevon* apparently—took a swing, but Trace dodged it easily, stepping back to watch his movements. Her uppercut had rattled him. He was slow now, his already dim eyes looking even more deadened. President Bell had spent a lot of credits over the years hiring PH City's most dangerous men and women to train her, and Trace had learned that sometimes it was better just to watch before pressing an attack. It wasn't as flashy, but it was how you won. Just like Mackie had taught her.

Jevon telegraphed his next punch, a sloppy haymaker, but watching his movements paid off and she sidestepped this attack, too, and then lashed out, catching Jevon in the ribs with devastating violence. She heard something crack inside his body and Jevon sucked in what sounded like a very painful breath. All the fight went out of his face—all the color, too. He looked into Trace's eyes, surprised, and then collapsed without a word to the grimy wooden floor.

Internal bleeding, Trace guessed. She'd been there. Not fun.

In the corner, Jonny stopped giggling and stared at his brother with dull, bloodshot eyes, his chin trembling now. He slid down the wall and landed unceremoniously on his ass.

Trace took a step to the left and retrieved her gun from the ground and then quickly surveyed the sparse apartment. A bed. A small table and two chairs. A tiny kitchen area with what looked like weeks of dirty dishes piled up. There was nothing here worth anything, nothing that could be bartered for credits. She shook her head and grimaced, trying to ignore the dull ache in her jaw.

When the president had tasked her with this job, she'd practically laughed. Another routine track-and-collect gig? Didn't Bell have anything better for her XN—her executive enforcer?

But Trace wasn't amused anymore.

She walked over to Jonny, slowly crouched down, smiled, and placed the SIG Pro against one of his knees.

The junkie whimpered and held up his hands in one last desperate attempt to save his own skin.

"*Please . . .*"

"Give me what you owe the president or I'm going to start blowing pieces off you, one by one . . . starting with your kneecaps." She spoke calmly as Jevon moaned on the floor behind her, underscoring the threat.

A tear spilled down Jonny's face. "Please . . ." he repeated. "Look around . . . I got nothing. I swear."

Trace cocked the gun.

"That's too bad."

"Wait, wait! Un-under the bed. There's a suitcase. It's all I got."

Trace's smile widened. She stood up, put the SIG Pro into the holster on her belt, and made her way across the room, kicking Jevon in his broken rib—or ribs—for good measure on the way. She knelt and peered under the bed.

Sure enough, there was a crappy old cloth suitcase under there, sporting a faded red-and-blue plaid design. She pulled it out cautiously, trying to ignore the throbbing pain in her nose and cheek. As she stared at it, wondering absently if the Nix brothers were sophisticated enough to booby-trap the case, she sensed movement—turning in time to see Jonny lunge forward with a knife. Trace brought her arm up, fast, but not fast enough. The blade was old, but it was still sharp enough to shred her trench coat and slice into her right arm. Trace bit back a scream at the intense pain and grabbed Jonny by the throat with one hand, the junkie's wrist with the other. She squeezed with both hands, causing Jonny to choke and the knife to fall to the floor. She brought her face close to his.

"*Bad. Move.*"

She headbutted the man, breaking his nose, and then let go. Jonny crumpled to the ground next to his brother.

Trace stared at them for a second, vaguely intrigued by the weird symmetry, and then turned her attention back to the suitcase. She squatted, unlatched and opened it slowly, and then sat back on her heels and let out an impressed breath. Jackpot.

Inside, there were some ancient stained containers—President Bell said they were used to hold "fast" food, which sounded disgusting, whatever it was—dozens of plastic spoons and forks, a ball of wadded-up plastic bags covered in what looked like dry mud, some crushed two-liter bottles with the tiniest hints of long-gone labels, and an old pink computer, probably some kid's toy from back before the Flu. Back in the days when people used actual computers.

It was a solid haul. Maybe it wouldn't pay off Jonny's debt completely, but it was still probably worth a few hundred credits, once Trace went through the bullshit negotiating ritual with PH City's pyro-techs.

She shut the suitcase, latched it, then wrapped her fingers around the thin metal handle and stood up. Both of the Nix brothers were writhing in pain on the ground, moaning, odd mirror images of each other. Trace wondered how many years apart they were and if their parents were still alive. If they ever even knew their parents.

She closed her eyes for a few seconds, thought about how she'd been born and abandoned in the garbage heaps twenty-seven years earlier, thought about the couple who had raised her. A flash of sadness threatened to encroach, but then she remembered her training and shoved that feeling away.

No empathy.

Trace opened her eyes and spat blood onto the dirty floor.

"Nice doing business with you, boys," she said, and then walked out into the night.

2

NINETEEN YEARS EARLIER

I made my way through the piles of garbage that rose above me on either side, following a path that most people would never be able to see.

I knew my parents were going to be upset.

It was past my curfew, and everyone knew Puente Hills got exponentially more dangerous after the sun fell behind the mountains of refuse—but I figured when they saw what I had in my pack, they would forgive me. Maybe even celebrate a little bit.

I moved the strap from one shoulder to another, fighting a smile as I moved quickly along the faint, jagged line beneath me. I was able to traverse that path with my eyes closed—literally—and few people were ever out this late, so I laughed silently through my nose at all the things I knew my parents were going to say when I got back to the makeshift house they'd built at the base of a particularly solid hill of garbage.

"You could have been robbed," my dad would say.

"You could have been killed," my mom would add.

I laughed out loud at that point, imagining their high-pitched voices when they got upset. They weren't my real parents, but I knew they loved me like they were, appreciated how good I was at finding plastic. Like the impressive, heavy load I was carrying.

I'd gotten wind of the cache while eavesdropping on some older kids. They didn't like me, constantly warned me away, found my eagerness annoying, but they were slow and sloppy and dumb—and it was a simple matter to follow them and listen in on everything they said, whenever I wanted. Usually, it was a pointless exercise, with the teenagers swapping gossip about the other Dwellers or fighting over scraps of plastic.

I suddenly stopped moving when I heard something behind me, then crouched down in the darkness and blended in with my surroundings. I always wore dark clothing, purposefully kept my face dirty, and my pack was black as well. I knew it was almost impossible to see me after dusk when I made myself small like this. Even before this, I'd watched as expert garbage trackers walked right past me, completely oblivious to my presence even though they were only inches from where I was hidden. I had trained myself to shift into the nearest pile of garbage as silently as possible.

But then a voice rang out, a voice I recognized.

"There's the rat! Hoping we don't see her. But a cornered rat is always easy to find."

It was Jasper. The de facto leader of the older kids—a nasty stain of a human, someone who delighted in torturing smaller kids and animals alike. When he could get his hands on them. But I'd always managed to steer clear of his dirty, grasping fingers. Had prided myself on it. I thought I was too smart, too fast. And as I stood up straight, knowing there was no way he and his smaller cronies could catch me once I took off, I allowed a smile to cross my face, hoping he would be able to see it in the haze of the growing evening.

"Why don't you come a little closer and see how hard this rat

bites, Jasper?" I called out, knowing my threat was idle. He was twice my size and could practically snap me in half if he managed to catch up to me. Which is why I assured myself that would never happen.

"You stole that plastic from us!" he screamed, ignoring my comment. I could see him literally shaking with rage. But I didn't feel guilty—it had never been his in the first place, and I knew that the unwritten law of Puente Hills was that the person who delivered the plastic to the brokers in PH City was the one who kept the credits. What happened up until that moment was irrelevant.

"Believe what you need to," I responded, turning and tensing to run. I was excited to get home and settle down. These idiots had no idea where I lived, and I aimed to keep it that way. "But this plastic is mine."

I started to move when a foot suddenly shot out from the shadows and caused me to tumble violently to the ground. I lost my grip on the sack, which fell forward as well and broke open. The numerous pieces of plastic, worth as much as a full week's normal haul, spilled out across the faint path.

I cursed under my breath and quickly got to my feet, ready to run again. I figured I might be able to grab a piece or two, but my larger plans had been thwarted. I'd gotten cocky, hadn't expected one of Jasper's friends to be hiding ahead of me.

As I began moving forward again, strong arms wrapped around my body and threw me back down to the ground. By the time I regained my bearings and looked up, I saw Jasper already standing above me, his crew circling around, cutting me off from any hope of escape.

For a moment, I thought about begging—but as soon as I saw his face, twisted in sick excitement, I knew it would be pointless. I just hoped that I could make it out of this situation alive.

"You're about to wish you were never born," he growled.

"I hear that's what your parents say about you," I retorted, forcing another smile onto my face, knowing I should have just kept my mouth shut. But his shocked reaction was worth it.

At least until the fists and boots started raining down, and I lost consciousness.

I stumbled through my front door hours later.

I had no idea how long I'd been out but had slowly awakened in the exact same spot where I'd been beaten down, now with a bloodied nose and mouth and, most likely, two black eyes. It wasn't the first time I'd taken a beating, but it was most certainly the worst.

My parents came running to greet me, their faces driving home how bad I must have looked. I tried to smile, hoping to make light of it, but immediately burst into tears. They ushered me over to my tiny bed.

"What happened?" my mother asked, looking me over. "We were so worried."

"I'm okay," I responded, forcing myself to stop crying, wiping away the tears with the back of my hand. The skin there was quickly darkened with dirt and blood.

"We thought you were out getting plastic, and then you just . . . you just never came home," my father added, confusion wrinkling his face.

"I was. And I got the biggest haul you've ever seen," I said quickly, hoping they wouldn't be upset. "But then the bigger kids jumped me. And stole all of it. I'm sorry. I'm so sorry." The tears were starting to fall again, and this time I couldn't stop them. I thought I saw disappointment on my parents' faces, but as quickly as I'd seen it, it was gone. I decided I'd imagined it as my mother

started unlacing my boots and my father helped me lie back down onto the straw-filled pillow.

"It's okay," he said, flashing me a closed-lipped smile. "You'll have better luck next time."

"Exactly," my mother said, looking up and making eye contact with her husband for a moment, then glancing back at me. "We're just glad you're still alive, that you came home. You're more important to us than plastic or credits or anything else in the world."

And I believed them.

The way a child believes in fairy tales, until they don't.

3

Abandoned by her mother within minutes of being born, Trace had been raised in Puente Hills, the human-made mountains surrounding the single-structure city—but even so, the stench of the ground level still got to her.

It had been a long time since she'd actually lived here, down amid the refuse, and she sure as hell didn't miss it.

Still, Trace sometimes wondered what had happened to the couple who had found her as a newborn and saved her from starving to death, then raised her as one of their own—at least until they had traded her to President Bell years later. Were they still out here somewhere? Did they know she was the president's top mercenary now?

Questions that she knew would never be answered.

As she walked past the mounds of garbage that made up Puente Hills, stretching out into the darkness on her right, she took a moment to stop and look up. She couldn't remember the last time she had seen PH City from below.

Above her, the giant structure rose into the night sky, its thousands of pale electric lights flickering. Even from down here, she could hear the generators roaring.

On the top two floors, President Bell was enjoying all the finest things that life had to offer, while the majority of her citizens toiled and suffered in poverty and obscurity on the lower levels of the city or out here in the hundreds of acres of refuse. You had to get at least five levels up to avoid the stench completely, and that's exactly where the pyro-techs worked and lived. High up enough that they didn't have to live in the filth they processed but not so high up that the elite had to see them.

Trace was probably the only person in all of PH City or the Hills who had been on almost every single level of the city and who had lived out among the Garbage Dwellers—the poor souls slopping around in piles of filth day after day, hoping to find enough scraps of plastic to sell to one of the half-dozen licensed brokers who handled the deals between the Dwellers and the techs.

Or sometimes they just melted the plastic down to huff it. Like the Nix brothers.

As Trace made her way toward the executive elevator, the few people who were out and about at this time of night gave her a wide berth. She was wearing the kind of black trench coat that marked her as one of the elite, even if she really wasn't, and the blood spattered across her pale face must have made her appear like some kind of vengeful wraith. Her dark hair had come loose from its usual ponytail during the fight, and the cut on her arm was still bleeding, though slowly. She knew she looked like shit, but at least no one would hit her up for any spare plastic.

She finally reached the elevator and entered her access code into the security pad. While she waited for it to descend from the upper levels, she looked out across the mountains of garbage. Puente Hills was almost beautiful in the dark—the decades' worth of refuse that had been dumped here, outside of what used to be Los Angeles, and had developed into a city of its own. Or, as Bell put it, had been *forged* into a city. One of the last six cities that remained on Earth—or *seven* if you believed those rumors about a floating garbage city called the Patch.

The elevator dinged and the doors opened, the rusted metal whining. She stepped on board, pressed a bloody finger against the glowing number five, and took a deep breath as she waited for the doors to close again.

Time to negotiate with the pyro-techs. Always an adventure.

"Jeez, I'd hate to see the other guy."

Trace stared at the bearded, bespectacled face of Brisby Frost but didn't crack a smile. Frost was the tech who annoyed Trace the least and was thus her go-to guy whenever possible—but she wasn't in the mood to joke tonight. Her jaw was feeling better, but her lacerated arm was still throbbing.

"The other *guys*. Plural."

"Well. Excuse me. *Guys*. I forgot what a badass you are," Frost said, raising an eyebrow. Trace just stared at him, unamused. "Okay, okay, I can see that you're in a bit of pain. Whaddaya got for me?"

Trace handed over the suitcase, and Frost unceremoniously dropped it onto a nearby table. Around them, other techs were making similar transactions despite the late hour, and behind them all, the giant pyrolysis machines chugged and belched, turning plastic back into oil, the lifeblood of Puente Hills and its five or six sister cities scattered around the world.

Metal chimneys arced out of the machines and fed the smoke into the air outside, internal fans forcing it as far away from the upper levels as possible.

Frost unlatched the suitcase and poked through its contents. "Hmmm . . . not bad. This computer is nice and dense, should have multiple parts that we can melt down. The other stuff is unremarkable but certainly worth a decent amount. I can give you . . . three hundred credits."

"Brizz, we both know this is worth at least five."

Frost stared at Bell's XN for a moment, seemingly weighing his options and perhaps also the statistical probabilities that the grim-faced woman in front of him would get violent.

"There isn't much here, Trace. I mean, I do like this computer . . . *I* might even buy it. My daughter would probably love it—but a handful of plastic bags . . . a few bottles . . . ? Four."

"Five. This is for the president."

"You know I can't let politics influence the amount I give, Trace. This is all regulated by the Guild, and I have to answer to—"

"Brizz."

"Okay. Four fifty. That's my final offer."

"Done."

Frost jotted something down onto a pad and then ripped off the top two sheets, giving the carbon copy to Trace, whose arm was really starting to hurt now.

"Okay, thanks. You're good to go," Brisby said, smiling. "Hey, have you thought any more about coming over for dinner one of these nights? I mean, no pressure, but Jenna keeps telling me to ask you and I think—"

Without letting Frost finish, Trace turned and headed toward the elevators. She needed some painkillers and a stiff drink.

Not necessarily in that order.

4

Trace settled onto the barstool.

The gauze she had haphazardly taped to her arm was itchy, and her jaw was starting to hurt again, but Bell's personal physician wouldn't be available until the morning. Might as well take her painkillers in whatever form she could find them in the meantime. Technically, this bar—*hell, any bar*, she mused—was illegal in PH City. The president didn't drink, and therefore no one else was allowed to either. But there were a few places that were hidden enough to find a drop or two of alcohol, and where Bell wouldn't come looking. This one was on the eleventh level and was Trace's favorite by far, even though it was small and dank. Maybe *because* it was small and dank.

Old Joe, the confusingly young bartender, walked over while cleaning a shot glass and gave Trace a long look, his eyes lingering on the slash in the right arm of her trench coat.

"Don't ask," Trace mumbled.

He nodded and filled the glass he was holding with shine. Trace knocked it down, then tapped the bar for another. Joe obliged.

"Quiet tonight," Trace said, downing the second shot and

glancing around. There was a young couple sitting at a shadowy table in the far corner, staring at each other and whispering. Otherwise, the place was empty. She looked back up at Joe. He wasn't exactly handsome, but he wasn't ugly either. And he knew when to talk and when to listen and when to leave her alone, which was a much more precious commodity than good looks. The scar above and below his left eye was kind of cool though. She had never asked about its origin, however, and he had never volunteered any info either.

"Well, it *is* three o'clock in the morning, Trace," Joe said, pouring another shot, even though it hadn't been requested. Trace considered the comment and the alcohol for a second, and then grunted and drank. "So, seriously, what happened to your arm? And don't think I haven't noticed that bruise on your jaw. This is the third time you've come in here over the past couple of weeks all beat up and bloody."

"Ah, you know, the usual. Bell sends me out to track something down. The person I find doesn't appreciate me showing up. Chaos ensues."

Trace realized that this was the first time she had ever mentioned Bell by name to Joe. Sure, they both knew who Trace worked for, but it wasn't something she had ever explicitly mentioned. After all, not everyone was a fan of the president.

Hell, I must be tired.

"Sounds fun," Joe said, pouring himself a shot and downing it. "Hey, I've been meaning to ask you . . ."

Shit. Trace had just opened a door and she knew it. She sighed and closed her eyes.

"Is it true what they say about Bell?"

"I'm not sure. What do they say, Joe?" she mumbled, then opened her eyes again and leveled her gaze on him. He didn't exactly take the hint.

"That she was a mobster before she ran PH City? That she used to be a hired killer? That she had her own husband taken out when she found out he was two-timing her? Come on, Trace, you know the rumors I'm talking about."

Tracer watched him as he downed another shot. There was a long moment of silence as she considered his questions, and then Trace let out a long breath, felt her entire body relax. She couldn't blame his curiosity. No one in PH City knew much about the enigmatic president, other than her propensity for violence and retribution. Trace knew more than most—hell, maybe more than anyone—but that was because she knew how to keep her mouth shut when in her boss's presence, how to almost literally blend into the wall.

"She was never a mobster, never a hired killer," Trace said quietly, leaning in a bit. Joe was the closest thing she had to a friend in this city, with maybe Brisby Frost a contender as well. Regardless, she wasn't close to either man, not even vaguely, had always shielded her truest self from everyone she'd ever met since being sold by her parents to President Bell. Maybe she was simply getting more comfortable around the bartender, or maybe it was the booze. She continued talking despite the small voice in the back of her head warning her to stop. "She was part of one of the original groups that decided to build this city. It started as a collective . . . everyone having a vote about how it would all happen, about each step. But she didn't agree with the way things were heading, you know? According to her, it was turning into some kind of bullshit bureaucracy, nothing was getting done. So, she took matters into her own hands. Got rid of the rest of the committee. One by one. Including her husband."

"Wow," was all the young bartender said after a long moment of silence. Trace berated herself. Why was she talking so much?

"And how did you end up working for her?" he asked, clearly comfortable enough to ask the kinds of questions he had never dared utter up until now. By way of an answer, Trace just stared at him, unblinking. "I . . . I'm sorry, Trace. That's none of my business."

"It's fine, Joe," she said, and forced a smile, her mind swimming slightly from the alcohol.

As Joe walked away from her for a moment, the nice moment having turned suddenly awkward, Trace realized that maybe she didn't understand what the word *friend* meant exactly.

Whatever. Mackie hadn't trained her how to interact with people, knew she came off as stilted and rude. And honestly she didn't really give a shit.

"So," Joe said, returning with a new bottle of shine, clearly trying to lighten the mood. "Do you think you'll—" But a ringing sound suddenly erupted from behind the bar, and he looked down, surprise creasing his face. "That's . . . *weird*," he murmured, reaching down and grabbing the phone receiver, the tangled cord hugging his arm. "Hello?" Skeptical. Cautious. Two things Trace respected.

She watched as Joe's face went pale. The person on the other side of the line said a few words, but Trace couldn't quite make them out. Then she heard a click. Joe held the receiver to his ear for several long moments after the call had already gone dead.

"What's the matter?" Trace said, even though, in her gut, she already knew the answer to the question.

"That . . ." Joe croaked, hanging the phone back up. "That was President Bell. She said she wants you in her office. *Now.*"

Trace stared at the shot glass, the alcohol in her stomach suddenly turning sour.

"How does she know about my bar, Trace?"

She looked up into Old Joe's face and saw, for the first time, really, how young he actually was. Probably even younger than Trace. Joe's nickname seemed more ridiculous than ever.

"I don't know. But you should probably shut down for a few days. I'll try to get some information out of her. I'll let you know when it's clear to come up for air." Trace stood and put her hand on her holstered SIG Pro, a gesture that calmed her whenever she felt anxiety creeping up her throat. "What do I owe you for the shots?"

"Shit. Okay, yeah, you're probably right. I'll just . . . close for a few weeks. And . . . no, no, of course not, don't worry about it. After what you did for me last month, the drinks are on the house."

"Joe, I can't live off that debt forever."

He smiled weakly and threw a dirty rag over his shoulder. "Maybe not forever, Trace," he said. "But certainly for a long time."

5

Bell's XO, her executive officer, an annoyingly tall, thin, and manicured sycophant named Gunnar, who wore almost exactly the same trench coat, ushered Trace into their boss's large office and signaled for her to stay quiet as the president finished reading a letter.

Gunnar had been purchased by Bell as an orphan, just like Trace—making them step-siblings of a sort—but the president had never treated her XO quite the same way she treated her XN. Trace had always wondered why that was, but it wasn't the kind of question she would ever actually ask.

There had always been a delicate thread of pending violence between Trace and Gunnar, but nothing had ever erupted between them other than sly insults and exchanged looks loaded with savagery. She knew in her gut that eventually they would go toe-to-toe and find out who was the more formidable fighter. But it hadn't happened. Yet.

It was shockingly bright inside the president's office, even though outside it was almost pitch black. In the distance, the buildings that had once upon a time made up downtown Los Angeles were completely dark except for a handful of campfires inside some of the top floors. Probably where the people whom Bell had banished from Puente Hills for any number of "crimes" had taken up residence.

"This is fucking *hilarious*," the president said and slammed the letter onto her desk. As usual, the desk was cluttered with an assortment of papers and random knickknacks that Bell had acquired during her tenure, including a small silver pistol she always kept close by.

The president finally noticed Tracer and smiled. Trace tried to smile back but couldn't quite pull it off. She'd never been called into Bell's office in the middle of the night like this. It was unsettling. At best.

Bell stood, ran a hand through her short hair and straightened her business suit, and then walked to a nearby window, one in a series that ran from the floor to the ceiling. This was the highest point in all of PH City, the fiftieth floor. On clear days, you could even see the outskirts of their territory from here—where dozens of guards patrolled the fence that surrounded the nearly seven hundred acres of landfill that made up Puente Hills. "Trace, come in. I just got the most amazing telegram. I mean, *amazing*."

There was a long pause. Trace could hear Gunnar breathing right behind her and had to fight an urge to turn around and break his nose.

Bell suddenly turned around and approached her XN, grabbing her gently by the shoulders. Trace ignored the pain radiating from her right arm as a result of her adoptive mother and boss's gesture and watched with satisfaction as Gunnar shifted uncomfortably in her peripheral vision.

"Let me look at you," Bell said, contemplating Trace's bloodstained and bruised face. "Ouch. I guess the Nix brothers gave you some trouble, eh?"

"You could say that," Trace muttered. She was suddenly

conscious of the alcohol on her breath. But if the president noticed, she made no indication of it.

"Gunnar," Bell said, sitting down on a nearby couch, "get Trace some ice and go get Dr. Webb. The poor girl's face looks like raw meat!"

"Yes, ma'am," the XO replied, his toothy smile barely containing his contempt. He exited silently, the door gliding shut behind him.

The president glanced at the love seat next to the couch, and Trace took the hint, sat down. Bell stared at Trace for a minute. Her face was impossible to read.

"I'm sorry to call you in at this time of night. Morning. Whatever. Especially right after you took care of that Nix situation for me." She licked her lips, raised her eyebrows. Trace took this hint, too. She reached into her coat pocket and withdrew the carbon copy, handing it over to her boss. Bell looked at it, then crumpled it up and threw it into a darkened corner. "Not as much as I'd hoped . . . but more than I expected. Thank you for that."

"There's no need to thank me, ma'am. Just doing my job."

Bell's face suddenly went serious. "It's more than just a job, Trace. We both know that. You're like a daughter to me." *Like*, Trace noted but didn't say anything, despite a sudden, annoying swell of emotion. Mackie had taught her *never* to reveal her emotions when on the job, even to Bell. *Especially* to Bell. She thought back to the techniques he had taught her, and the feeling subsided.

Instead, she nodded, still unable to read the president's mood, and the moment of silence stretched on until Bell smiled, inscrutable, and stood up. She headed back to her desk and picked up the piece of paper she'd been reading. Trace stood, too, not comfortable being lower than any given person in a room, even if there wasn't a threat. Yet another lesson that had been drilled into her by Mackie during the training that had lasted her entire childhood.

"I just got a message from Frank Stewart, who runs Apex City. I've mentioned him before, right? Doesn't call himself President—I think he makes them call him Chancellor—which seems ridiculous to me, but okay, fine. To each their own, right?" Trace didn't answer. She knew a rhetorical question when she heard it. Bell held up the telegram. "Seems like Ol' Frankie Boy has a bit of a problem and he needs my help. He needs *our* help."

"Whatever you need me to do, I'll do it," Trace said, and she meant it. She was tired, yes, she was in pain, and the pain was getting worse, but she was a good soldier and she owed her life to Bell. A fact the president had been reminding her about since the day they met.

"I know you will, Trace. I know." Bell looked up and smiled, then turned her attention back to the telegram. She stared at it for a long moment, a strange smile crossing her face. Trace had never seen a look quite like that before, and her training kicked in yet again. She had been taught how to predict possible outcomes based on things as simple as smiles. Something serious was about to go down.

Gunnar reappeared with a plastic bag filled with ice, and Dr. Webb, a pale, mousy man in a lab coat and holding a medical kit, trailed behind. Gunnar stared into Trace's face as he held the bag of ice out, his envy and hatred on full display while Bell's attention was diverted.

"Here you go, *Tracer*," Gunnar whispered.

Trace snatched the ice faster than the XO expected and let her grasp linger, crushing the man's fingers within her own for the shortest moment. Gunnar was tall and dangerous as hell with a gun, but he wasn't as strong as Trace. Dr. Webb averted his gaze. Gunnar's eyes bugged out of his balding head, and he pulled his hand back more quickly than Trace expected, his jaw working left and right.

"Everything okay, kids?" President Bell said, looking up. Gunnar's face shifted immediately, contorting into the role of obedient son and employee. Trace stared at the XO as he nodded at Bell and exited. The president sat back down on the couch while Trace held the bag to her face and sat down, too. She couldn't stand Gunnar but damn if the ice he had given her didn't feel good.

Dr. Webb placed his kit on a nearby table and opened it, removing several instruments. Trace sighed, put the ice down, and slowly removed her trench coat, the blood sticking and pulling painfully. She *hated* on-the-fly surgery.

Bell stared at Trace for another long moment and then murmured, "Brisby Frost. Pyro-tech. You're friends with him, yes?"

Trace was surprised to hear Frost's name but nodded, hoping to get this over with as soon as possible and collapse onto her bed in her bare-bones apartment. Webb approached, pushed up the sleeve of Trace's black T-shirt, removed the gauze she had applied, and plunged a needle into her arm, near the knife wound. Trace grimaced. Somehow, it hurt more than anything that had gone down in the Nix brothers' apartment.

"I think using the term *friend* would stretch the definition of the word," she grunted.

"But you do business with him on the regular," Bell insisted. "He was the one who processed the plastic you procured from Jonny Nix earlier this evening, right? Wasn't that his signature on the credit receipt?"

"Yeah, I know him," Trace admitted. She didn't like where this was going. "He's okay, I guess. Less annoying than the other pyro-techs. Why, what's going on?" Part of her arm had already gone numb and now Webb was sewing the skin together. Even though she could barely feel it, Trace felt sick to her stomach. Take a knife, take a bullet during a mission? *Fine.* Have a needle pulling thread across your flesh? *Nope, no thank you.*

"Nothing to worry about," Bell said, looking up and smiling again. But the smile was different. Sly, conspiratorial. Trace had seen this look before. And she didn't like it. Never had. It was the same smile when the president had first introduced her to her "brother," Gunnar. The same smile when she told a very young Trace that her training was about to begin. The same smile she flashed before sending a teenage Trace out on her first retrieval mission. "But I do have a new job for you."

Trace grabbed the ice while Webb worked and placed it back against her face, staring at the president. The silence stretched out until Trace gave in, lost the game of verbal chicken.

"Of course, anything you need."

"That's my girl," Bell said, leaning forward and clapping Trace on the shoulder. A totally intentional move, she knew. A way to remind her of who was in control in this room. The shock of the gesture ran down Tracer's arm, through the painkiller, and into the cut from earlier, and she sucked in a breath, silently. Webb pulled back momentarily, unsure of what to do, and then proceeded with the surgery.

Bell stood again, walked over to her desk, and sat down behind it, holding up the telegram.

"So, Frank Stewart . . ." She laughed, shook the piece of paper. "My mistake . . . *Chancellor* Stewart has a problem. And seeing how we're the closest city to Apex, he wrote to me, looking for help." Bell slapped the paper down onto the desk. "Wait, did I say *looking*? I meant *begging*."

Trace heard the slight shift in Bell's voice and felt her stomach tighten. This was the moment when Bell went from benevolent benefactor to vicious tyrant. Trace had witnessed this dozens of times since she'd been adopted, maybe hundreds. And she'd seen people receive countless blows, if not outright torture, shortly after this kind of tonal switch in the woman's voice. Sometimes even Trace was the one who was at the receiving end of the president's wrath in these moments. She clenched her jaw and waited.

"Are you done or what, Doc?" Bell said, staring at Webb with a sudden intensity. The president's personal doctor clipped the thread and nodded, not making eye contact with his boss. Webb nodded at Trace, a sad look in his eyes, and then shuffled out of the room. Bell didn't even seem to notice. Trace had hoped the doctor would have had time to check out her jaw, too, but she was willing to settle for just getting her arm stitched up. After all, how long could this new mission take? It was the middle of the night. Not much going on in the city itself or even out in the Hills.

Trace dropped the ice again and rotated her arm, poked at the stitches. It was weird not to be able to feel the cut or any of the flesh around it. She knew the pain would return, but for now, she welcomed the numbness. She grabbed her jacket and put it back on. She didn't feel quite right not wearing it while still on the clock. Even though she should have been passed out in her bed by now.

"So," the president continued, "this idiot . . . Chancellor Stewart . . . he told me that they only have *one* pyro-machine! Can you fucking *believe* that? I mean, sure, apparently it's huge . . . just fucking dwarfs any of ours. But if that one *giant* machine breaks down, he is royally fucked, right? And guess what happened, Trace?" Bell laughed, clearly enjoying the moment. "Yep! His big, stupid machine broke down. Which means no more new oil for him. Which means . . . that when he runs out of fuel—and he said it's a matter of days, the way they burn it—the proverbial shit is gonna hit the not-so-proverbial fan. You following me, Tracer?"

Trace's stomach dropped further. Bell rarely called her by her full name—the name the president herself had given her.

"Yes, ma'am," she answered.

"Yes, ma'am," Bell repeated. She stood up again, came around the desk, and sat down on its edge. She stared at Trace for another long moment.

"You've never left Puente Hills, have you, Trace?"

"No, ma'am," Trace answered, starting to understand where this was going. And hating it already.

"Well then, this is your lucky day. You are going to escort Mr. Brisby Frost to Apex City, where he will fix their broken pyro-machine. Then you will return to PH City and go back to kicking ass and taking plastic for me. Is that clear?"

"Crystal, ma'am." Bell had shown Tracer a crystal when she was young, a year or so after she'd been adopted. Had promised to give it to the young woman after she completed her first mission. And after that first retrieval had been accomplished, Trace stood in front of her boss, waiting for that crystal, forcing herself not to mention the promise that had been made.

And she was still waiting.

"Great. Frost is already waiting for us downstairs. I know you're exhausted but I need you to leave immediately. The *chancellor* is kind of . . . how would you put it . . . *freaking the fuck out.*" Bell laughed at her own joke.

Trace felt her heart sink. *Immediately?* She was pretty sure she was moments away from passing out due to an acute case of pain and exhaustion.

"Before you leave, though, there's something I want to show you," Bell said, her eyes glowing preternaturally.

"What's that, ma'am?"

Bell stood up and clapped Trace on the shoulder again, pain echoing up and down her arm.

"Goldie."

Trace's jaw nearly fell open as she stared into her boss's eyes. Bell had mentioned Goldie—one of the only working cars left from the Before Time—over the years, but Trace had never actually seen the vehicle. She'd never been allowed anywhere *near* it. Trace tried to fight back an excited smile and for the most part failed. This was most likely just another promise that her boss would fail to keep.

But if not . . . ?

Well, at least *some* good would have come out of this shit situation.

6

FOURTEEN YEARS EARLIER

Mackie threw a punch toward my face, and I leaned back as fast as I could, avoiding the blow. Barely.

I'd been training with him for two years, and his attacks were just as vicious as they'd been since I was introduced to the man by President Bell. Back then, though, he was a lot better at landing his attacks. I was smaller than him—much smaller—but I learned fast. Was *fast.*

While I was regaining my balance, Mackie kicked out and swept my legs, causing me to stumble back and tumble along the floor. I used the momentum to roll and spring back up to my feet, barely missing a follow-up kick from my mentor.

"Not ba—" he started to say but was interrupted by my rabbit punch that connected with his nose, snapping his face back with a spray of sudden blood.

"Oh!" I cried, lowering my fists, stepping forward. "Mackie. I'm sorry."

He looked up, smiling, the blood from his nose already seeping between his teeth. His face was red from the blow, almost as red as his close-cropped hair, and it looked for a second like he was about to say something, but instead he kicked out again, catching me in the stomach. The breath exploded out of my lungs, and I collapsed to the ground, trying desperately to suck some oxygen into my suddenly empty lungs.

"What did I tell you?" he asked, standing over me and wiping his nose with the back of his hand.

"No . . . mercy . . ." I barely managed to utter.

"Hearing my instructions is one thing," he said, offering his hand. "But it's more important to listen to them."

I fought back my anger at him. Used the techniques he'd been teaching me on a daily basis. Emotion never helped in combat. I had let my guard down, and he had taken advantage. It was that simple. Nothing else mattered. Especially my feelings.

I took his hand, and he helped me back up to my feet.

"Let's go again," I said, forcing my breathing to normalize—in through the nose, out through the mouth. Just like Mackie had trained me.

"No," he responded, smiling at me. "We've been going for hours. You've earned a break."

"I want to keep going," I demanded.

"And I'm telling you that you need a breather," he countered, his face growing more serious. Unlike Bell, Mackie had a core of kindness, which he sometimes displayed when the two of them were alone, but when his eyes narrowed like this, it was in many ways more frightening than Bell's bouts of gleeful sadism. I held up my hands in mock surrender.

"Fine," I teased. "I finally land a punch and you want to quit. I get it."

Mackie stepped closer, face darkening further. "It was a good punch, Trace. Hurt like a motherfucker. But you still lost the fight. You should have pressed the attack. You show mercy like that in the real world? It'll be the last thing you ever do."

"I won't make that mistake again," I mumbled.

"I know you won't," he said, then placed a hand on my shoulder. "You're the best student I've ever had. By far. But go easy on yourself. This stuff takes time to learn, and even longer to master."

I knocked his hand off my shoulder and raised my fists. "So let's go again, old man. Unless you're afraid."

Mackie barked a laugh, a huge smile spreading across his bloody face. "Far be it from me to disagree with my star pupil. And we have a few minutes before Gunnar gets here anyway. I'll tell you what. If you manage to—"

Before Mackie could finish his challenge, the door to the training room opened, and President Bell sauntered in, eyes cold steel as she took in her two employees.

"Sorry to interrupt!" she said, too loudly and not even vaguely apologetic. "I need to borrow Tracer here. If that's okay with you, Mack."

The man blinked at his boss, his entire demeanor changing. I hated to see him like this but knew he was just as scared of the president as everyone else. He had been in debt to her for years after borrowing credits on multiple occasions. I wasn't sure why he needed the money so bad, and had never asked. Apparently no amount of plastic in the world would ever make up for what he owed—so instead she'd hired him to train her soldiers—and her adopted children as well. Based on what Trace knew, his contract would end on the day he drew his last breath.

"Of course, ma'am," he replied, keeping his eyes on the floor.

Bell looked at me and then nodded at the door. I wanted to say something to Mackie but simply moved past him and toward the exit. Bell glanced at Mackie before following. "How's she doing?"

"Honestly?" he replied. "Trace is the most gifted pupil I've ever worked with. Stubborn but gifted."

I fought back a smile as Bell laughed at the man's comment.

"I fucking love it," she exclaimed, glancing at both of us. "And of course I'm not at all surprised. Did I ever tell you why I named her Tracer, Mack?"

His eyes lit up. "No . . . no, you have not."

"Well, it's a great fucking story," the president responded, stepping closer to Mackie. "So, the first time I ever saw her . . . a few years ago . . . this innocent-looking little girl . . . she was in jail!" Bell laughed, and Mackie did so as well. I wondered if he was faking it to make his boss happy, or if he was honestly finding the story funny. I wished I could ask him—and thought maybe someday I would—though I never did.

"They caught her trying to steal plastic from one of my barter shops on the ground level. I'd heard about her. She was only ten but it took five guards to get her locked up. Five!"

I knew from memory that it had been only three, but I didn't correct her. Bell loved to exaggerate, and regardless, correcting the president was a very dangerous proposition.

"She wasn't scared of me," Bell continued. "I think that's what impressed me the most. It was obvious she knew who I was, she called me President before I even opened my mouth. Sure, she called me other things, too, things I woulda killed other people for saying, probably with my bare hands. But coming from a ten-year-old . . . ? Well, let's just say it gave me a good laugh. I liked her right away."

Mackie looked like he wanted to say something but kept his mouth shut. He was well trained himself.

"The people who had found her, the ones who raised her, came looking for her a few days after she was arrested. And you know what, Mackie? That surprised me. I was shocked that a couple of Dwellers would give a shit about some garbage rat they had found. I think . . . I think maybe they actually loved her. Or maybe they just loved all the plastic she stole for them! But it didn't matter. I already knew. I knew she was destined to work for me. And I

handed over enough credits for them to walk away without ever looking back." Bell glanced over at Tracer. "Sorry if that's hard to hear but it's the truth."

I grunted. Every time Bell told this story, it hurt, but Mackie had taught me to push pain—both physical and emotional—down deep into my stomach and then forget it was even there. The body figured out how to heal itself. And so did the soul.

Still, as I glanced over at Mackie, I thought I saw sadness there. Or maybe it was pity. Either way, I hated it. Hated that I loved him for feeling it, and for treating me with more kindness than maybe anyone else ever had in my thirteen years. And the fact that he would probably disappoint me eventually. Just like everyone in my life always had. I convinced myself it was impossible that he would be any different.

Bell turned back to Mackie, whose eyes had hardened again.

"When I told her back then that I was adopting her, that she was basically going to be the president's daughter, guess what she said to me?"

Mackie raised his eyebrows, clearly unsure if this was an actual question. After a long, painful moment of silence, he said, "Thank you . . . ?"

Bell laughed and clapped him on the shoulder. "You'd think, right?! No, Mack, she said, 'Big deal.' Big deal! Hahaha! How amazing is that?!"

Mackie laughed and I could tell it was genuine this time. I hated this story, but hearing my trainer laugh for the first time elicited an unexpected smile from me. I fought against it and, after a moment, succeeded.

"She didn't like me right away, that was for sure," the president continued. "But she did what I told her. And I had a feeling about her. I just knew. And she proved me right within a week. Do you remember, Trace?" Bell didn't even bother to look back at me,

so I didn't bother to answer. "Someone had stolen a baseball from my office. Signed by Steve fucking Garvey. I mean, fuck, I know baseball hasn't even existed for . . . what . . . a hundred years? But that ball was special to me. A relic from the old days. A reminder of the way the world used to be, and the way it will be again. And someone stole it from me. Totally fucking unacceptable."

Bell's tone had shifted, and both Mackie and I held our breath. The president was known for unbelievable acts of violence in moments like this, even against people who worked for her.

"I'd had her for a week and she wouldn't tell me her name. For all I knew, she didn't even have one. It was driving me crazy. I called her every name I could think of, just to see if she'd react. Do you remember that, Trace?"

There was a long moment of silence. This question wasn't rhetorical.

"Yes," I whispered.

"But she wouldn't tell me, Mack. She was too pissed off to give in. And I respected that. I mean, she had just been dumped by the people who had raised her! I'd be pissed, too! But I just had a feeling about her. And sure enough, after that baseball was stolen, she stepped up. Big time. And I didn't even have to ask her! To this day, I still don't know why she did it. But she tracked that ball down—traced it to the guy who used to train my guards." Mackie's eyebrows shot up ever so slightly, but otherwise he didn't react to what was clearly new—and vaguely threatening—information. "When she told me, I didn't believe it. How the hell would some ten-year-old even know that? And on top of that, why would that guy even take it? It had no value anymore. Most people have never even heard of baseball! But sure enough, when we searched his apartment—there it was."

I hated this part of the story.

"I didn't enjoy torturing him, Mack. I didn't. But an example

had to be made. And even though it was a dark day for my administration, it was a necessary one. But still, it was . . ." Bell paused, her face tightening as she thought about those hours spent in a room covered in thick, expensive plastic. "Dark."

Mackie shifted uncomfortably but didn't say anything. Waited for his boss to continue her story.

"And when I visited her the next day, to thank her, it came to me. She was a finder of things. A kid . . . a young woman who would stop at nothing to fulfill a mission. A tracer of clues, of facts." Bell turned and looked at me. "My Tracer."

Another moment of silence filled the large room. Mackie opened his mouth to say something, but before he had a chance, the door opened and Gunnar walked in. He took in the scene, and when he saw me standing there with the president and our teacher, his face darkened into a nasty scowl. But he didn't say anything. He was well trained, too.

Bell clapped her hands together. "Anyway! I'll leave you and Gunnar to it. Trace, let's go. I'm having trouble finding something I misplaced, and I can't think of anyone better suited to finding that fucking thing."

I fell into step behind her and headed for the door. Just before I exited the room, I glanced back. Gunnar was stretching, his back to us, but Mackie was watching me, a deep sadness etched into his face. I had never seen him look like that before.

But I would, one more time, years later.

On the day he died.

7

Bell and Trace stood in the elevator.

The dim lighting made the president look even deadlier than usual, her eyes hollow sockets. The silence was painful but Trace welcomed it. She just wanted to be on her way, get this mission over with. She didn't allow herself to think about all the steps it would require to do that—compartmentalizing missions was always the surest way to success. Especially a monster job like this one.

The elevator slowed and shuddered, and then the doors opened on the second floor, groaning slightly. Bell walked out first and Trace trailed. She'd had no idea Goldie was kept down here. Come to think of it, Trace realized she had never actually been on this level before. This fact made her even more uneasy than she already was. Despite her exhaustion, she took in every detail as they walked. Mackie had drilled into her the importance of being alert in unfamiliar surroundings.

They continued down a long, bare hallway. Yep, Trace had definitely never been down here before. It was unnerving. She'd thought she knew this city inside and out and was further shocked that she couldn't even smell the garbage while being this low in the city. How the hell had the president pulled that off?

Finally, they reached a door at the end of the hallway, and Bell stopped for a moment, looking at her XN. "Here we are," the president said quietly, as if imparting a secret.

She slapped Trace gently on the cheek and smiled, an act of affection tinted with violence, then turned and opened the door, ushering her XN into Goldie's cavernous room.

Even though she knew he was going to be there, Trace was shocked to see Brisby standing next to Goldie, his fingers pressed against her.

Trace took a closer look at the man. She'd been doing business with him for years but had never really seen him, she realized. His hair and beard were wispy, and his clothes looked old and baggy on his thin frame. He pushed his glasses up his nose, and she found herself wondering how much plastic they had cost him, how much he made doing his job. Questions she had never bothered to contemplate before because he was just a function of her job and not a real person. Not really.

He smiled at her, his fingers resting on the car, and the sight of it sent a shock wave across her body. It wasn't the first smile she had ever seen on Brisby's face, but it had always reminded her of someone—and she had never been able to place it. Until now.

It was the same kind of lopsided grin that her Garbage Dweller father had. It was a smile she had loved deeply and then hated, just as deeply. The realization broke her heart, but she didn't allow the emotion to show on her face. She'd been too well trained to allow that kind of tell.

Bell flashed an enraged look at the pyro-tech, and Brisby quickly snatched his hand away from Goldie, smiling sheepishly. Gunnar stood nearby, and the silence in the room was painful.

"You must be Brisby Frost," Bell finally said, approaching the man with her hand extended. Brisby hesitated and then shook hands, staring at his shoes.

"It's an honor, Your Majesty," he mumbled awkwardly.

"Your *Majesty*!" Bell yelled, looking over her shoulder at Trace. "Can you believe this fucking guy? I *love* it!"

"I-I'm sorry," Frost stuttered.

Bell punched him softly on the shoulder. "Call me President Bell, please. None of this 'Your Majesty' stuff. I'm not a queen! Just a humble servant of my constituents." She looked around at everyone as if waiting for someone to contradict her. They all knew she hadn't been voted into office. Far from it.

"Now," she continued, "Trace, come here." The XN did as ordered. "This is your first time meeting Goldie, right?" Trace nodded. "Well? What do you think?"

Trace looked the car over and had to admit—it was even more impressive than Bell had made it sound.

A 1972 Dodge Dart. Its gold paint was chipping away in a thousand places, but it was still a gorgeous reminder of the world before fossil fuels ran out. Before 99 percent of the world's population was wiped out by the Jar Flu.

Goldie had clearly been cleaned and polished recently because the paint that remained glimmered in the large room's harsh overhead lighting. Trace took a few steps and ran her fingers along the car's frame, the slight squeaking sound echoing up at her. She knew she probably shouldn't touch Goldie—she'd seen the way Bell had narrowed her eyes at Brisby when they walked in—but she couldn't help herself.

Part of her training with Mackie had involved fixing engines and driving shitty little ATVs on the insane Puente Hill roads—if they could even be called that—tracking down thieves and runners, and delivering them, sometimes literally kicking and screaming, to the president. But she had never seen a car like this before.

She peeked into the window. The leather seats were just as beat up and beautiful as the exterior of the car. As her breath fogged the window, she heard Bell clear her throat behind her.

"Sorry," Trace said, standing and turning around. Brisby was still staring at the floor, his face pale. He looked terrified. Gunnar now stood behind and slightly to the left of Bell, and the president's face was serious. Trace nodded slightly.

Right. Mission time.

"There are a couple of bottles of water in there, and I put a map in the glove compartment," Bell said. "It should only—"

"Wait, we're leaving right now?" Trace interrupted.

Bell's eyebrows knitted together, and an expectant smile crossed Gunnar's face. Even Brisby looked up at the sudden silence. *Shit.* Trace *knew* the president hated being interrupted. Why the hell had she done that? She *must* have been tired.

But Bell just smiled and stepped closer to her XN. "That's cute, Trace. *Yes*, you're leaving right now. We don't want to keep the poor chancellor waiting. We all have needs." The president placed her hand on Goldie's hood and smiled. "Now, as I was saying, it's about a six-hour drive to Apex City, the way the roads are these days, and assuming you don't make any stops along the way. Now, when you get there—"

"What about the Nomads?" Brisby said quietly, his eyes fixed on the floor again.

The air seemed to be sucked out of the room. Gunnar took a step toward the pyro-tech, but Bell warned him away with the slightest shake of her head, then walked over to Brisby and placed a finger on the man's chin, slowly raising it so their eyes were locked.

"The *Nomads*? Come now, Mr. Frost, surely you know that's an urban legend. Do you really think there's a group of *barbarians* roaming around what's left of the United States, preying on the weak and the helpless?"

There was another long moment of silence. *Shut the hell up*, Trace thought, staring hard at Brisby.

"I . . ." the pyro-tech started to say but then stopped. Bell indicated with her eyes and a painfully false smile for Frost to continue. "I heard a story. About the Nomads. I heard that they once caught a family trying to make it to Puente Hills and that they . . . they ate them. All of them. And then used the bones to kill the next family they came across."

Bell looked cockeyed at Brisby for a moment, and Trace wondered if this mission was about to end before it had even started. She had heard stories about the Nomads, too, everything from the mundane to the terrifying, and wasn't sure what to believe. People who left PH City and Puente Hills—voluntarily or otherwise—never came back. So all they had to work on were rumors that had drifted in over the years. And Trace preferred working off facts and things she could hold in her hands. Like her SIG Pro. And soon . . . Goldie's steering wheel.

Laughter suddenly burst out of the president's mouth, and she nearly doubled over, placing a hand on the pyro-tech's shoulder to steady herself.

"That's fucking *amazing*," Bell said, wiping a tear away from her eye. "And just precious. No, you're not gonna get eaten by a bunch of savages on your way to Apex City, Mr. Frost. I give you my solemn word. Cool?"

Brisby glanced nervously at the hand on his shoulder.

"Um . . . yes, cool. Very cool," he muttered.

"Besides," the president continued, dropping her hand and glancing at Trace, "I'm sending my best soldier with you."

Out of the corner of her eye, Trace saw Gunnar tense. She fought a smile at the sight.

"Trace has been in more firefights than I can count. More fistfights than everyone in this room combined. She can certainly handle a little trip to Apex City. Now . . ." Bell pulled a key from her pocket and walked over to her XN.

"Take care of her," Bell whispered, staring into Trace's eyes, then handed the key to Goldie over. She smiled briefly and then shifted her gaze to Brisby.

"One more thing, Mr. Frost . . ."

"Yes, ma'am?"

"If you ever fucking interrupt me again, I will personally choke you to death and then cut your corpse into tiny pieces and mail them to your widow. Cool?"

She grinned again as the pyro-tech's face went even paler. Gunnar smiled, too, directly at Trace, and the two sized each other up, not for the first time. They'd both been trained extensively by Mackie when they were young, were probably equals in combat when all factors were considered, but they had never gone toe-to-toe, not really. *Inevitable*, Trace thought.

The XO reached into his pocket, and now it was Trace who tensed—she couldn't help herself, and the fact bothered her to no end. It was exactly what Gunnar wanted, and she knew it. But he just removed a thin, folded sheaf of papers and handed it to Trace, that eerie smile never leaving his face. The XN took hold of them gently, in contrast to the violence in her eyes. Another agonizing moment passed. Brisby shifted uncomfortably.

"Let's go," Trace finally said.

PART 2

THE ROAD

8

The heat and silence were killing her.

They were close to the east gate now, having wound their way through the narrow roads of Puente Hills, the seemingly endless mountains of garbage shoved back just enough to allow a vehicle to navigate through. It was early, the sun not even up yet—only a few random, desperate Garbage Dwellers could be seen here and there, in the distance—so it was especially quiet outside, making the atmosphere in the car that much worse. But the stench outside was unbearable, and Goldie's air-conditioning was long defunct, so they had no choice but to keep the windows up and swelter.

Trace kept her eyes locked on the road, pretending she was having trouble driving in the dark. Frost was looking out the passenger-side window. The way he was gawking at everything they passed, Trace wondered if it was his first time outside of PH City and surmised it was definitely his first time in a car. She let out a long breath, shook her head. She was exhausted, couldn't believe this was actually happening.

The silver lining to this absolute shit situation was finally being able to drive Goldie. The car handled beautifully.

"Have you been to Apex City before?" Brisby finally asked as they approached the gate, a guard suddenly appearing from the shadows, stepping into the headlights with a submachine gun resting against his shoulder.

"No," Trace grunted.

She pulled to a stop inches away from the guard, who didn't flinch. *Impressive*, Trace thought.

The guard, who wore a face mask and goggles, approached the driver's side, and Trace rolled down the window. The smell wasn't as bad this far out, but it still wasn't pleasant.

"Papers," the guard's muffled voice demanded, a little too aggressively, the gun now held a bit more tightly. Trace eyeballed him—based on the sound of his voice, he was probably fifteen or so. She wondered if this kid knew he was talking to Bell's XN and then decided not to even mention it. She nodded at Brisby, who opened the glove compartment, reached in, and handed over the signed presidential forms that Gunnar had given Tracer.

She proffered the papers to the guard, who stared at them through his dirty goggles.

Bet he can't even read the signature through that gunk, Trace thought.

The guard stared closer at the papers, and she saw the kid tighten his grip on the gun. The XN sighed, too exhausted to even contemplate fighting one of Bell's hired thugs. Which, she supposed, she was, too. Bell had an uncanny knack for pitting her own people against each other. An annoying—but surprisingly effective—way to further ensure loyalty. Despite being aware of that irony, Trace slowly reached down, undid the clasp on her holster, and withdrew the SIG Pro without looking—a skill that Mackie had drilled into her over and over and over again. As she waited, the tension slowly ratcheting up in the car, she held the gun down in the shadows.

"Okay, you're good to go," the guard finally said through the face mask. He lifted his chin at someone else, someone unseen, and the gate lumbered open, a horrible metallic shrieking noise filling the early dawn air.

With the teenage guard still staring at her, too tired to even follow her own rules, Trace dropped the gun onto the floor of the car and hit the gas gently, resisting an urge to kick up a bunch of dust in his face. She'd overheard enough of Bell's conversations over the years to know it was a shitty, low-paying job patrolling the edges of Puente Hills, one of the two most sought-after—and thus dangerous—places in what used to be North America. The last thing the guard needed was some jerk adding insult to injury.

"Well, that wasn't bad. I guess this won't be too awful after all," Frost said, that lopsided smile crossing his face. Trace ignored him and focused on driving.

As they made their way along a dirt road and then eventually onto a paved one, Frost rolled down his window, raising his nose to the rushing air and breathing deep. He scratched at his beard, and Trace fought back a chuckle.

Despite the way his smile made her feel, the pyro-tech looked like a little kid with that big dumb grin on his face.

Trace guided Goldie along the rubble-strewn streets for a few miles. It was a shock to see the world outside of Puente Hills for the first time. Husks of burnt-out cars and destroyed buildings were everywhere.

No sign of a single person. Disconcerting at best. Then again, there were only about seventy million people left on Earth, based on the stories Bell had told her and Gunnar over the years. Sometimes the stories changed, ever so slightly, either intentionally or not, so she was never quite sure what was true. Still, seventy million sounded like a lot to Trace—but it was a big planet.

Bell had also told her two "children" about the way things were outside the relative safety and stability of Puente Hills, had described the devastation in sometimes stomach-tightening detail. But stories and reality were two very different things. What she was seeing felt infinitely worse than what she had imagined.

Brisby was wrong.

This was going to be awful.

Minutes of welcome silence were interrupted by the pyro-tech, who murmured as he gazed out of the window.

"I didn't get a chance to say goodbye to Rachel."

Trace stared through the windshield into the slowly lightening darkness, glancing occasionally down at the map half-unfolded between her and Brisby, hoping to see a sign that would lead her to the road that used to be called CA-60.

She knew from her conversations with both Mackie and Bell that during the years when conventional oil dried up and the Jar Flu flourished, resulting in the collapse of society as humanity had known it, things like road signs hadn't been a top priority. But despite Trace's concentration on driving, Frost's words echoed in her ears.

She glanced over at Brisby, hoping he'd been talking to himself, but he was now staring back at Trace, seemingly waiting for a response.

Crap.

"Who?" was all she could manage.

"Rachel," Frost repeated. "My daughter. She's five. And she's going to be a wreck tomorrow morning . . . *this* morning. She was already asleep when I got home from work last night.

I mean, Jenna said she would explain . . . said the computer I bought from you would help . . . but still . . ."

Trace knew she should say something else, something comforting, but she didn't have training in this area. And talking about a five-year-old girl made her think about herself at that age, when she still believed her adopted parents loved her, would do anything for her. She was having trouble ignoring her emotions, so she just focused on her breathing, something Mackie had always said was key to self-control.

Part of her wished that she was back in the Nix brothers' apartment, fighting two guys at once. That would be easier than talking to this poor, depressed pyro-tech about his wife and daughter.

Much to Trace's relief, she saw a tilting, broken green sign up ahead, part of which revealed a smudged "60" and an indication to turn right.

"Here we go," Trace said, feeling her body fill with some much-needed adrenaline. She knew she would have to sleep soon. And that would involve stopping, a dangerous proposition. She assumed Frost had no idea how to drive Goldie, which had a manual transmission, or any other car for that matter.

"I've never been away from them," Brisby continued, and Trace felt a stab of anger. She was still in pain, and she didn't want to be on this mission, and she certainly didn't want to be force-fed any guilt about the family of a man she barely knew.

"Yeah, well, life sucks," she said, pulling onto CA-60 and working around a half-dozen ancient, empty cars.

She could feel Frost's eyes on her and knew the pyro-tech was pissed off. Hell, she didn't blame him. She'd be pissed off, too.

"My daughter looks up to you," Brisby snapped.

"What?" Trace responded, grateful for the rising sun, which helped illuminate all the burnt-out cars in her way. She maneuvered around them like she'd been born to do it. "How is that possible? I've never even met her."

"Yeah, well, believe it or not, most people who bring plastic in to be processed aren't the most interesting or ethical, Trace. I mean . . . I'm sure you're aware that I'm not a fan of most of the brokers. Wait, strike that. I'm not a fan of *any* of the brokers. The way they look at me . . . I swear, if they thought gutting me would get them a few extra credits, they wouldn't hesitate. You're the only one who doesn't look at me that way. You know that, right?"

Trace glanced over at Brisby again and then pulled her eyes back to the road. She couldn't afford to get distracted. There were way too many dead cars on the highway. Too many shadows where things—*people*—could be hiding.

But no. She *didn't* know that.

"I'm aware that you don't really . . . have a family, Trace. But *I* do. And I tell them about my day—during dinner—the way families used to do . . . before the world turned to shit. Do you even know anything about that? The way families used to be?"

She had a flash of memory as a very young girl, walking on a path through the mountains of garbage, holding her adopted parents' hands, looking up at them and feeling safe, like nothing could ever hurt her.

"Nope," she lied.

She pulled around a particularly blackened corpse of a car and then was pleasantly surprised to find a long stretch of clear highway. She opened Goldie up a bit, hitting fifty-five and reveling in it. Even Brisby stopped sniping at her for a few moments, sticking his head out the window, letting his longish hair flow in the wind.

"She thinks you're cool," Brisby muttered, his eyes closed, the rushing air pushing against his face. "You work for the president. You bring bad guys to justice. You protect PH City. I mean . . . both you and I know that's not exactly accurate, but she's young. She still believes the propaganda Bell spews on the radio. How she's forging a new world, how she cares about all the little people. Your name is never mentioned on the broadcasts, admittedly, but when I told Rachel that I know Bell's 'executive enforcer,' she lost it. She thought it was the most amazing thing in the world. I know she thinks I'm a little square, making her finish her lessons at night when I get home in time. Jenna is too tired to enforce the rules after homeschooling her all day, you know?"

Trace sighed. This was, possibly, the most painful conversation she'd ever had. But the concept that a five-year-old girl thought she was cool was annoyingly satisfying. Despite this, she simply grunted by way of an answer.

"Anyway," Brisby continued after a moment of enjoying the fresh air, "that's why I'm always asking you to come over for dinner. It's not really Jenna asking. It's Rachel. But I thought it would be weird to mention that little fact while I'm processing the plastic you bring in. 'Hey, my daughter thinks you're rad, wanna come eat some shitty stew?'" He erupted into maniacal laughter and leaned his head even farther back, going as far as to reach his arms out into the wind. "This is an awesome feeling, Trace. I've never felt anything like this."

Trace pretended she wasn't listening. But then, after a minute, she put her own hand out the window. Felt the wind. And smiled.

It *was* pretty awesome.

9

Trace pulled the car to the side of the road. After following Route 60 for about twenty minutes, they'd turned onto a major highway, I-15, the path that would take them almost directly to Apex City. They'd been driving for about an hour on 15, the world slowly turning from destroyed civilization to hints of the oncoming desert. The map indicated they were in an area that had once been called Cajon Pass.

"What are you doing?" Brisby asked, peering at the shrub-pocked hills as if the answer to his question was out there. The conversation between the two had trickled into silence. Frost had apparently taken the hint: Trace didn't want to talk about the pyro-tech's family, or anything else for that matter.

"Nature calls," Trace said, and that was enough to elicit an understanding nod from Brisby.

Trace pushed the door open and unfolded herself from the seat, standing and stretching. She could hear Brisby doing the same but didn't bother looking over. The exhaustion was washing over her in waves now, as if she'd been downing shots of shine all day or had a fever. Or both.

Still, as she looked out across the landscape, she was amazed by the beauty of the surrounding mountains. *Real* mountains—not ones composed of garbage. After a moment of taking in the scene, she snapped out of it. Mackie hadn't trained her to admire the scenery while on a mission.

She headed over to a particularly dark spot near a large cluster of tall bushes. She wasn't exactly shy—but hell, she still wanted some privacy.

As she found a sufficiently shady spot, she heard Brisby mumbling something, but she decided that the eccentric pyro-tech was just talking to himself, probably freaking out about how beautiful nature could be. But even if he wasn't, Trace didn't want to hear it. She reached down to unbuckle her belt, wondering if she should just try to stay awake and finish the drive, or get a few hours of shut-eye now before—

The shape came from nowhere.

A large tree branch crashed down on Trace's back, hard, knocking the breath from her lungs and making her see stars. She fell to her knees, tried to clear her head. She could hear the shape as it circled her, realized it was a man, someone intent on doing her further harm, and she swore out loud when she realized she'd left her gun on the floor of the car. She'd never been so careless in her entire life.

The man hit Trace in the side of the head with the branch, and the wood snapped in half, both pieces clattering to the ground next to her as she fell over. Flat out on her back, Trace tried desperately to breathe, failing, blackness crowding her consciousness. The man got on top of the XN and wrapped his hands around Trace's neck, which didn't help matters much.

Trace stared at her attacker for a second, taking in his features. He was old, maybe even older than Bell, and both his head and face were covered in gray stubble. Deep lines were creased into his skin, especially around his haunted eyes, which he narrowed as he tightened his grip on Trace's throat. He wore a dirty dark-red hoodie and baggy jeans, which made him look like some kind of wrinkled teenager.

Ridiculous, she laughed to herself. *What kind of Nomad is this*?

Trace smiled despite the fact she was being choked to death, causing her assailant's forehead to furrow in confusion.

"Hey!" Brisby shouted from nearby. "Get off her!"

The old man looked over, loosening his grip ever so slightly, either stupid or surprised, or both, and the momentary distraction was all Trace needed. She brought her legs up and wrapped her ankles around the man's neck, pulling her assailant down and away with a pained growl. The man's fingers slipped away from Trace's neck, and he fell back, gurgling. Still fighting for breath, Trace let go and shakily got to her feet. When Trace's vision came back into focus a second later, she saw the old man was already on his feet, too.

Damn . . . he's pretty good.

The two circled each other warily.

"Guys, I think we should talk this over!" Brisby shouted. "There's probably just been a misunderstanding. We can—"

"Shut the hell up!" Trace yelled. The old man lunged at her, but if he thought Brisby's voice was going to distract her, the way he had been distracted, he was in for a rude awakening. The man threw a quick rabbit punch—she realized at that moment he was a lefty—and he was fast, sure, but he was still a few decades older than Trace. Not nearly fast enough.

Trace blocked the punch with her right forearm, glad that Webb's stitches held, and punched the guy in the nose with her left, admittedly her weaker arm but strong enough to cause blood to spout forth almost immediately, running down into the old man's mouth. He staggered back, clearly rattled.

Trace didn't give him a second to recover. She hit the guy in the nose again, this time with her right fist, and the man yelled in agony, instinctively cupping his face. Trace quickly grabbed his left arm and snaked it around the man's back, moving behind him as well, then pulled it up in a violent gesture, snapping it immediately. He screamed louder, all the fight going out of his body.

"Do . . . do you know who you're messing with?" he huffed, trying to wriggle free from Trace despite his obvious agony. "You are going to *die*. Very fucking slowly. You know that, right?"

Trace stood behind the man, holding his arm, but the guy was strong for someone so old and with a busted arm. He was pushing his weight back against Trace—testing different ways to get free, and if he managed *that*, who knew what would happen next?

Not interested in round two of this particular fight, still out of breath and in extreme pain, Trace kicked down hard onto the man's lower right leg, and that bone snapped, too, a wet, popping sound. He gasped, in too much pain to even scream, and collapsed into a writhing pile of blood and shattered limbs. After a moment, the man caught his breath and yelled, a strange collection of swears and incoherent ramblings, until the pain overwhelmed him and he passed out, his body shuddering even in unconsciousness.

Trace rose to her full height and stared down at what was left of the old man, and then slowly turned her gaze to Brisby.

"I guess the Nomads are real after all," she muttered.

Brisby, apparently done talking for the moment, just stared, mouth agape. Silent. And suddenly very aware of just how dangerous this trip was going to be.

"What do we do now?" Brisby finally whispered as the sun continued its slow movement in the sky above.

"We finish our damn mission," Trace snapped, frisking the

old man's prone form, and pulled out a gun, an old pistol. She checked the chamber.

"No bullets," she mumbled, throwing the gun into the distance, and then started walking toward the car. "Good thing, or we'd already be dead. Let's get out of here before his friends show up."

"How do you know he has friends?" Brisby asked, following.

"I don't. But do you want to stay here and find out?"

Frost considered this for a moment and then sped up and got into the car. Trace slid in next to him, reaching down and grabbing her gun, shoving it back into its holster. She quickly turned the key, and Goldie roared to life. Brisby looked over his shoulder and out the rear window at the man, whose body was bathed in the red brake lights.

"What about *him*? Do you think he'll survive?"

"Don't care," Trace answered and peeled off, covering the quivering old man in dirt.

Brisby kept glancing back at the road behind them.

He couldn't help himself. They'd already been driving for ten minutes, were miles away from the unconscious man, but he couldn't stop looking.

"Do you really think he was one of them? I mean . . . do you think he was a Nomad?" he said, knowing Bell's XN didn't want to talk but unable to stop himself.

"I have no idea. And it doesn't matter anyway. We're gonna go to Apex City, you're gonna fix their machine, and then we're gonna go home. Maybe if you fix it fast enough, Chancellor Stewart will give you a nice fat tip for your service. Hell, you might make some money off this trip after all."

"But did you see his hair . . . and that sweatshirt? What kind of Nomad is *that*? I always thought they were . . . you know . . . *animals*. But then, President Bell said they didn't even exist."

"*Brisby*. Maybe she was telling the truth. Maybe she was lying to mess with your head. Which is pretty much standard operating procedure with her. But even if there really are Nomads . . . and even if that guy *is* one . . . he probably met some nosy pyro-tech, killed him, and stole his stylish red hoodie."

"Ha ha," Brisby responded, deadpan.

The faux laughter echoed in Trace's ears as her vision blurred and she heard a distant pounding sound. The blow to the side of the head had rattled her more than she'd realized. She tightened her grip on the wheel, tried to keep focus, but the road went dark, and then went altogether black.

10

NINE YEARS EARLIER

Mackie poured two drinks, took one, and held it up.

"Happy birthday, Trace," he said, a rare smile appearing on his face.

I looked down at the small glass of clear liquid, then back up at my mentor. A part of me wondered if this was yet another test. Alcohol was, after all, illegal in PH City, and I didn't actually know my own birthday, so I found myself completely confused, especially by the odd sight of Mackie's grin. We were sitting in his small office area just off the large training space—a room I had never been invited into before. We'd just finished hours of combat exercises, and I was sweaty and in pain, but all of that slipped from my mind as I stared at the drink on the desk in front of me.

"Birthday . . . ?" I asked, looking up at my trainer.

"Well," he responded, lowering his glass slightly. "I realize that no one knows when you were actually born, but the president adopted you eight years ago today. So, happy adoption day, then."

I knew there was plenty of illegal alcohol in the city, had seen it now and then ever since Mackie had started taking me with him on retrieval missions, but it had certainly never been presented to me like this. After a moment, I took hold of the glass and lifted it, taking a nervous breath. I'd been learning to handle myself in real-world combat situations, had fought men much larger than me—and usually won—but for some reason, the idea of tasting this illegal substance made me more nervous than any of those encounters.

What if the president walked in at that very minute?

"Don't worry about Bell," Mackie said, as if reading my thoughts. "She's in a meeting that's gonna have her tied up for at least another hour."

I nodded at that information, then reached forward and took hold of the glass. I held it up close to my mouth and hesitated for the slightest moment.

"Happy adoption day," Mackie said again, then swallowed his drink in a single gulp.

Pushing what felt suspiciously like fear out of my mind—like he had been teaching me to do during our arduous mental agility sessions—I mirrored his action and felt the liquid burn as it slid down my throat. I saw him watching me and tried to smile but immediately burst into a coughing fit, which made the burning even worse. Tears rolled down my face as I tried to get control of myself.

"Delicious, ain't it?" he said, and poured us two more.

"That . . ." I managed to say after another minute. "That is terrible."

"Yeah," Mackie replied, then downed his shot. "But it turns into delicious eventually. Help yourself."

I eyed my glass, felt a vague pressure to drink it quickly, to make him happy. But as the uncomfortable sensation in my throat slowly subsided and my head grew slightly fuzzy, I let out a breath and smiled slightly at him. Something as rare as his own.

"Maybe later," I said, staring him directly in the eye.

Mackie didn't say anything for a long moment, and I wondered if I had insulted him, but then he reached forward and downed my shot, then twisted the top back onto the bottle. "Good. It's important to know when to hold yourself back . . . when it comes to liquor, yes, but in all things. Moderation is the key to a successful life. Never too much of anything. Letting yourself go is how you lose control. And losing control, in this world, is how you die."

"I understand," I said, and I did. I had let myself go once in my life, had believed that the Garbage Dweller couple who had raised me actually loved me, but I knew I wouldn't make that mistake again. Moderation. Control. I had committed to live my life based on those two tenets, make Mackie proud, and maybe even President Bell, too.

"Speaking of moderation," Mackie said, standing up. I started to stand, too, as I'd been trained to do, but my mentor waved me back into my seat. "I have a birthday gift for you. But you have to promise me that you'll always be careful with it, use it only when absolutely necessary."

"I promise," I said without having to think the request over. If Mackie thought I should be careful with something, or in any given situation, it was something I took very seriously.

He nodded, then turned to a nearby filing cabinet and carefully withdrew an object. My eyes went wide. I'd seen this item before, knew how important it was to my teacher.

Mackie handed me the SIG Pro, a perfectly maintained weapon, and I carefully turned it over in my hands.

"Are you sure?" I said, almost a whisper. "You love this gun."

"More than sure," he responded, sitting back down across from me. "I can't think of a person who deserves it more. But I want you to listen to me. I've only had to shoot it a few times in actual combat situations, and I clean it regularly—which you should do, too—so it should last you a good, long time. You just need to know when it's necessary, and when it's not."

I looked up into his eyes. "Moderation," I said.

"Moderation," he confirmed.

"Thank you, Mackie. This is—"

A sound from the training room interrupted my train of thought, and I stood, terrified that President Bell was about to walk through the door and see the illegal substance on the table. Mackie, however, didn't move, that enigmatic smile still on his face. He was always impossible to read, and that grin made it even harder to get a sense of the man.

But it wasn't President Bell who appeared in the doorway. In some ways, it was even worse.

Gunnar looked at me, at the gun in my hand, then at Mackie, and finally at the bottle of alcohol on the table. I realized I was holding my breath and slowly let it out. Control, *I reminded myself, despite my lightheadedness.*

"I'm sorry, sir," Gunnar said quietly. "I thought we had a training session scheduled."

"No apology necessary," our mentor responded, standing up. "I was just having a little chat with Tracer here. Would you like a drink, Gunnar? Who knows . . . maybe it'll loosen you up a little before we train."

Gunnar worked his jaw as he considered the question. I knew my adoptive brother well enough to suspect he was trying to guess the right answer, was most likely wondering if this was a test, just like I had. Finally, he shook his head and said, "No, thank you, sir."

"Fair enough," Mackie responded.

"I should go," I said, taking a step toward the door, wondering how I would get through it without knocking past Gunnar. I'd always wondered why Mackie had never pitted the two of us against each other.

"One second," our teacher said, his voice shifting. His tone was no longer playful, the way it had been only moments earlier. Now

he was our instructor again, someone who expected the absolute best from each of us.

He stepped around the table and looked at both of his students, standing equidistant between us.

"I'm not stupid," Mackie said. "I know there's no love lost between the two of you, and that's fine. That's the way President Bell wants it. If I was running things, it wouldn't be like that, but I'm not, so it is. But I'll tell you this: Whether you like it or not, you are siblings, and there may come a day when you realize how important that is. No matter what Bell tells you, or the way she treats you. Or the way you treat each other."

Gunnar and I glanced at each other, but neither of us said a word. For a moment, I thought I saw the look in his eyes soften, but I figured it must have been a trick of the light, and he looked away before I could really get a read on it.

Mackie grunted and started cleaning his desk, hiding the contraband once again. "Trace, get outta here. Gunnar, help me clean up here and then go stretch."

As I turned to leave, still feeling a little lightheaded, I tried to catch a glimpse of Gunnar's gaze again, curious what I'd find. But my "brother," never shy and always aggressive, seemed to be avoiding eye contact.

I pushed the confusing emotions away as I walked through the large training space, tucking the gun into my pants beneath my shirt. By the time I exited the room, my emotional walls were back up, and I refocused on being the best soldier possible for President Bell.

11

Tracer woke with a start, shocked that Goldie was still moving.

She sat up quickly and reached for the steering wheel before realizing she was now in the passenger seat. She looked to her left, shocked to find Brisby driving. Brisby, who had never even seen a car before today.

"How the hell—?" Trace began.

"You're awake!" Brisby said, smiling, barely taking his eyes off the road. "Good. I was getting worried about you."

"How . . . how long?"

Brisby shrugged. "I've never been the best at keeping track of time. But I'd say . . . two hours? Maybe three?"

"You never mentioned that you know how to drive," Trace said, rubbing her face and feeling the pain once again from where the Nomad had smashed her with the tree branch.

"Well, I don't . . . I mean, I *didn't.* But I was watching you do it. Earlier. And I guess I picked it up pretty quickly."

"You *guess,*" Trace said, irritated, more at how shitty she still felt than at Frost's uncanny learning curve. "What the hell happened?"

"Well," Brisby said, "we were talking . . . you made that joke about some pyro-tech getting killed, and then the car started veering off the road. I looked over and you were unconscious. I mean, totally asleep or unconscious, I couldn't tell which. I grabbed the wheel, and kind of . . . just . . . pulled you off the accelerator until we eventually stopped. It took me a little while, but eventually I was able to push you into the passenger seat. And then I . . . I just experimented with the car . . . with Goldie . . . until I got the hang of it. Kind of."

Trace cleared her throat. "Thanks," she said reluctantly. She wasn't used to owing anybody anything, felt vaguely embarrassed about having passed out and put them in potential danger.

They sat quietly for a few minutes as the world blurred past them.

"So . . . do you want to take over?" Brisby said, risking a glance over, clearly worried that he'd somehow offended Bell's XN.

Trace almost accepted the offer but then sat back and closed her eyes. She wasn't exactly tired anymore, but the darkness felt good. It helped keep some of the pain at bay.

"No, it's fine. Just don't hit anything."

"Yes, ma'am."

After a few minutes, Brisby started humming, and Trace opened her eyes.

"Seriously?"

"Sorry. Habit. It drives Jenna crazy. Rachel kind of likes it though. She does it, too, when she's concentrating. Like her old man."

"Hmph," Trace grunted.

Another long moment of silence ticked by, and Brisby started humming again, and then immediately stopped.

"It's so *weird* out here, right?" he said to fill the silence. "All those burnt-out buildings but no people. It's like some kind of insane nightmare. Do you think people back in the day ever expected anything like this would happen? I mean, back when there was oil still coming out of the ground and there were billions of humans, people who lived normal lives?"

"What does that mean?" Trace replied.

"Huh?"

"*Normal.* What does that even mean?"

"I don't know," Brisby murmured, staring at the highway snaking out in front of them. He'd gotten good at downshifting when they had to move around broken-down cars, then accelerating and upshifting. It was impressive. "You gotta admit that our 'normal' is a lot more messed up than theirs was. I mean, people used to wake up and drive to a job, work eight hours, maybe nine, then go home and be with their families. Have dinner. Watch TV. Have you ever heard about TV?"

Trace opened her eyes, glancing at the pyro-tech. She didn't want to admit that she hadn't, so she didn't answer. Just looked back out the passenger-side window at the desolate landscape. They were driving through the desert now, and she could see heat vapors rising off the sand.

"TV was a big rectangular screen that had music and dancing and all kinds of other stuff on it. Apparently, every house had one. And some people had two. Three. The size of this car, from what I hear. Hanging on the wall . . . maybe the ceiling? I'm not sure if I read that or I'm making it up . . . but still, a giant screen . . . and there were these things called 'shows' and some were made up and some were . . . I guess . . . real? Where real people would play games, I think, or even just a show about a bunch of strangers living in a house together or going on a road trip . . . kind of like us."

"Sounds stupid," Trace said.

"I think it sounds amazing. That people had the kind of

luxury and freedom to sit around for hours on end and watch made-up stories. With their families. Have you . . . ever thought about that?"

"Thought about what?" Trace said, even though she knew exactly what he was talking about.

Brisby hesitated and then forged ahead. "You know . . . finding someone. Getting married."

Tracer shook her head and then looked away, but somewhere deep inside of herself, in a place she had abandoned as a young woman, she *had* thought about it. A small sliver of herself dreamed of meeting someone, of losing herself to him. Of building a life away from President Bell and being an XN, and all the violence those things entailed. She'd even had a crush on Mackie for a minute but had quickly realized how silly that was, for so many reasons. He had trained her in the exact opposite direction, had warned her that losing yourself to emotion could get you killed. Falling in love, at least for her, was just a fantasy, a childish thing that she had closed the door on years ago.

"No," was all she said in response to Brisby's question.

"That's too bad."

After a moment, Trace glanced over at Brisby, but the pyro-tech was lost in thought as he took a slight curve in the highway. He looked even sadder than before—obviously missing his wife and daughter.

When she was younger, Trace had often found herself missing the couple who had raised her, and she'd then remind herself—repeatedly—that they had sold her for a handful of credits. *You don't miss them*, a voice in her mind echoed. *And you never will. Because you never actually knew them.*

But now that the pyro-tech had introduced the idea, Trace genuinely wondered what that was like. Missing someone. Being missed.

She shook her head and looked away again. No. That wasn't in her job description, and all she'd ever done was her job. Trace didn't have a life outside of that. Didn't want one. Every single day, she woke up, followed orders, maybe had a drink or two after she did whatever it was Bell needed her to do, and then she went back to sleep. That was it. She didn't love anyone, and no one loved her.

Simple. The way she liked it.

But this mission? It was anything but simple. And they hadn't even arrived at Apex City yet.

Trace sighed and closed her eyes, leaned her head back against the seat, and slowly slipped off into dreamless sleep.

A merciful and yet somehow terrible blackness.

12

"Trace! Trace, wake up!"

Her eyes fluttered. The last time she'd woken up, in the car earlier, it was sudden and she'd been immediately, acutely aware of her surroundings. This time, she felt like she was climbing out of an inky darkness, clawing her way out of some kind of thick web, and it was awful. Her eyelids felt glued shut.

"Trace!"

"Calm down, I'm awake!" she shouted back.

"Look," Brisby said, slowing the car and then stopping, the idling engine the only sound now.

Trace forced her eyes open and looked out the windshield, sitting up as she did so. She had slumped painfully as she slept, and her whole body ached. If she thought sleep was going to heal her injuries and overall exhaustion, she was woefully, laughably wrong.

"What the hell . . . ?"

"I saw her as we approached," Frost said. "I mean, barely at first, but she was kind of moving back and forth across the road, so I slowed down as we got closer. I didn't think it would be a good idea to . . . you know . . . run her over. Not to mention the damage it would do to Goldie. And the damage President Bell would then do to me."

Pacing in front of the car, in the middle of the highway, was a twenty- or thirtysomething woman with a shock of black hair and clothing that could only be loosely described as such. It was more like a large burlap sack that covered her flaccid body. She stared at them through button-hole eyes, her wrinkled face impossible to read.

"How far are we from Apex?" Trace asked.

"Can't be more than an hour at this point," Brisby answered, glancing down at the folded map on the seat between them.

"All right, let's see what this crazy person wants."

Trace opened the door and stood. It felt amazing to move her muscles after sleeping for so long in the car, and she had to stop herself from stretching her body entirely, realizing how ridiculous that would look. She approached the woman as she heard Brisby opening the driver-side door behind her.

"Hi there," she said, forcing a smile onto her face. "You're in our way. Is there a problem? Can we help you with something?"

"Can I help *you* with something?" the stranger responded through a mouth full of yellow teeth, stopping in her tracks and staring at them.

"Well," Trace said, keeping her voice calm. Brisby was right. The last thing Trace wanted on her conscience was some random dead lady. "We're trying to get to Apex City and you're kind of in our way, like I said. So, can you please move?"

"Apex City?" she asked, bursting into a half cough, half laugh. "You're in luck! I can help you!"

Trace's smile transformed into a genuine one. Yep. A crazy person, just like she'd thought. Harmless.

"I appreciate that but we don't need any help. I thought *you* might, but since it seems like you're doing just fine, we're going to get in the car and finish our trip. I just ask that you not get in the way. We don't want to hurt you."

The woman laughed again, which devolved into a vicious coughing attack, and she doubled over, her arms clutching her stomach as if she were in pain.

Trace looked over at Brisby, who was grimacing in empathy for the woman. The pyro-tech's eyes were pleading. He obviously wanted to help her, probably wanted to give her a ride to Apex City, see if a doctor could check her out. Trace shook her head and sent a message to Frost with her own eyes.

Don't get emotionally invested. We have a job to do.

Exactly what Mackie would have told *her*.

As the woman continued to cough, Trace turned away, ready to get back to the mission, and then to her routine in PH City. She was starting to realize just how unhappy she was outside of her comfort zone.

Trace heard a shuffling sound and then Brisby shouting something inarticulate. She felt the skinny pyro-tech shoving her, hard—harder than she would have expected possible—and maybe it was the fatigue or she was just losing her edge, but she went down onto the concrete and felt the skin on her right palm opening, felt the blood already beginning to flow.

"What the *fuck* are you doing?!" she shouted, looking up just in time to see the woman plunging a shiv into the pyro-tech's shoulder. The blood that immediately spurted out made the scratches on Trace's hand look like a joke, a child's wound. The woman sneered at Frost as he crumpled soundlessly to the ground. Somehow his glasses remained perched on his nose.

"Brizz!" Trace shouted, a deep and surprising rage flashing across her entire body. She was on her feet instantly, rushing the woman, who was already bringing the blade down for a second time toward Frost, a killing blow.

Trace landed a right hook across the woman's jaw with a sick cracking sound, and she fell back, her makeshift weapon clattering onto the concrete. The XN walked slowly toward her with purpose, withdrawing the gun from its holster.

"D . . . don't . . ." she heard from behind.

She turned and saw Brisby raising his uninjured arm, the other one limp at his side, blood spilling everywhere.

"Don't . . ." Brisby repeated.

Trace turned back to the woman, who hadn't moved but stared up at the trench coat–wearing XN with terrified eyes. The stranger looked innocent, confused, as if she had no idea what she'd just done. Trace raised the gun, aimed it right between the woman's eyes, and took a deep breath.

After a long, silent moment, she lowered the gun and leaned down, staring into the woman's eyes.

"If you're still in our way when I get behind the wheel of that car, I'm going *straight through* you. You hear me?"

The woman's face transformed, the confusion slipping away, and she began to crawl toward the side of the road. Tracer watched her for a moment, then holstered the SIG Pro, turned around, and hurried over to Brisby, who stared at the sky, a bemused look on his face.

"It doesn't hurt," the pyro-tech said as Trace lifted him up into her arms. "Is that weird? Does that mean I'm dying?"

The XN inspected the wound as she carried Frost back to the car. "You're fine. Just in shock. Luckily, it was only a flesh wound, and the bleeding is already slowing down. I've treated worse cuts than this—sometimes on myself. Think of it this way, you'll have a great story to tell Rachel."

A huge smile crossed Brisby's face.

"What?" Trace asked, standing in front of the rear passenger door, trying to figure out how to open it without dropping Frost.

"You remembered my daughter's name."

Trace balanced the pyro-tech against the car with one arm and quickly opened the door, then awkwardly slid the wounded man feetfirst into the back seat.

"Yeah, well, let's not make a big deal about it. It's not that hard of a name to remember."

Brisby was clearly starting to feel the pain, so Trace went to the front and opened the glove compartment, searching for something to clean and stitch the wound.

Despite everything, Frost didn't stop smiling.

Tracer welcomed the silence.

Ever since she'd entered the Nix brothers' apartment a day earlier, she'd felt like she was surrounded by chaos and noise. Now, as she navigated Goldie around the increasing number of burnt-out and broken-down cars, the silence greeted her like the best friend she'd never had in real life.

Brisby was unconscious in the back, having passed out halfway through surgery. His smile hadn't lasted very long once Trace had found a small medical kit in the back of the glove compartment and started sewing. But Frost didn't scream or even cry. He just gritted his teeth and then passed out, his head clunking against the door. Trace gave the pyro-tech credit for his nerves.

The dead vehicles were growing thicker and thicker, like some insane blackened metal forest. Trace squinted as the sun rose higher in the desert sky, the heat waves more pronounced now, rising ghostlike off the sand. She was thirsty. She'd sacrificed the last of their water to keep the wound clean during surgery and to keep Brisby hydrated. And Trace was hungry, too. She couldn't remember the last time she'd eaten something.

After another long few minutes, she saw something in the distance, something hunkered and flickering.

Apex City.

Her mouth went even drier somehow. She tried licking her lips but it was pointless. They were like old sandpaper—it was painful to even try.

The road was opening up now. Someone had clearly done some work to keep the final leg to the city as clear as possible. Trace sped up and glanced back. Frost's eyes were fluttering, soft moans coming from the back of his throat.

"Brisby!"

The pyro-tech's body tensed at the shout, but his eyes remained closed. Trace sighed, tried to swallow, failed.

"Frost! Wake the hell up!" It hurt to yell, but unfortunately for Frost, the time to rest had come and gone. The mission was all that mattered now.

Brisby sat up as if he'd been electric shocked, his hair and eyes wild. He looked around through smudged glasses, uncomprehending, trying to figure out where he was, what he was doing. Finally, his vision seemed to focus, and he gripped his shoulder, grimacing.

"Ow. Jeez, that *really* hurts. Where . . . where are we?"

"We'll be at Apex in about fifteen minutes or so. I'm gonna pull over in a minute and I want you to get in front. I don't think we should show up with you sprawled out in the back seat."

"Oh. Yeah. Right."

Trace kept driving for about thirty seconds, then pulled over. She could see the walls of the city more clearly now, despite the film of dust over the windshield—hell, over *everything.*

"Come on," she muttered, low, her throat still scratchy and painful.

Without another word, Frost shakily opened the back door

and stood on the side of the road, breathing deeply, fighting back what Trace assumed were waves of pain. The pyro-tech removed his glasses, eyes closed, and turned his unseeing gaze to the bright blue sky. She looked up, too. It would have been beautiful in another context.

"Come *on*," Trace insisted, and Brisby snapped out of it, shuffling the few steps needed, opening the passenger-side door, and crumpling in, a barely audible echo of pain accompanying his rearrival in the front.

Trace peeled out as soon as the door was closed, and they sped forward, relentless now in the otherwise pristine silence.

PART 3

APEX CITY

13

Even under the harsh brightness of the sun, the city's lights stood out.

Driving down a large hill, Trace and Brisby both stared in awe. Neither of them had ever seen anything like it. President Bell rationed electricity like the precious lifeblood it was—but there didn't seem to be any such frugality here. Apex, its many buildings shorter but more spread out than those in PH City, blazed with abandon. Despite how alien it looked after a lifetime in Puente Hills, how indulgent, Trace was impressed.

Locked away behind a first wall, then their own considerable mountains of garbage, and then another wall, the city looked as if it had been built in a spiral, with several levels of buildings running along a single road up to a final, flattened level, which housed a single, large structure.

Probably where Chancellor Stewart lives, Trace mused. *Not so different from Bell after all.* In fact, the two leaders were probably more alike than the president had let on. Then why had she talked so negatively about the chancellor? Trace tried to make sense of this mission, why Bell had been in such a rush.

For the first time in a long time, probably since the last time she had seen Mackie, Trace found herself wondering how much she could really trust the president.

"No wonder they're almost out of oil," Brisby muttered as he stared at the twinkling city, pulling Trace out of her thoughts.

Trace floored it, and as they finally approached a gate, which was much fancier than the one in their home city—with the words "Apex City: Home Is Where the Plastic Is" stretched across the front—Trace reached down and once again undid the clasp on her SIG Pro. Theoretically, Apex knew they were coming. But she didn't like to take chances.

"You know they're going to frisk us, right?" Brisby asked, looking at Trace skeptically.

"Why don't you just stick to fixing your damn machines and let *me* do *my* job," Trace growled, locking back into her soldier persona, as she pulled to a halt in a cloud of sand. As it slowly dissipated, she found herself looking at a guard who had appeared seemingly out of thin air. Unlike Bell's thug at the Puente Hills gates, he wore a gray-and-maroon uniform—crisp and clean—with two white stripes on his left shoulder. Trace was even more impressed than she'd already been, which was starting to annoy her.

"What's the purpose of your visit?" the guard said, not unfriendly, but not exactly friendly either.

"I've been sent by the president of PH City to assist Chancellor Stewart." She almost added, *"and fix his broken pyrolysis machine,"* but realized that part of the mission might not be for public consumption. The last thing she wanted was to get back home and face Bell's wrath.

The guard contemplated Trace's words and then pulled a walkie-talkie from his belt, punched a few numbers into a keypad on its face, and pressed the button on its side. A harsh, garbled voice said something, and the guard whispered a response, something Trace couldn't make out. A long moment of silence followed. Brisby shifted uncomfortably next to her, from pain or awkwardness at the situation she wasn't sure. Then the garbled voice barked something else, and the guard replaced the walkie-talkie to his side.

"Okay," he said, nodding at Trace, keeping his gaze locked on hers. "You're good to go. At the next stop, you'll get your instructions."

The gate in front of them began to open—no horrible screeching noise like back home—and Trace put Goldie into Drive but kept her eyes on the guard's. Her nerves calmed somewhat as she realized he had a kind face, unlike most of the guards back in her home city.

She mirrored his nod and pulled through the gate.

Goldie rolled along a paved, well-tended road toward Apex City. Its lights glowed even brighter as they drew closer. On either side of them, mountains of garbage circled into the distance, enclosing the circular territory. Trace could see a multitude of small dark dots amid the refuse: dozens and dozens of people on the hunt for precious plastic, some alone, some in groups. She wondered if they were called *Garbage Dwellers* here, too.

"Wow," Brisby murmured. "This is *really* different."

"Yeah," Trace said. "Almost looks civilized."

"It does," Frost responded, squinting out at the scavengers in the distance. "But honestly? No matter what it looks like, everything comes down to the same thing it always has, even before the Jar Flu. People doing anything necessary to survive. No matter how glamorous they make it look."

"I don't know," Trace responded. "This place is way bigger. Way nicer. Maybe they figured it out." She thought about the kindness in that guard's face, about her growing confusion regarding Bell. "Maybe not everyone here is living in absolute fucking fear like back home."

"Maybe," Frost muttered. They continued driving. Frost shook his head as they passed a group of waving scavengers standing on a nearby pile of garbage. "It's hard to believe that people used to throw away plastic so casually before oil ran out. They were discarding their salvation the entire time and didn't even know it."

"Very poetic," Trace deadpanned.

Brisby chuckled and they regarded the seemingly endless piles of garbage on either side of the road until, at last, the next gate came into view ahead.

"Here we go," Trace said as the new set of doors opened for them as they approached. She slowed Goldie, and they rolled through the city's inner wall and into a scene unlike any they'd ever seen before.

People were everywhere, walking along a wide road that did indeed slope up and around, circling toward the apex they had seen a distance. She wondered if Stewart was watching all of this from a window up at the top, like Trace had seen President Bell do more times than she could count.

Maybe Brisby was right. Despite any surface differences, it was all the same—people were just people, with the same pride and ego, wherever you went.

A skinny man in a pristine white suit surrounded by a small phalanx of guards approached. The guards all wore the same gray-and-maroon uniform with two white stripes on the shoulder that the guy at the front gate had sported.

The man in the suit approached Goldie, but the guards held back, forming a perimeter around the vehicle. The man tapped on the window, and Trace rolled it down.

"Miss Tracer, I presume . . . ?" the man lilted.

Trace cocked her head back at hearing her own name spoken

from the thin, bloodless lips of this stranger. She didn't like to be caught off guard. An uncomfortable moment passed. She wondered how this joker kept his suit so clean in the middle of a desert.

Brisby's elbow in her ribs brought Trace's attention back to life, and she cleared her throat, still seemingly unable to produce any saliva.

"Yeah, I'm Trace. Who are you?"

A smile slid like silver onto the man's face as he held out a neatly manicured hand.

"*Fantastic* to meet you, Miss Tracer. I'm Trevor Albright. I'm what you would call Apex City's . . . welcoming committee. And we are *very* excited that you're here. I trust your trip was uneventful?"

Trace glanced over at Brisby, at the jagged circle of blood that had stained the pyro-tech's shirt.

"Yeah, sure, whatever you say, Trev."

The man visibly bristled at the sudden nickname, a strange facial tic attacking his left cheek, but he settled down quickly, smiling again.

"Well . . . yes . . . anyway, Chancellor Stewart is expecting you. If you'll just drive forward, the guards will show you the way. You'll be parking in Section 83, which will get you as close to the central hub as possible. Of course, there are always safety concerns, so there will be a bit of a walk. I hope you don't mind. It's—"

Trace smiled and rolled the window up, the tic returning to the white-suited man's face. Brisby laughed into his hand, attempting to conceal his amusement at the situation.

"And here I thought I was the only one you liked to piss off."

Following the hand signals of the stone-faced guards, Trace pulled forward, fighting a smile of her own.

Apex was a behemoth. As they got up close to the heart

of the city, they found the sheer number of lights and people staggering. Trace had been trained to keep her cool under all circumstances, but as they slowly followed the guards, who walked ahead of Goldie, keeping pedestrians out of the way, Brisby could barely keep his jaw off the floor.

"Jenna and Rachel wouldn't *believe* this," he murmured.

"Could these guys walk any slower?" Trace responded, desperate for some food and water and a bed. Those few hours of sleep in the car felt like months ago.

Finally, the phalanx approached a building, and the guards suddenly stopped, causing Trace to press down hard on the brakes. After a moment, a man with a buzz cut strode out of the structure and approached the car, his eyes locked on Tracer's. He wore the same uniform as the others but had three white stripes on his shoulder rather than two. *Boss man,* Trace thought as he stepped up to the driver's-side window.

"Please shut off the engine and step out of the car, ma'am," he ordered, his words more polite than his tone.

Trace squeezed the steering wheel so hard, her hands turned an almost bright white. She knew what came next—they were about to disarm her—but wasn't sure she could, or should, do it. She had never been more than a few feet away from her SIG Pro since she'd received it as a gift from Mackie as a kid.

A long moment passed. The man standing outside her window was completely still, almost unnaturally so.

"Trace?" Brisby's voice sounded distant, as if she were at the bottom of a hole and he was calling down to her.

Finally, Tracer nodded, more to herself than to Frost, and then shut off the engine. Hoping to throw the man outside the car off balance—another thing she'd learned in training—she suddenly opened the door and quickly stood.

She noted that the man didn't budge, didn't even flinch,

despite the fact that the door had come less than an inch from hitting him.

Okay, not bad, she admitted to herself.

Trace closed the door behind her and stood right in the guy's face, nose to nose, staring right back at him. They were about the same height, but the guy was wider, looked like the kind of person who spent every spare minute lifting weights. He stared at her with the same look she'd seen a million times in her life: a man who didn't think much of a woman, of any woman.

The man's eyes flicked toward the holster on her hip, then back up at Trace.

"We'll have to confiscate your weapon," he said in a low voice.

"I figured," she responded, slowly unholstering her gun and holding it up. He grabbed it, slightly rougher than necessary, she thought, and then handed it to the nearest guard. Despite wanting to keep her eyes on her weapon, she continued to stare directly at him. "Also? If anything happens to this car . . . a dent, even a tiny little scratch . . . I'm going to find you and we're going to have a very unpleasant conversation," she added quietly.

"I look forward to it," he said, just as quiet.

Trevor suddenly appeared, inexplicably fitting himself into the sliver of space between Trace and the man. He was smaller than both of them, so their eye contact was uninterrupted.

"I see you've met Captain Janus. He's going to escort us—"

"My friend needs immediate medical attention," Trace interrupted, looking over at Brisby, who now stood sheepishly on the other side of Goldie, his face gaunt and pale. "He was stabbed by a vagrant right before we reached Apex. Anything else we need to do can wait."

"Of . . . of course," Trevor sputtered. "Captain, please escort Mr. Frost to the infirmary while I show Ms. Tracer to her room."

"It's just Trace," she stated, then pushed past both of them and walked around the car. Brisby stared at her with huge eyes. She could see how terrified he was.

"Trace?" he said as she stepped close to him.

"It's okay, Brizz, go with them. You need to get that wound looked at by a real doctor. I'll meet up with you after and we'll complete our mission and then get the hell out of here."

"Okay," Brisby answered after a moment.

Captain Janus appeared next to Frost and wrapped his meaty fingers roughly around the pyro-tech's thin arm. Trace fought back an urge to protect Brisby, but that was ridiculous. They were here as allies. Janus might be an asshole, but he was just doing his job.

"Let's go," the captain said, pulling the smaller man away.

Frost looked back as he shuffled forward, and Trace forced a smile, hoping to reassure him. Even though she knew it wouldn't work.

And then Brisby Frost was lost from sight.

14

Trace walked slightly behind Trevor, marveling at the sheer number of people passing them.

She was suddenly aware of how dirty and bloodied she was compared to everyone she saw. In fact, pretty much anyone from PH City would look unwashed compared to the citizens of Apex, with the notable exceptions of President Bell and Gunnar. The Apexers' clothes were nicer, too, their hair styled in ways that Trace had never seen before. She also became painfully cognizant of the bruises on her face. She probably looked as deranged as the vagrant who had stabbed Brisby.

Bell had always bad-mouthed Apex, had made it sound like some kind of shithole, but the reality was very, very different. Trace didn't know what to believe anymore.

The open-skied sidewalk they traversed was wide, larger than any public area Trace had ever seen, with kiosks every several hundred feet, selling food and wares. She noted that they were walking in a slightly upward, meandering circle, heading away from where they had left Goldie and toward the upper levels of the city.

"Impressive," she grunted.

"Yes." Trevor beamed. "We take great pride in our concourse!"

A group of children stared up at Trace, slack-jawed and wide-eyed, and then burst into laughter once they'd passed. She realized that a lot of people were staring.

"No one seems very worried that your oil is running ou—"

"And this is our dance hall!" Trevor nearly shouted, grabbing Trace's arm and pulling her close while using his other hand to point at a nearby building.

"No one knows that our pyrolysis machine is broken," he hissed into her ear. "And it is *essential* that they never find out. The last thing Chancellor Stewart wants is for people to panic, for a . . . a *riot* to break out."

Trace pulled her arm away and kept walking. She had kept her voice purposefully low, but the foppish man's outsized reaction confirmed they were trying to keep their situation very, very quiet. And that it was even worse than Stewart had let on to President Bell. Or Bell had let on to her.

"I don't know . . ." she finally said. "I get the sense that your boy Janus wouldn't mind cracking some skulls."

Trevor gave her a shocked look, but Trace could sense the truth in his eyes. She smiled and took another look around. Everything really did seem so perfect, but she had been trained to see past the surface, and sure enough, she could see literal cracks in the walls' foundations, could see some faces here and there that were gaunt from hunger. Not exactly a shithole, like Bell had said, but not perfect either.

She had to admit . . . Apex City threw off a pretty damn convincing *sense* of perfection, something that her boss never bothered to attempt, but Trace was more sure than ever that the two cities were more alike than Trevor, or anyone else here, would care to admit.

As if in response to her thoughts, a young girl, face streaked with dirt, came running up to Trace and pulled at her trench coat. "Can you spare any plastic?" the girl said, eyes light brown and huge.

Trevor opened his mouth to rebuke the girl, but a glance from Trace shut him up. She knew it was probably hopeless, but she quickly patted her coat's pockets. There was nothing there, just like she knew there wouldn't be. She was about to apologize to the girl, who reminded Trace so much of her younger self, when she decided to try a little harder. She reached into one of the inside pockets of her coat, empty, then tried the other side, a last-ditch effort. To her surprise, her fingers wrapped around something. She smiled and withdrew the object, whatever it was.

A plastic fork. Cracked. Stained. But definitely worth some credits—if Frost was able to fix Apex City's machine. Trace must have put it in there during one of her repo missions—she couldn't even remember which one it had been. Which scars corresponded.

The girl's eyes went even larger as Trace held the fork out. Trevor started to reach out, saying, "By law, you can't—" but Trace slapped his hand away. There might be rules about this kind of thing in Apex, but she wasn't bound by them.

"Can I . . . ?" the girl said, barely a whisper.

"Of course," Trace said. "But keep it safe. Don't let anyone take it from you."

The girl nodded, her face hardening, a look Trace knew well from reflective surfaces in Puente Hills decades earlier, and then she sped off, the fork already hidden somewhere within her ripped and dirty clothing.

As she watched the girl disappear into the crowd, she noticed a man hidden in the shadows of a doorway. Even from this distance, even partially hidden from sight, it was impossible to miss his light-brown eyes. His messy hair. And an odd, mischievous smile.

"I'll have to report this," Trevor said, and Trace glanced at the man as he strode forward, back stiff and stringy hair flowing in his wake.

Trace glanced back at the doorway, but the man was gone.

"Good for you," she said to Trevor's receding back, following after him. And for the moment, she didn't feel quite so tired anymore.

The living quarters were small but were cleaner and more brightly lit than her apartment back in PH City, and the bed was larger than any Tracer had ever seen before. She stood in the doorway and could feel Trevor hovering behind her, could feel his hot breath curling out against the back of her neck.

"This is perfect, thank you," she said, turning around to face him.

"Once you've"—he waved a hand at her in a large circular motion—"washed up, please come back out into the hallway immediately. There will be a guard posted here, and she can bring you directly to the—"

"No," she interrupted, attempting to stay calm but feeling the violence in her voice. "I need sleep. And then food. And Brisby needs just as much time, if not more. Your chancellor and your pyro-machine and whatever else will have to wait. I'm sure you have enough oil to survive a few more hours."

"But I was told to—"

Trace took a single step backward and closed the door on his face. She could hear him still talking through the wood, but she didn't care. Her body was shutting down.

She slowly removed the trench coat and threw it in a corner, then sat down on the bed. An inadvertent sigh escaped from her lips. The mattress was as soft as it looked. The softest thing she had ever felt. Tears formed in her eyes, but she fought them back. She hadn't cried since the day Mackie died.

"You *must* be tired," she murmured to herself.

Reaching down, she shakily untied and removed her combat boots and lay back onto the bed slowly, savoring every moment.

Trace stared at the ceiling. It was painted a peculiar shade of gray, and she felt herself falling into the color, being completely encompassed by its blandness, a feeling she welcomed, and her eyes closed and her entire world drifted into darkness.

15

SIX YEARS EARLIER

I sat in my apartment, cleaning the SIG Pro.

It was possible I cleaned it far more than I needed to, but Mackie had told me to keep it in good condition, and I found that the methodical routine of the exercise calmed my nerves, particularly after missions—whether I had used the weapon or not.

I hadn't needed to fire the weapon in several weeks, but I was starting to run low on bullets. Once I finished cleaning the gun, I would head down a few floors and see how the armory was looking, if the most recent scavenge mission into what used to be Los Angeles had bolstered their supplies at all. If not, perhaps I'd request to join the next one. Bell always said no, but perhaps it would be different this time now that I was finally in my twenties.

A knock at the door pulled me out of my thoughts, and I checked the clock on the wall. Eleven o'clock at night. Who would be calling at this hour? I was almost done cleaning the gun anyway, so I reattached the slide, stood up, holstered the weapon, and headed toward the door.

As I swung it open, slightly annoyed with a surprise visitor—I was not a big fan of surprises—I was shocked to see Gunnar standing there. I couldn't remember him ever visiting my apartment before, and I had never been to his, which was two floors lower. I had always assumed we lived in similar types of accommodations, but secretly wondered if that was true or not.

"Gunnar," I said, keeping my voice flat. "What are you doing here?"

"President Bell called and told me to come get you," he responded, mirroring my tone. "She wants to see us in the training room."

I cocked an eyebrow at my adoptive brother, and I could tell by examining his face that he was just as confused as I was. Anyone else would think of his expression as a passive blank, but I'd been taught by Mackie how to read people, especially people I spent a significant amount of time with. Gunnar was almost as hard to read as President Bell, but I could see the subtle hints that something had him slightly on edge.

I nodded, then reached over and grabbed my trench coat off its hook. He turned and started walking to the elevator, and I hustled to catch up.

As Gunnar made his way down the long hallway, he slowed slightly and looked over at me. "She's never called us in like this," he said quietly.

I worked to mask my own surprise at his conversational tone. I wondered briefly if it was some kind of trick, but dismissed it. Gunnar had been trained in the exact same way I had, and he had nothing to gain by pretending to be congenial. Maybe he was letting his guard down, even slightly, because of the odd late-night request.

"Except that one time," I said, surprised by my own response. It almost felt like a surrender, in some way, speaking to him like this. "That night in the pyrolysis bay."

Gunnar sucked in a short breath and glanced over at me as the elevator came into view down the hallway. "I forgot all about that," he murmured.

It had been years earlier, when I was eleven and Gunnar was twelve. Bell had woken us up in the middle of the night and brought us down to the floor where the pyrolysis machines were held. The essential machinery was run by a skeleton crew at night, the perfect time to explain to the president's two wards how the technology worked.

I remembered being in awe of the process as the pyro-tech explained exactly how they turned the scavenged plastic back into oil, which would then power the entire city, including the machine itself. Gunnar and I had looked at each other in amazement. This was in those early days before Bell had really started pitting us against each other emotionally—creating a rift that went from competition to hatred.

I found myself missing those days, even though they'd been short-lived.

We reached the end of the hallway, and Gunnar pushed the button, both of us listening as the unseen elevator began rumbling in our direction. I tried to think of something to say, something casual or even friendly, but I felt like all those interpersonal instincts had been worn down into almost nothing after my years of training. Making small talk with my rival felt like a betrayal. But the words came out before I really had a chance to think them through.

"This elevator is terrible," I said, the words and even the sound of my voice ringing false in my ears.

Gunnar flashed the slightest smile, odd and awkward, and I realized it might have been the first time I'd seen anything other than a scowl on his face.

"It really is," he confirmed.

The elevator arrived, its doors squeaking open, and we stepped inside. Silence reasserted itself, and both of us went rigid again as we headed toward our destination.

Within minutes, we were approaching the door that led into the large training area, a space we had spent hours and hours and hours in but had never entered together. In fact, the last time I could remember being inside with Gunnar was the day Mackie had given me the SIG Pro three years earlier. I had always wondered if Bell ordered our training to be completely separate to widen the emotional distance between us. If so, it had certainly worked.

"After you," Gunnar said, holding up his hand slightly. For a second, my instincts kicked in, and I thought this might be a trap. And then common sense reasserted itself. If Gunnar, or Bell for that matter, wanted me dead, there were far easier and less complicated ways to make that happen. No, it appeared that Gunnar was simply being polite.

First time for everything, *I thought, taking hold of the knob and pushing the door open. Maybe things are finally mellowing between us.*

But those thoughts were wiped violently away as I took in the scene before me. I heard Gunnar gasp softly as he stepped into the room behind me.

Mackie was tied to a chair in the middle of the room, beaten raw, blood trickling from countless wounds on every visible spot on his body. His eyes were shut, and the floor beneath him was covered in plastic, where the liquid pooled in various abstract shapes. My hand instinctively went to my SIG Pro as I moved forward, unlatching the holster's clasp as I scanned my surroundings. I assumed Gunnar was doing the same, but he was silent, just like me.

My rattled nerves settled slightly when I saw President Bell walking out of Mackie's office, wiping her hands on a bloody rag.

"Ma'am . . . ?" I said, barely more than a whisper, my gaze moving back toward my mentor, whose eyes fluttered open at the sound of my voice. As he slowly focused on me, a sad smile crept onto his battered face.

"Hey, Trace," he croaked.

"Shut the fuck up!" Bell screamed, striding forward, and I had to keep myself from flinching at the volume and the rage in the president's voice. Gunnar stepped up and stood next to me, and the two of us watched as Bell backhanded Mackie, a fresh stream of blood shooting out of his mouth and landing on the plastic. He blinked against the pain and then made eye contact with me again, the smile diminished but still there.

I had no idea what to do, racked my brain, tried to figure out a next step.

"You two have any idea what this traitor was up to?" Bell growled, pacing behind the restrained man like a starved predator. When neither of us answered, the president shouted, "Do you?!"

"No, ma'am," we both answered, monotone, unmoving.

Bell grabbed Mackie's hair, pulled his head back so he was forced to look into her eyes. "This little shitbag was plotting to take me out. Take over. Can you believe that?! After all I've done for him."

"You killed my wife," Mackie said quietly, and I thought I saw a tear roll down the side of his face.

Wife.

I hadn't known he'd been married, and I realized I had never bothered to ask the man anything about his own life. I silently berated myself, then shunted the guilt aside. I had to focus on the situation, figure out a way to make it right, to save Mackie's life. There must have been some kind of mistake.

Bell let go of the man's hair and laughed, a deeply incongruous sound in the echoey space. "Prove it," she said calmly, as if she were making a casual request during an ordinary business transaction. Mackie spit blood but didn't say anything else, kept his eyes on the floor. I glanced over at Gunnar, but his eyes were locked on the scene playing out in front of us. I had to give him credit: He had wiped all emotion off his face, and I had no idea if he was as unsettled as I was. I worked to do the same, breathed slowly, calmed my nerves.

Just like Mackie had taught me.

"That's what I thought," Bell said, circling her prisoner and moving toward me. "Shoot him, Trace."

Mackie looked up, the smile gone now, his eyes widening slightly. He was clearly as surprised by the president's words as I was.

"Ma'am?" I said, forcing the word out, forcing strength into my voice.

"You heard me," Bell insisted. "Shoot. Him."

I unholstered the SIG Pro with a trembling hand. Took aim at my mentor's chest. A moment passed, the room silent except for Mackie's labored breathing.

"He betrayed us!" Bell screamed. "He was going to kill me, and probably both of you, too. If I hadn't been tipped off, I'd be dead right now. We all would. Do it, Tracer. That's an order!"

I flinched at the yelling in my ear and began to pull the trigger, then paused, fighting against myself, my brain screaming unintelligibly, louder even than Bell's voice.

"It's okay, Trace," Mackie said quietly, and now tears were flowing freely down his face. "It's okay."

There was what sounded like an explosion, and a hole erupted in his chest and blood exploded out, and Mackie fell back, the chair collapsing to the ground, his feet sticking into the air.

Shocked, confused, I looked over and saw smoke trailing from Gunnar's P226 MK. His eyes were filled with water, and his mouth was open slightly, as if shocked at what his own hand had just done.

"God fucking damn it!" Bell shouted, pushing past me and grabbing the gun out of Gunnar's hand. "Did I tell you to shoot him, you dumb piece of shit? No. I didn't. I told her to shoot him."

"I . . . I'm sorry, ma'am," Gunnar responded, looking at the floor.

"Bunch of imbeciles . . ." she muttered, then handed the gun back to him and turned to me. "I saw your finger tightening on

the trigger, and I'm sorry your dumbass brother took that away from you."

"That's okay," I said, forcing my voice to stay calm.

"Ugh!" Bell retorted, throwing her arms into the air. "It's not okay! That's what I'm saying. Fuck. You two both need a lot more work. Two complete badasses who are also total idiots. For fuck's sake."

She stared at both of us as we holstered our weapons, then looked at Mackie's unmoving form, still bound and sprawled out on his back.

"Get out of here. Both of you. I'll have someone else clean up this mess. But tomorrow, I want you in my office at 9 a.m. You're both going on missions for me. This whole thing has me pissed off, and I need a lot of plastic to make me feel better. There are a lot of people . . . too many people . . . who owe me. And it's time they paid the fucking piper."

"Yes, ma'am," we both said, just as synchronous and monotone as before, and headed toward the door. I couldn't bring myself to look at Gunnar, and he didn't look at me either. When we were in the hallway, I wondered if he was going to say anything, but instead, he turned and walked away toward the stairs. Whatever moment we had shared during our trip from my apartment to the training room was gone now, and I knew on some level that it would never happen again. That door had opened slightly and then been slammed shut. I watched his back recede into the shadows, then began to make my own way to the elevator.

It took every lesson Mackie had ever taught me not to absolutely break down once I was inside its claustrophobic walls.

16

Trace awoke in absolute panic, sucking down huge gulps of air.

She sat up and swung her legs over the side of the bed. It was dark in the room, darker than she remembered it being, and for a second, she couldn't remember where she was. Then it all came rushing back—President Bell, Brisby, Apex City.

She rubbed her face with her hands. Her face still hurt but nowhere near as bad as before she'd slept. Trying to clear her mind, she found the grogginess to be almost unbearable. How long had she been asleep?

She reached over and clicked on a small lamp, wincing at the sudden brightness that followed. Blinking, she looked around the room. On a nearby dresser sat folded clothing, and Trace swore. The lights. The clothes. Someone had been in the room while she'd slept. They could have easily hurt or even killed her. She hadn't even thought to see if the door locked before passing out. First leaving the gun on the floor of Goldie right before being attacked by the Nomad, and now this. This mission had thrown her completely off her game.

Letting out a frustrated breath, Trace stood and walked to the door. Sure enough, there was a button in the center of the handle. She pushed it, then swore again, promising herself she would be smarter going forward, would rely on the lessons Mackie had spent years teaching her.

She turned and took in the sparse room more carefully than when she'd first entered, noting the small bathroom to her left, then inspected the clothing, which included a white shirt and black jeans—all of it looking brand new. She picked them up and, after a moment, raised the shirt to her nose and inhaled. It smelled amazing.

She dropped the clothing back onto the dresser and headed to the bathroom. Flipping on the light switch, she saw a shower stall next to a small sink beneath a mirror and a wooden table, which held a single white towel.

She quickly made her way to the sink and turned the right handle, lowering her face as she did so. She lapped up the cold water, drinking deeply for several minutes. She wasn't sure if the water here was better than PH City's, or if she was just suffering from dehydration, but it was the most refreshing drink she had ever had.

Finally, she'd had her fill, and she shut the tap off, then stood straight and looked over at the shower. Her stomach tightened with excitement. She didn't have her own shower back in PH City. She shared one with the rest of the people on her level and hated using it. It was never clean, and the water was barely lukewarm. Tentatively, she turned the knob on the left and waited. Seconds later, steam filled the bathroom. She quickly shucked off her filthy, bloody clothes, pulled her hair out of its ponytail, and stepped into the stall.

The hot water felt unlike anything else she had ever experienced. She could literally feel her body relaxing, an odd sensation given her situation, and found herself chuckling. Apparently relaxing was another skill she'd have to practice.

She stared up into the water, ignoring the fact that it was so hot it actually hurt. Eventually, it cooled a little, and she turned, allowing the water to hit the rest of her body. There was a small bar of soap on a mini-ledge, and she washed herself slowly, enjoying the moment, the water at her feet turning brownish red and then eventually going clear again once she'd scrubbed all the muck and grime off herself. She waited for the water to turn cold, but it never did.

Finally, after her fingers were long puckered and she had washed herself multiple times, even after she was already clean, she shut off the water, standing there while the stream tapered off and droplets fell off her and down the drain.

Trace stepped out of the shower and began toweling off vigorously, almost angrily. An image of the little girl she had given the fork to suddenly appeared in her mind—how thin and desperate and hungry she had looked, huge hopeful eyes looking up at Trace.

The hot water had felt so good, but now she felt guilty about it. She didn't deserve that kind of luxury when so many people, so many Garbage Dwellers and poor people, suffered in obscurity all day, every day.

Like that little girl. Like Trace, when she was the same age.

She took the few steps to the sink and ran her hand across the now-fogged mirror, then regarded her smudged reflection. Hair wet and hanging down past her shoulders, face clean, she looked younger than she had in as long as she could remember. It was startling. She could see the traces of the child President Bell had adopted all those years ago. It made part of her want to cry.

She turned away from the mirror and exited the bathroom, flipping off the light as she did so. These Apexers didn't seem to give a shit about wasting electricity, but Trace had been conditioned to use no more than was absolutely necessary. Even the long shower she'd just taken now seemed excessive.

Shoving down those feelings, she looked at the clothes on the dresser, folded so perfectly, and then back to the floor of the bathroom, where her dirty, bloodstained outfit lay in a disheveled heap. She didn't like the idea of donning strange clothes. But she liked the idea of putting on her old attire even less.

Trace lifted the shirt off the dresser and held it up to her nose again, inhaling deeply. It had a very particular smell, a nice one, and it reminded her of the time Bell had let Trace sniff a flower that the president had somehow acquired. It was the only flower Trace had ever seen. She had no idea how Bell had gotten her hands on something so rare but was sure it had involved violence or a lot of plastic, or both.

Trace put on the new clothes, fighting back another wave of guilt.

The softness of the material was alien to her, but she acclimated quickly. She walked back into the bathroom and looked at herself. The jeans were nice, fit her style, but she had never worn white clothing before. The shirt wasn't fancy, but she liked the choice—wondered if they'd chosen white specifically to mess with her head.

Or maybe it was just what they had on hand.

Stop overthinking, she berated herself.

Realizing she was still exhausted, Trace lay back down on the bed and stared at the gray ceiling again, waiting for sleep to come. It seemed like no one was actively waiting for her at this point, and who knew how long it would be until they informed her that Brisby was all patched up and had fixed their pyrolysis machine. She should rest while she could.

But she felt wired. Painfully awake and aware, despite being so tired. And *hungry*.

This city had an almost literal kinetic energy, and she could feel it running up and down her spine. She wasn't sure what time it was, but she did know there was no way she was falling back asleep anytime soon.

She sat up, swung her feet over the side of the bed, then rose and walked back to the bathroom, grabbing her hair tie from where she'd dropped it on the floor. Then she headed over to her trench coat. Putting her hair into a ponytail and then slipping the trench coat back on made her feel more like her true self, even with the new clothes. Lacing up her combat boots made her transformation back into President Bell's top soldier complete.

She glanced at the door. Wondered if anyone was on the other side.

Regardless, it was time to go for a little walk.

17

When Trace stepped into the hallway, the young guard leaning against the wall stood up straight and then spoke, a rushed jumble of words.

"Ms. Tracer. I didn't realize you were awake. I'm supposed to report to HQ when you get up, so if you don't mind, just hold on one second while I radio in."

The young woman fumbled for the walkie-talkie on her belt, started punching numbers into the keyboard on its face, but Trace strode over and quickly placed her hand over the guard's, stopping the guard's actions.

"Wait," Trace said, not unkindly, but she realized she was giving an order, which the guard obeyed. Tracer looked down into the woman's eyes, forced a smile. Part of her just wanted to take off, figure out this maze by herself, but she was good at sizing people up immediately. She suspected this young woman would help her.

"What's your name?"

The guard blinked several times, clearly debating her next move, then lowered the radio. "Lieutenant Jones, ma'am."

"Your first name," Trace insisted.

The woman faltered, then said, "Darcy, ma'am."

"Great. Darcy. It's nice to meet you. I'm Trace. We can cut through the ma'am stuff and the lieutenant stuff. Just for now, okay?"

"Um . . ." the younger woman responded, looking up and down the hallway. They were the only ones there, and Trace noted there were no cameras either. *Good.* That asshole Janus wouldn't come storming down after her, at least not right away. "Sure," Darcy finished.

"Do you know if my friend, Brisby, the one I came here with . . . do you know if he's done . . . doing whatever it is he came here to do?"

The guard regarded Trace, both of them trying to figure out what the other one knew.

"I believe he's still working," was all Darcy said.

"Okay," Trace responded. "That's fair. Now, look, I realize that you're supposed to report in, that you have a job to do, and I respect that. But I'm starving . . . haven't eaten in a *really* long time. Can we just go grab some food real quick, and then we can come back here and you can call whoever you need to? I promise it won't take long and that I won't cause any trouble."

Darcy opened her mouth to respond and then clamped it shut. The woman was clearly having a moral crisis, but Trace decided to up the ante. "Please?" she added softly, widening her eyes slightly.

In her service to Bell, she had often found herself required to adjust her personality while seeking out people who owed the president money. Those encounters almost always ended with violence, but they always started with Trace being whoever she needed to be to get the door open.

Darcy let out a breath and then nodded, placing her hand

on her holstered gun, a seemingly unconscious gesture that Trace noted. *Smart girl.*

"Yeah. Fine. I don't think anyone would mind because they said they were going to call me when they were ready for you, if you didn't come out first. Just stay close to me and don't engage with anyone. It's rush hour out there."

With that, Darcy's face hardened back into the soldier she was, young or not, and she headed down the hallway to her right. Trace followed, slightly annoyed with herself for already liking this young woman so much.

They took several turns, Darcy perhaps unconsciously increasing her pace each time she did so, and Trace kept up. The movement felt good. Although the rest and the leisurely shower had been nice, relaxation was foreign to her core while on a mission, and she appreciated the guard's expediency.

Trace wondered if they would run into Captain Janus or Trevor Albright, which was the last thing she wanted right now. She just needed time to get some nourishment, then grab Brisby, and get the hell out of there.

Eventually, after passing what felt like an endless number of closed doors, a long hallway led them to an elevator bank. While it was similar in many ways to PH City, everything here was just nicer, cleaner.

Trace cautioned herself not to get used to it.

Assuming she was on the sixth floor based on a number stenciled on the wall, Trace watched as Darcy pushed the down button, and one of the sets of doors immediately opened, dinging its availability. They stepped in, Darcy pressed the number one, and the doors slid shut. Tinny music played while they descended—another stark difference between Apex and PH City, where elevator rides were usually marked by their silence.

After a moment, they came to a halt, and the doors slid

open. Trace and Darcy stepped out into a glass-encased room with a single door that led outside, where it was clearly nighttime despite the number of lights that illuminated the street. Dozens of people walked past soundlessly, in every direction possible, mouths moving, their faces showcasing a myriad of emotions.

Trace had never seen anything like it. She could feel Darcy looking at her but didn't glance over, wiping the surprise from her face.

To their left was an unattended desk. The overhead lights were bright but flickered once as they made their way toward the exit. Darcy didn't seem to notice. It was something most Apexers wouldn't notice, Trace surmised, but she knew it was a sign that the city's oil was slowly running out.

Stepping outside, Trace was surprised to discover how loud it was after the silence of the building's apparently soundproof foyer. Another impressive element of this strange city.

"Come on," Darcy instructed. "The best place is this way."

As Trace followed the young guard, people bumped past her: a man intent on getting wherever he was going as fast as possible, a group of rowdy teenagers, a woman holding a baby. There was nothing like this in PH City. The only outdoor area she'd experienced in her home territory was Puente Hills, which was an extremely dangerous place—and only the Garbage Dwellers and city folk desperate for plastic spent time there. Even the ground-level homes and businesses—like where she had found the Nix brothers—were considerably less than safe.

But this—a place where people meandered and socialized. It was intoxicating.

But also a mirage, she realized, noticing more lights that flickered as she glanced around. There was no way there was enough easily findable plastic in the surrounding landfill to keep this going forever. Not at the rate they were burning fuel.

Then again, she was here to help fix the problem at hand, at least temporarily, and any larger considerations were simply not her problem.

She scanned faces and buildings as they walked, memorizing all of it in case it came in handy later, until Darcy leaned closer and said, “Here,” pointing at a building with a flashing neon sign promising food and alcohol. Trace nodded and followed the woman inside.

The place was packed. Trace’s first instinct was to turn around and walk away. She didn’t have her weapon and had no idea how many people in here might be hostile to an outsider. But then she checked herself. That was ridiculous. In a place this busy, no one would care who she was or where she was from. She felt her body relax slightly, but she still swept the entire establishment with her eyes as she followed Darcy deeper inside. She noticed a flash of bright color through a group of people and realized that Trevor Albright was in the establishment as well. Hopefully, he wouldn’t notice her. He was harmless, but sometimes annoying was worse than dangerous.

They made their way around and through drunk, rowdy groups and eventually found a small table in a corner with two wooden chairs. The previous occupants’ empty glasses remained, but Darcy grabbed them and placed them on a ledge that ran along the wall behind them.

“We got lucky,” she shouted over the din. “It’s usually impossible to get a table in this place. I normally just eat at the bar, which is fine, but guys tend to think that gives them permission to hit on you. Not sure what that’s all about.”

Tracer grunted her understanding but actually had no idea what the younger woman was talking about. As President Bell’s XN, Trace found that men—or women, for that matter—never approached her socially, just saw her trench coat and regarded her at best with caution, and more often with naked fear. As far as she was aware, she had never been "hit on" in her entire life. Or maybe she had been, and had been completely unaware. She started running through previous encounters in her mind, dissecting the interactions, when an older woman approached their table, a paper pad in hand.

"Hey, Ellen!" Darcy said loudly, a big smile sliding across her face. "Busy tonight!"

"Eh, same shit," the waitress said, deep lines etched into her face. She eyeballed Trace, who gave the stare right back. "Who's this?"

"A visitor from PH City!" Darcy said, excited to share this tantalizing info, but Ellen's face remained passive.

"Great. What can I get you?"

"Beer okay?" Darcy said, and Trace raised her eyebrows in surprise. She'd heard of the drink but had never had it before. It didn't exist in PH City.

"Sure."

"Two beers, and a couple of the house sandwiches, please," Darcy finished. Ellen grunted and moved off into the crowd. The guard laughed. "That's her in a good mood, if you can believe it."

Trace found herself grinning, despite being on guard in this strange, chaotic place. It was hard not to like Lieutenant Darcy Jones. But then she forced the smile away, reminded herself not to trust Darcy.

Not to trust anyone. Just like Mackie had taught her.

18

"So, what's PH City like?"

Trace heard the question that Darcy had asked over the increasing din in the bar but took a long moment to answer. She was savoring the final bites of her sandwich, even though she wasn't entirely sure what was in it, didn't really care—it tasted *so* much better than the gruel President Bell served to her employees.

Perhaps not *literal* gruel, Trace allowed, but compared to what she was eating right now . . . ? Not much better. And she knew that people in the lower levels of PH City suffered through even worse food. It simply wasn't a priority for the president.

"It's a wonderful place to live," Trace said, and then realized she was just parroting Bell's propaganda from the radio and cursed herself for doing so. She knew it wasn't true, at least not most of the time. "I mean . . . it's fine," she admitted, putting what was left of the sandwich she had practically inhaled back down onto the metal plate. She took a swig of beer—not enjoying the taste yet, but not hating it as much as when she'd had her first sip minutes earlier. She'd taken off her trench coat when the food arrived, and it currently hung on the back of her chair. "Nothing like this. We don't—" She almost finished with *waste our oil like you do*, but instead commented, "We don't have all the amenities that you do. This place is pretty incredible."

Darcy smiled at the compliment—an affectation that was almost contagious. Trace took another bite, felt herself relax further. The sensation felt amazing, and totally bizarre.

"Yeah, I guess we have it pretty good," the younger woman said, looking around appraisingly. "I mean, this used to be a dumping ground for a city called Las Vegas. People played games there. For credits, I think . . . ? I don't know. It doesn't make a whole lot of sense. But based on what they teach us, it was apparently a lot of fun. And people came from all around the world to see the lights. Which is part of the reason Chancellor Stewart puts so much effort into keeping Apex City lit up like it is. He says it's in honor of our past. Which I think is pretty great."

Trace grunted at the sentiment. Sounded like its own version of propaganda to her. But she liked Darcy too much to get into politics. She took a big gulp of beer, then another. It was tasting better and better the more she drank it. She might even get a second one.

"You got family back in PH City?" Darcy asked, and Trace sat back, considered the question. Thought about her first set of parents out in the garbage heaps. Then Bell. And Mackie. And Gunnar.

"Not really," was all she said.

"Oh," Darcy murmured, then pressed on, clearly determined to fill the awkward silence between them. "Well, I was raised by my mom. We were super close. Just . . . you know . . . best friends from day one. My dad, whoever he was, took off right after she told him she was pregnant, so we really relied on each other. She really, really took care of me. And I tried to do the same for her. Then she got sick. She's been gone about a year. And I . . . I really miss her, you know?"

Trace found her mind turning to Mackie, his final moments. It was too much for her, so she pushed it all away, just nodded. Took another sip of beer.

"My girlfriend has made it a lot easier," Darcy continued. "She's helped me process my grief. It helps to have someone to talk to."

"I'm sure," was all Trace was able to manage.

"So . . . Puente Hills," the guard said. "That was the garbage depository for Los Angeles, right?"

Trace blinked at the question. Maybe it was the young guard talking about her loved ones, or the conversation switching back to Tracer, but she felt her defenses going back up. She didn't mind talking about the logistics of Apex City—its lights and its origins, and whatever else this likable young woman wanted to brag about—but she sensed the conversation was heading in a direction that made Trace increasingly uncomfortable.

"That's what I've been told," she responded.

"And they made movies and shows there and people traveled from all over the world to go there, too," Darcy continued, oblivious to her dinner companion's growing discomfort. "Have you ever gone to the LA ruins? I've only been to the Vegas ruins once—part of my training—but it was *very* cool. Scary. But cool."

The mention of "shows" made Trace think about Brisby, and she wondered how he was feeling, if he was already fixing the city's broken pyrolysis machine—or had already done so and was waiting for Trace to come back so he could get home to his wife and daughter. Suddenly, similar to how she'd felt after the hot shower, the food and the beer and the raucous barroom seemed excessive and indulgent, and the rest of her walls went up.

"Thank you for all of this," Trace said, her tone clipped. "But I think it's time to leave."

Darcy blinked, clearly confused. "Um. Yeah, of course. Whatever you want. Let me just get—"

At that moment, a figure pushed through a small cluster of people in front of them and made a beeline for their table.

Captain Janus.

Wearing his still-crisp uniform and sporting the same nasty look on his pinched face. A small glass of brown liquid was clutched tightly in his right hand. Tracer instinctively reached for her SIG Pro but cursed when she remembered it had been confiscated. By the very asshole who was aggressively approaching.

"Jones!" he shouted, two of his guards materializing out of what seemed like thin air and flanking him as he reached the corner where they sat. "What the *fuck*!"

"Captain!" Darcy said, abruptly standing and saluting at the same time, her knees almost knocking the table over as she did so. Trace remained seated, coolly scanning the room for potential weapons and exits. The three men were all big, clearly schooled in violence based on the way they were standing, but there were only three of them. Mackie had taught her to take on twice as many.

Still, she had come here on a mission—she couldn't afford to compromise what was expected of her by President Bell. So, she breathed slowly through her nose, told herself not to get involved, no matter what happened.

"I thought you were supposed to radio me as soon as our guest left the holding area," he growled.

Holding area? Trace thought. *Interesting.*

"I know, sir, but Tracer was famished, and I knew you would call me as soon as Mr. Frost was—"

"And are you *drinking* on the job, and doing so while *going rogue* with an important guest of the chancellor's?"

Darcy's eyes shot down to the alcohol grasped in her

commanding officer's hand, and her face contorted in confusion. "I thought we were allowed to—"

"That was your first mistake," Janus hissed, voice slurring slightly, taking a step closer and pointing a meaty finger directly into his subordinate's face. "You *didn't* think. You dumb little *bitch*."

Trace took a deep breath, leaned into what she had been trained to do when emotions threatened to take over. But then she saw the look on Darcy's face, how all her enthusiasm from moments earlier was gone, replaced by absolute fear of her imposing boss, and she felt all her carefully curated training suddenly vanish like it had never been there in the first place.

Tracer's fist hit the side of the man's face with a bone-crushing impact that made everyone standing nearby flinch, while several people in the crowd oohed collectively. The large drunk man went down in a heap, and somewhere nearby, whoever was handling the music must have noticed, too, because it abruptly cut out, the multitude of conversations dying as people slowly started to realize what was happening in the corner.

"*Fuck*," Tracer said quietly. She hadn't meant to do it. Had told herself in the past she would *never* do it, would never let pure emotion win, no matter what. But she had been called a bitch before. *So* many times. And the look on Darcy's face when Janus had said it had just been too much for Trace to bear.

To his credit, and despite clearly being extremely intoxicated, Janus was on his feet within seconds. He glared at Trace with naked hatred, and his two friends closed ranks, excited smiles curling on their cruel faces.

At that moment, the lights overhead flickered—just for a second—but Trace and Janus both looked up. No one else seemed to really notice.

Don't say it, Trace told herself. *Don't.*

"You wanna tell everyone what that means?" Trace said quietly, looking back at the stone-faced captain. "Or shall I?"

"Shut your fucking mouth," the man ordered.

"Why don't you shut it for me?" she responded, knowing she should stop, that she shouldn't even have started. It was a bad habit, her impulsiveness. One that often worked in her favor.

Not tonight though, she surmised.

"You've made a huge mistake, girl," he said, nothing more than a harsh whisper. "Under Apex City law, I'm not allowed to strike a guest of the chancellor—unless they hit me first."

"Then what are you waiting for, old man?" Trace challenged, keeping her eyes directly on his.

Darcy took a half step between them, raising her arms in clear desperation. "Please, don't. I can just take her back to her quarters and you can write me up, even report me directly to Chancellor Stewart. You don't have to—"

With a growl, Janus shoved Darcy into the wall with one arm and threw a punch with the other. It was an impressive move, on some level, one full of considerable strength, but a terrible way to start a fight, as far as Trace was concerned. In that moment, his concentration was split between two objectives, and she used it to her full advantage.

Blocking his sloppy punch with her left forearm, she threw out a lightning-fast uppercut that connected with the big man's chin, effecting another nasty crack and causing Janus to fall back into one of his two friends, who then fell back into a group of people at the bar. Their drinks went flying, and Trace watched as one of them splashed into the shocked-looking face of Trevor Albright, who had been grinning maniacally only seconds earlier. The yellow liquid oozed down and stained his once-pristine suit. She fought back her own smile at his outraged look.

As the two men attempted to untangle themselves from

each other on the floor, the third tried to grab at Tracer. But he was even slower than his boss, so she simply stepped inside his clumsy grasp and rewarded him with a headbutt that instantly shattered his nose. He fell to the ground screaming.

Stepping back, taking in the entire situation and her surroundings in an instant, Tracer noticed several things:

Darcy had slipped away. Trace figured she was calling for backup, but it didn't matter.

The music had started up again, louder than before, as had a series of pulsing lights, adding to the frenetic energy already suffusing the bar.

The crowd had gotten a taste of bloodlust and was pushing in, waiting excitedly and desperate to see what would happen next.

Tracer's opponents were all on the floor, but she knew it was only a matter of seconds before they regrouped and attacked again—and perhaps with more organization this time since they now knew they weren't dealing with an amateur.

And finally, there were multiple streaks of blood on her new shirt.

This is why I don't wear white, she thought.

As Trace clenched her fists and glanced quickly around, she realized there was no quick or easy way out of the corner, so she readied herself to take on Janus and his goons for a second round. But as the growing crowd continued to close in, she suddenly felt a hand wrap around her upper arm and heard a voice whisper in her ear, "Come with me. I can get you out of here."

She assumed it was Darcy, but when Trace looked, she found herself looking into the face of the man she'd seen in the doorway back in the concourse. The one with light-brown eyes and messy hair. And that same inscrutable smile.

"I'm a friend of Darcy's," he added as the noise in the room grew even louder. "Come on. Now or never."

Out of the corner of her eye, Trace could see the three men gathering themselves, beginning to push through the increasing crush of drunken people. While she loved a good fight, she knew this conflict could very well compromise her mission.

And the mission always came first.

"Fine," she conceded, grabbing her trench coat off the nearby chair. "Let's go."

Trace followed the man through a side door and out into a dark alleyway.

The increasing noise of the crowd and the music died away instantly as the door shut with a loud clank behind her. She blinked rapidly in the sudden darkness after the bright lights of the bar, trying to clear her senses. Darcy had warned her at the outset the beer in that particular establishment was strong, which Trace had waved off, explaining the strength of Old Joe's moonshine. But she had apparently been a little overconfident and now found her senses swimming from the unexpected combination of alcohol and adrenaline.

"Come on," the man said, throwing her that lopsided smile again, and walked deeper into the alley. Without looking back, he reached into the air and hoisted himself up onto a ladder that hung several feet above their heads. He began climbing into the night's undulating shadows.

Trace watched him go, amused. This man was crazy if he thought she was going to blindly follow him into what could easily be a trap.

But . . . then again . . . there was something about him, about that stupid smile, that intrigued her. Plus, he was smaller than her, and she suspected that if he had wanted her dead, she'd be on her way to a shallow ditch out in the garbage heaps by now. Plus, he had name-dropped Darcy, which made Trace feel slightly better about the situation. Maybe the young guard was waiting wherever this man was leading. After all, Trace had started the fight, no matter how much it may have been justified, so she owed it to Darcy to try to make things right again.

Sighing and shrugging on her trench coat, Trace made her way down the alley and climbed up after her mysterious benefactor, who was now only a splotch of darkness against the roiling night sky.

When she reached the top of the ladder and climbed to the other side, Trace found herself on a large ledge. Across the cracked pavement, the man stood, holding open a door and waiting patiently for his guest to catch up. As Tracer approached, he started to move into the building, but she grabbed his upper arm, a mirror of his own action in the bar a few minutes earlier. He looked down at her fingers, then back up at her face, still showcasing that annoying smile.

"Yes . . . ?" he asked.

"Your name. I don't follow complete strangers to unknown locations. Ever. It's an occupational hazard."

"Fair," he said. "My name is Ezra. And yours is Tracer. But you prefer Trace. Now follow me. Please. I think you're gonna want to see this."

Ezra pulled his arm from her grasp, which she allowed, and he headed inside, toward a nearby elevator bank with blue tape crisscrossed in front of it. He hit a button, the doors opened, and he nimbly stepped through the tape and into the waiting car.

Confused but also kind of amused, Trace watched, contemplating her next move. In the few seconds since he'd introduced himself, she had read his body language, sized him up, and she knew he was no threat. This was someone who obviously didn't know how to fight, how to handle himself in conflict. There was no question in her mind about that. Plus, she had nowhere else to go, other than the room to which she had been assigned.

The holding area.

And she figured Janus—and probably his goons—would probably be waiting there for her anyway. She literally had nothing to lose by following Ezra wherever he was attempting to lead her.

Trace entered the building, bypassed the tape the same way he had, and then entered the elevator, leaning against the wall like this was just a day like any other. Ezra stared at her appreciatively.

"Well? What are you waiting for?" she said, allowing the slightest smile to appear on her own face. "Let's go."

19

Tracer couldn't believe her eyes.

In the distance, the desert unfolded into complete darkness, flanked by the purple-black sky overhead like a pinpricked ceiling. The seemingly endless lights shone up from below, on all sides of where she stood, and just past the first wall, she saw the ring of garbage that encircled the entire city. Seen from this angle, the amount was breathtaking, dwarfing the mountains of Puente Hills, probably hiding tons and tons of hidden plastic treasure despite how much had already clearly been plundered. And beyond the second wall, through which she and Brisby had driven who knew how many hours earlier, the desert began and then extended out into what seemed like infinity. There was something unsettling and yet peaceful about her inability to find the line where the desert ended and the dark sky began.

"Pretty amazing, isn't it?"

Ezra stood next to her but seemed to intentionally give her enough space so she wouldn't feel uncomfortable. Part of her wanted to answer his question, but it was a small part, and she felt those carefully curated walls go up again as she turned slightly to face him.

"Where's Darcy?"

"I'm not sure. But you're safe here. You can figure out your next move. There's no way Janus and his goons would ever look up here. Most people think that elevator's been out of service for months. I may have been the one to start that rumor." Again with that little smirk.

"Who are you?" Trace asked, and then preemptively interrupted him as he opened his mouth to speak. "And don't say Ezra. I already know that part."

He nodded and sat down on a nearby ledge that jutted out near the door leading to the elevator. There was more than enough space for Trace to sit as well, but she resisted the urge. She wanted answers.

"Well, I'm not a city guard, but I'm sure you've figured that out by now. Still, I do work with some of the guards now and then, if they're looking to do something outside the parameters of their job. Hell, I'll work with anyone who's got credits to spare. Running errands, tracking down information, getting my hands on sought-after pieces of plastic, even when those pieces are already spoken for. It's not very glamorous, but I'm very, *very* good at it."

Trace was taken aback by how similar the job description was to her own but kept her face blank. She wasn't going to give this guy anything if she didn't have to.

"Okay," she said. "That's all well and good. But why did you help me? And why were you staring at me when I first got here, back on the concourse?"

Ezra sat back against the brick wall and raised one foot onto the ledge, wrapping his arms around his leg. He smiled again. "I'm not going to lie to you, Trace. News of your arrival spread like wildfire. You're the first person to ever visit us from PH City. The chancellor had to work very hard to . . . *convince* people not to seek you out or bother you. And Janus had fun making sure that everyone listened to the chancellor." He placed a fist into his other hand, indicating the violence that apparently preceded her visit. "Maybe a little too much fun."

Trace took in this information. It made sense, but it still surprised her.

"And yet . . . despite all that, you still took a chance to get a look at me right when I arrived. And then brought me here. Right from under the captain's nose."

Ezra shrugged. "What can I say? I like to take chances."

She laughed, and then stopped herself, surprised. She couldn't remember the last time someone had made her laugh. In fact, had anyone *ever* made her laugh like that? She wasn't quite sure. But there was something about this man—about the casual manner in which he spoke to her, the way he looked at her when *she* was speaking—Tracer had never met anyone quite like him.

And the realization made her uneasy.

She stepped back toward the edge of the roof and looked down at the city far below, at its sparkling lights and tiny people as they made their way from one building to another despite the late hour. The height was dizzying, and she found herself experiencing what must have been vertigo. She'd heard of the sensation but had never felt it while looking out the windows of PH City, even on its upper floors. Protected by metal and glass, there was no sense of how far Puente Hills was below, of how deadly a fall from that height would be.

It was a terrifying feeling, and an exhilarating one.

"It's so . . . *different* here," she said, barely more than a whisper.

"I can only imagine," Ezra responded after a moment, still

seated across the roof. Trace was somewhat surprised he had even heard her over the din of the night. She suspected there was a lot more to this man than he was letting on. "How so?" She turned to look at him, took a few steps closer. He didn't move—just kept his eyes locked on hers. "If you don't mind telling me," he added. Trace took a deep breath, looked around the roof. It was clear they were the only ones up there and that no one could step out of the allegedly broken elevator without her being aware of their arrival. She was safe. And she felt her body physically relax at the realization.

Tracer walked the rest of the way across the rooftop and sat down next to Ezra, leaving a few feet between them. She kept her eyes locked on his the entire time. There was something . . . comforting about them—about the light shade of brown she had never seen before, about the way they were inquiring without being aggressive.

She had no idea what was happening, felt like she was betraying all her instincts, all of Mackie's training, but she spoke anyway.

"There are so many differences," she said softly. "But I think the garbage is the biggest difference. I . . . I *grew up* in it, and even when you've *made* it, when you're safe from the trash in the security of PH City, it's never very far away. You look out the windows and there it is. Or if you have a job to do outside the city itself—which is really just a single building, not like this, even if it is a *huge* building—there's not much distance before you hit the piles of garbage. A ring of smaller buildings . . . where people work or live . . . a big road beyond that. And then the trash begins. And it's just endless. Oppressive. Or at least it feels that way."

"You grew up in the garbage?" he said, and she flinched, her defenses working their way up again, but she realized that the question was tinged with curiosity, not judgment.

"I'm guessing by your question that people don't do that here," she replied, not answering the question, keeping her voice level.

"I mean . . ." he said, stammering slightly, probably realizing she was uncomfortable, "some people do, out of their own choice, really, but it's not a regular thing. Don't get me wrong, lots and lots of people work out there, digging for plastic. Day and night. But the majority of the citizens live within the city limits. But not everyone has a lot of credits or even a place to live. In fact, I didn't exactly have the most . . . *normal* childhood either."

"No?" she said, glad to no longer be talking about herself.

"I didn't grow up in the trash heaps—not that I would ever judge anyone who had," he quickly added, holding up his palms in supplication. "But my family was poor. *Very* poor. At first, when I was young, they tried really hard to be plastic scavengers. We'd leave early in the morning, even before the sun came up, and head out to the in-between—"

"The in-between . . . ?" Trace echoed.

"Sorry. It's what we Apexers call the area between the two walls. Where all the garbage is . . . and thus all the plastic."

"Understood," she responded. "Please, continue."

"*Anyway,*" Ezra continued, pretending to be annoyed by the interruption, "I spent a lot of time in the in-between. A *lot* of time. At first, I tried finding plastic, but I was as bad at it as my parents were. It didn't help that there was so much competition. The other kids were merciless. And I'm not exactly the biggest of individuals. So, I gave up on that pretty quick. And yeah, maybe I wasn't the tallest or the strongest kid out in the in-between . . . but I was the fastest, by *far*, and I was the best climber."

"So you climbed over the outer wall," Trace guessed.

"So I climbed over the outer wall," Ezra confirmed. "The first time was basically an accident. I was trying to get away from a bunch of scavenger kids who were pissed off because

I'd stolen a plastic bottle from them. I was surprised how easy it was to scale the wall, and there was no way those kids could follow me. First off, they could *never* get over that wall. Second, they were a bunch of cowards."

"I'll bet," Trace said, smiling slightly. She was confused by how comfortable she felt around this stranger.

"I'm nothing if not brave, Ms. Tracer," he said, returning her smile. "And that was the first of many, many, *many* trips outside of Apex City. All on foot, all by myself. Eventually, of course, my parents gave up on scavenging, but not before I had become very familiar with the desert, had all kinds of adventures, and spent more than one night learning how to build a fire and sleep under the stars. Which is basically the best way possible to spend a night. Have you ever done it?"

Trace considered the question. She grew up amid the garbage piles of Puente Hills, but she had no memories of ever spending a night around a fire, looking up at the stars. It was the kind of thing she would remember.

"No," she said.

"Well, it's amazing," Ezra murmured. "You should try it sometime."

"Unlikely," Trace responded. "Okay, so your family eventually gave up on scavenging. Which I get. It's not easy. What happened next?"

"Next? Well, my parents didn't really have any skills that they could barter. So, they would head out into the city . . . all day, and all night honestly, trying to scrape enough to keep the three of us from starving, however possible. And at that point, I was old enough to know that I was fucked if I depended on them to survive. I had realized out in the in-between that I was good at stealing. And I mean, *really* good at it. My parents were disappointed in me when they found out what I was doing, but that didn't stop them from taking what I gave them. Funny how morals slip away when you're starving."

Ezra suddenly stood up and walked toward the edge of the roof.

"I didn't want to spend my life digging through garbage for a few credits' worth of plastic here and there," he said quietly. "Or doing manual labor for a handful of food or credits here and there. I dreamed of doing something bigger. Something better. But when it comes right down to it, I'm just a common street rat, I guess."

Tracer took in his dark silhouette against the lights of the city. She could tell from his body language that he was upset—it was clear that despite all his words, his jokes, he didn't enjoy talking about his past either. She rose and walked over, stood next to him at the edge of the roof. They stared down into the lights for a long moment, the incessant sounds distant and tinny.

"Another difference between PH and Apex is the people," Trace finally said.

"Oh yeah? How so? We're way more annoying?"

She laughed again and let herself do it this time. It felt good. Better than she ever would have expected. "No, the opposite, actually," she admitted, turning her head to look at his face. "Everyone seems very kind . . . other than Captain Janus, of course. Even that fop Trevor Albright seems generally harmless."

Ezra's face clouded over for a second, and he glanced down at the ground.

"I'm sorry," she said, confused. "Did I say something wrong?"

He looked up, and the mischievous smile returned to his face, the momentary darkness fading away almost instantaneously. "No. Not at all. Not everyone in this city is as nice as they seem . . . but overall, everyone here would bend over backward to help you. I mean . . ." He swept his hand over the city as if he had built it himself. "It's hard to be an awful person when you live in a place this beautiful." Trace inhaled a deep breath and exhaled it slowly. Apex City really was a technological marvel.

As if in response, dozens of nearby lights flickered, went out, and then quickly came back on. Trace glanced over at Ezra, who looked at her at the exact same moment.

"Nothing is ever exactly what it seems though," he said.

She stepped closer to him, feeling the heat coming off his skin. She realized her fingers were trembling—which was ridiculous. She wasn't in danger.

"What do you mean by that?"

"I know why you're here," he whispered.

"Why am I here?" Her words were just as quiet as his.

"To save the city."

Their faces were inches apart now. Tracer was confused, deeply, but also felt a strange calmness washing over her. She had been in more life-and-death struggles than she could remember, and had felt this kind of calm before: when she gave in to her primal instincts and allowed her truest nature to take control. It had saved her life countless times. But why, this time, was there also a layer of fear lurking just below the usual sheen of calm?

"Which everyone appreciates," Ezra continued, turning back to look at the lights. "Even if they don't know it."

Trace swallowed, shook her head, took a few steps away from the edge of the roof. What the hell had just happened?

After a moment, she looked over at Ezra, who was already looking back at her, a sad look in his eyes.

"It's late," he said. "And I know you have a job to do. Let's get you back to your room."

20

To Tracer's surprise, Darcy was waiting outside the door to Trace's room—but she wasn't alone.

The young woman stood talking in low tones to another guard as PH City's XN approached.

Ezra had shown Tracer back to her building as dawn rose in the distance, saying his goodbye at the front door. He said he was tired, that he had a lot to do the coming day. Their conversation after leaving the rooftop had been limited, a few words here and there as they made their way through the thinning crowds—a marked change after their previous exchange. Trace felt her usual stoic personality reasserting itself and even silently berated herself for revealing more than she should have.

That won't happen again, she thought as she approached her quarters and took in the two guards in front of it.

"Trace!" Darcy nearly shouted, pulling away from the other guard, a man who somehow looked even younger than his counterpart. The sound of her voice echoed in the otherwise empty hallway, and Trace stopped in front of them, an awkward moment of silence playing out.

"Um . . . Nick, can you give us a minute?" Darcy said, flicking her eyes toward the other guard, then at Tracer, then back again.

The man shifted uneasily, looked up and down the hall. Trace could see him battling internally against his orders and his obvious crush on Darcy, and almost felt bad for him. But ultimately his feelings triumphed over duty, and he nodded and walked away, turning a corner, the sound of his footfalls diminishing and then fading completely.

Darcy looked at Tracer's face, clearly had trouble getting any kind of answer there, and then whispered, "Are you okay?"

"I'm fine," Trace responded, wishing she could shove past this Apex City guard and go back into the room—get some peace and quiet before they came to collect her and let her go home.

But no, she liked Darcy. She forced herself to relax. To act like a human.

"You?" Trace asked. "I figured Janus would have thrown you in jail or something after what happened."

"Yeah, I'm . . . fine. I'll probably get written up . . . maybe even demoted. Who knows? But he has a tendency to forget about the things he does to people . . . sometimes *horrible* things . . . when he's drunk."

"Lovely," Trace said quietly.

"But what happened?" Darcy asked, eyes running across Trace. "The last I saw, you were fighting Janus and Tobias and Franklin—kicking their asses, to be honest—and then I got swept up by the crowd for a minute, and by the time I got back, you were gone. Ellen told me that you rushed out of there with some guy . . . ?"

Trace cocked her head. Something wasn't right here, and she thought back to that look in Ezra's eyes on the roof. She took a deep breath, let it out through her nose.

"Your friend helped me. Ezra."

Darcy blinked several times. "Ezra? I don't know anyone named Ezra."

"*Fuck*," Trace whispered, berating herself yet again. What had the thief—if that's even what he was—been after? Why lie about knowing Darcy? *To get you to leave with him, idiot*, her mind responded. It was so obvious. But he hadn't tried to hurt her . . . hadn't asked for anything at all, when it came right down to it. None of it made any sense.

"Never mind," Trace said, taking a step closer to the door. "It doesn't matter. Like I said, I'm fine. And I'm sorry I started that fight. I just didn't like the way that Janus was talking to you."

"*Why* are you apologizing?!" Darcy said, voice suddenly loud, stepping closer to the door, too, keeping her eyes locked on Tracer's. "That was the greatest thing I've ever seen. Janus has been bullying everyone for . . . *forever*! And not just the people in his command. Citizens. And especially plastic scavengers. He's *ruthless* with them. *Everyone* hates him, but they're just too scared to do anything about it. And then *you* just . . . you just *fuck* him up. In front of the entire bar. It was glorious, Trace."

"Well, I wasn't trying to be *glorious*. But I also wasn't going to let him treat you like that. Not on my watch."

"No matter what you meant, or why you did it . . . thank you," Darcy said, an appreciative smile on her face. Trace wasn't sure, but it almost looked like the younger woman's eyes were watering. All of it made Trace very, very uncomfortable. She glanced at the door, wanting to go inside and decompress, but Darcy didn't take the hint.

"I want to return the favor," the guard said, reaching down and rummaging in one of her uniform's many pockets.

"No, seriously, Darcy, it's okay, you don't have to—"

But Trace stopped talking when she saw what the other woman had withdrawn. It was a walkie-talkie, similar to the ones all the Apex City guards carried but smaller—the kind of item that was easy to hide in a fold of clothing.

"I want you to have this. It's an older model . . . the first one I got when I was hired . . . but it still works."

"I don't know what to say," Trace confessed. "You don't have to do this."

"I know I don't," Darcy responded, her voice hard, and Tracer loved to hear it. It was the kind of strength this younger woman would need to survive the Captain Januses of the world. "But it's important to me that you take it. I mean, you probably won't even need it. But just in case you do, you can call me on this *anytime* you need to. Just punch in my personal call number—130503—and I'll come running, day or night. It'll only work within Apex City, and I know you're leaving soon, but if anything happens and you need me . . . well, now you know how to make that happen."

Darcy held out the radio, and after a moment, Tracer took hold of it and looked at it appreciatively. She had never really had a friend before, other than maybe Old Joe, but even that wasn't a whole lot more than a transactional relationship. Whatever she had with Darcy, which was something she would never, ever be able to put into words, felt deep and real, and she was surprised by how much the relationship already meant to her.

"Thank you," was all she managed to say. Darcy nodded, and Trace put the walkie-talkie into the inside pocket of her trench coat.

"Anyway, I'll let you be," the guard said, taking a step away. "I'm not even supposed to be here. Luckily, Nick is an old friend and will keep his mouth shut. But like I said, Janus will probably forget I was even at the bar tonight. I'll report to duty tomorrow and it'll be like nothing happened."

"I hope so," Trace said.

Darcy winked at her, making her somehow look even younger than she was. They both turned at the sound of someone walking down the hallway toward them. It was the guard who had left minutes earlier, and he had a grim look on his face.

"What's up, Nick?"

He stopped in front of them and cleared his throat, his posture entirely more rigid than when he'd been standing in the exact same spot moments ago.

"I've been instructed to escort Ms. Tracer to Chancellor Stewart's office. Apparently, Mr. Frost has completed his work."

His tone was clipped and to the point, and he didn't look either woman in the eye.

"Do you . . . do you need to get anything from inside the room before you head over?" Darcy asked.

Trace thought about her soiled clothes on the other side of the door. Other than that, there was nothing else of hers inside, and she wasn't exactly desperate to get her hands on them again.

"No," she replied, voice low. "I'm good. Let's do this."

Darcy hesitated and then took a step closer to Trace. "In case I don't see you again . . . it was great to meet you. Thanks for . . . just, thanks."

Trace nodded. She wanted to say a lot of things, but didn't know how to get the words out, and was painfully aware of Nick's eyes on them.

"You're welcome," was all she managed, and then she gently pushed past the younger woman and followed the other guard down the hallway and toward whatever came next.

21

The elevator ride felt interminable.

Standing next to Tracer, Nick showed no emotion, but she noticed that he kept his hand on top of his sidearm the entire time—and knew she would have done the same in his position. She was sure that word of her violent interaction with Janus had spread around the city, and this young guard wasn't taking any chances.

At length, the elevator shuddered to a stop, and the doors slid open, revealing yet another hallway—one that looked almost like every other hallway she'd seen in this city. Back in PH, every corner of every floor looked different, like it had been cobbled together with whatever resources had been on hand at the time—which is exactly how it had happened, at least according to President Bell.

"After you," Nick ordered, his face still stony. Trace moved forward, not loving having an armed guard behind her, but she didn't have much choice at this point.

She reached a single door at the end of the hall and waited as Nick reached around her and held a card up against a security panel. It beeped, and after another moment, the door clicked.

"Go ahead," he instructed.

Trace opened the door and entered a huge, brightly lit room. She realized after a moment of blinking against the brilliance that most of it was coming from an array of differently sized windows. At first, the sheer number and random shapes of the windows seemed odd and off-putting, but as Trace took the entire room in, she realized there was a symmetry to it, that it had been planned and constructed very carefully. Another difference from the extremely basic design of her home city.

The early-morning sunlight cascaded in, reflecting off every surface, making the room feel almost like a desert mirage.

As Trace's vision settled, she realized there were multiple people on the other side of the room—sitting on several different chairs and couches. A half-dozen guards were stationed throughout the room, blending into the surroundings as much as possible, with large guns resting across their forearms. Unoccupied desks and tables were scattered throughout the room, a smaller hallway led to a darkened doorway up and to the right, and a bar had been built along the wall to Trace's left. As she quickly took in her surroundings and memorized as much as she could, she surmised that this was Chancellor Stewart's office—the kind of opulence that made Bell's seem miserly in comparison.

"Ms. Tracer!" a voice shouted, and a man rose from one of the couches, striding toward her quickly. He was tall, one of the tallest people Trace had ever seen in her life, and older than she had expected, with long graying hair, and his huge strides brought him close to her more quickly than made her comfortable. She forced herself to remain calm. She was a guest; she wasn't in danger.

At least that's what she kept trying to tell herself.

The man stuck out his large hand, and Trace took it. He shook vigorously, a big smile plastered onto his face.

"It is *so* great to meet you," he said, looking down at her with what seemed like admiration. "I've heard a lot about you. I'm Chancellor Stewart. But please, call me Frank."

"It's very nice to meet you, too . . . Frank," Tracer said, forcing the final word out of her mouth. She'd been raised by Bell to be polite to a fault. Still, she figured it would be ruder to ignore his request.

Trace noticed that the other people behind the chancellor had stood up and were now approaching as well. She recognized two of the other four.

The first was Captain Janus, who looked at Tracer with unadulterated hatred. She could see a large red-and-black bruise creeping up onto his chin—the exact spot where she'd landed the uppercut the night before.

And the second was Brisby Frost. She fought back a huge smile at seeing her traveling companion and instead took in his appearance. His arm was in a sling, and he looked pale and exhausted—but she probably appeared the same. But when she made eye contact with him, he nervously pushed his glasses up his nose, blinking rapidly, and Trace immediately knew that something was very, very wrong.

She recognized panic when she saw it.

Trace cocked her head in a silent question, and he responded only by shaking his head, barely perceptible—but she knew exactly what he was trying to communicate.

Something bad is going down.

Fuck. She felt her entire body tense up but tried to keep her outward appearance completely unchanged.

"I believe you know Captain Janus," Stewart was saying,

clapping his officer on the back and gently forcing him forward. "And I know the two of you had a little . . . incident last night. Which happens. I myself used to get into a bit of trouble when I was a younger man."

He laughed, not an entirely unpleasant sound, but it rang discordantly in Trace's ears as she engaged in a death stare with Janus. Despite the chancellor's words, it was clear that neither she nor the captain considered what had happened a "little incident."

"Go ahead, shake and make up," Stewart ordered.

The air in the room seemed to fill suddenly with an electric charge. Trace noticed the two strangers' eyes go wide while Janus began working his jaw, his rage bubbling just below the surface.

Knowing it would make the man even angrier, Trace forced a smile onto her face and stuck out her hand. "Of course. It was nothing. Just a bit of fun."

Considering she had kicked the shit out of Janus and his two friends, it had absolutely been a lot of fun for her.

The captain hesitated for a moment, but then the chancellor cleared his throat, apparently getting annoyed at his top officer, so Janus reached out, briefly shook, and then pulled his hand away as if he'd been forced to handle a dead animal.

As Stewart introduced the two other men—the top two officials in his cabinet—Trace eyeballed the guards, who stared right back at her, tightening their grips on the weapons. They were clearly taking no chances when it came to the safety of their city's leader.

Trace turned her attention back to the chancellor.

"And of course, this young man needs no introduction!" Frank nearly shouted, clapping Brisby hard on the back. The pyro-tech winced at the contact but kept his mouth shut. "He is nothing short of a miracle worker!" the chancellor continued.

"He knew exactly how to get our machine humming again. And not a moment too soon!"

"I'm . . . glad to hear that," Trace said, trying to figure out how to get more information out of Brisby. He was currently looking down at the floor, and his face had gone even more ashen.

"I just figured you'd want to say goodbye to him before you headed back. And of course to finish the trade."

Trace heard the words but felt herself stiffen as she tried to process them.

Goodbye.

Trade.

"What the *fuck* are you talking about?" she said in a low voice, almost a growl.

By the time she realized she shouldn't have said that, it was already too late—the words had come spilling out in a tumble of anger. She'd lost control. *Again.* Just like in the bar. It went against everything Mackie had taught her, but something had shifted in her over the last day, something she didn't fully understand.

A slick smile spread across Janus's face—as if he had hoped this was coming, as if he *knew* it was—and the guards all took a step or two in her direction, the guns slowly being brought to bear.

"What did you just say to me?" the chancellor asked in a hushed tone, a look of absolute confusion crossing his face.

Trace breathed slowly, calling on Mackie's training to calm the blood that was pounding in her ears. She didn't have her SIG Pro, and she couldn't fistfight her way through a hail of bullets.

"I'm . . . sorry," she replied, slowly raising her hands, attempting to lower the temperature in the room. "You just caught me off guard. I'm afraid I don't know what you're talking about.

I thought Mr. Frost and I were heading back to PH City now."

Chancellor Stewart huffed his amused indignation and shook his head. "Seriously? President Bell didn't tell you? That woman is a mystery wrapped in an enigma. I hope I get to meet her someday!"

Trace tried to make eye contact with Brisby again, but the man wouldn't look at her, and she could see that he was shaking.

"Go ahead," Stewart said, nudging Frost with his elbow. "Tell her."

"I am honored to remain in Apex City and become their lead pyro-tech," he said robotically, the words clearly memorized.

"But . . ." Trace began, trying to figure a way out of this situation.

"But *what*?" Janus demanded, stepping forward, goading her into doing something stupid. "Is there a problem?" She knew the unspoken part of his comment was *Please let there be a problem*.

"Nothing," she finally said, knowing there was nothing else she could do. At least not right now. "And what's this about a trade?" she continued, almost spitting the words out. She could see how much Janus was enjoying the moment, and compared to Brisby's defeated posture, it was killing her.

"Bring him out!" the chancellor shouted.

Everyone turned to look as someone entered the room through the side door, out of the dense shadows. Tracer, who had spent her life learning how to rein in her emotions, fought hard not to literally gasp.

It was Ezra.

His smirk, which seemed almost omnipresent when she'd last seen him, was long gone. Instead, he stared at the floor as he moved toward them, stopping once he was inside the circle of guards, his hands clasped in front of him.

"I don't understand," Trace admitted, looking back at Stewart.

"You don't need to," the chancellor responded, any pretense of civility now gone. Janus beamed, loving every second of Tracer's discomfort. "And with that, our business is done here. Have a very nice life, Ms. Tracer. I don't expect we'll ever be seeing each other again."

Stewart turned to leave, nodding at Janus as he did so. The captain went to grab Brisby, but the wiry pyro-tech slipped through the man's grasp and nearly fell into Tracer, who wrapped her arms around him—primarily so the two of them wouldn't go tumbling to the ground.

"Please," he hissed into her ear. "Please take care of Rachel."

Before Trace could even respond, several guards grabbed Frost and dragged him away. He didn't fight, and he didn't look back, but Tracer could see tears running down his face as he was pulled down the hallway and into the room from which Ezra had just appeared.

Tracer's mind raced, and she ran through options, wondering if it was feasible for her to attack the men and women in the room, attempt an immediate rescue. But no. She knew it was ridiculous. She was completely at the mercy of whatever the hell was happening here. She shot a nasty look toward Ezra, but he still had his eyes locked on the polished wooden floor.

"Time for you to leave, *Ms.* Tracer," Janus insisted, grabbing Ezra by the arm. "And take this street garbage with you."

Trace squared up in front of Apex City's captain, even though she knew that multiple weapons were trained on her. Still, she looked directly into the large man's eyes. He stared back, silently daring her to make a move.

"This isn't over," she said quietly.

"Oh, but it is," he replied immediately. "Time to go crawling home with your tail between your legs. You PH City trash."

It took everything in her power not to throw a punch, but she didn't give in, simply turned and headed back toward the door through which she'd entered. She heard Janus and Ezra following, but it was a distant sound, her mind filled with the white noise of violence and regret.

22

Tracer and Ezra were roughly escorted down the city's spiral and toward the front gate.

It was midday at this point, and the citizens of Apex City took great interest in the bizarre procession—Captain Janus and several armed guards escorting a foreigner and a criminal through the streets. Despite the fury raging behind her eyes, Trace kept her gaze focused on the ground in front of her, cycling through options—which were limited.

Any immediate attack on Janus or his troops was pointless. She was unarmed and barely knew the city. She also had no idea where they were holding Brisby, or exactly what deal had been struck between Stewart and Bell. For all she knew, her life had been a bargaining chip as well—there was nothing to say that Janus wouldn't put a bullet behind her ear if she caused too much trouble. She was far too familiar with how President Bell operated—the woman cared about people, but only in terms of how their existence benefited her. As soon as someone became a liability, that person no longer needed to breathe oxygen, as far as Bell was concerned. Just look at what happened to Mackie.

Yes, Trace was the president's "daughter," but she knew deep in her heart that she was more slave than progeny—even if she had always avoided thinking of their relationship like that.

Trace had *no* options at this point. Her next steps had been carefully plotted by her mother—her boss—and Tracer had to go through the motions in order to save her own life, and Brisby's, at least for now.

She glanced over at Ezra, who walked next to her, but his eyes were still glued to the ground. As they made their way to the gate, a few people in the crowd shouted his name, mocking him. It was clear that he had made enemies of his own during his years in this city. Trace wondered if the story he'd told her—about growing up, about his family—was even true.

After what seemed like hours, but was probably only minutes, they reached the first gate. A large crowd still followed them, which Janus finally seemed to notice.

"Disperse!" he shouted, waving an arm toward the amassed Apex citizens. "Unless you'd each like an immediate five-hundred-credit fine!"

That was all it took. The people hurried away in every direction, and soon only Janus, his troops, Ezra, and Tracer remained. She looked directly into the captain's eyes, wishing she could show the man what she really thought of him—for a second time.

"Your piece-of-shit car is waiting for you on the other side of this wall," Janus said, stepping closer to Trace, his bad breath curling out across her face. She didn't move a muscle, just kept her gaze locked on his. "I hope you have a wonderful trip home with this absolute gem of a human being," he finished, shoving Ezra for good measure.

"Thank you," Trace responded, smiling. "I look forward to seeing you again."

Captain Janus laughed, an awful sound, and instead of responding, he simply walked away, back up the spiral and toward the city. Trace stared daggers into his receding back.

One of the guards raised his chin as the gate opened, signaling that she and Ezra should make their way out, that her time in Apex had come to an unceremonious close.

She saw Goldie waiting, and a slight feeling of relief washed over her. Even though everything that could have gone wrong had done exactly that, seeing the Dodge Dart filled her with a sense of comfort, reminding her of the world she had left behind only a day or two earlier. It was insane to her how quickly everything had changed. She wished none of this had ever happened. Life had been so much simpler forty-eight hours ago.

"Let's go," she barked at Ezra, moving forward without bothering to see if the rattled man was following.

To her pleasant surprise, her SIG Pro was on the front seat. She begrudgingly appreciated Janus for not confiscating it or throwing it in a nearby trash heap. But her appreciation quickly evaporated when she discovered that the rounds had been removed from the weapon.

"Fucking asshole," she muttered as she turned the key and Goldie roared to life. Ezra slid into the seat next to her, head still down, hands in his lap.

Without another word, she shoved the car into Drive and peeled out, leaving the guards in a cloud of sand and dust. It felt amazing—a small comfort, she admitted, but she'd take it.

As the gate closed behind them and they drove down the paved road and past the mountains of garbage, she glanced at Ezra, who was now staring at her.

"*What?*" she demanded. "You ready to apologize?"

"Apologize for what?" he said, his tone matching hers, his meek demeanor from moments ago having completely vanished.

Trace slammed on the brakes, and Goldie came to a screeching halt on the asphalt. There were no other vehicles on this road between the gates—the in-between, as he'd called it—and in the distance, she could see small figures searching for plastic amid the piles of refuse.

"Who the *fuck* are you?" she said quietly, her rage a ragged baseline beneath the words.

"I'm exactly who I said I was," he responded. "I'm a thief . . . a criminal. Nothing less, nothing more."

"You lied about knowing Darcy."

"I *didn't* lie," he insisted, throwing his arms up in exasperation. "I've met her before. She just doesn't remember me, apparently."

"How did you meet her then?"

He paused for a moment, seemed to be contemplating his words carefully.

"She . . . arrested me once."

"Of course she did," Trace responded, letting out a frustrated breath. "Why am I taking you to PH City?"

"Trace," he said, his voice suddenly softer, sounding more like it had when they were on the roof together. She felt something shift deep inside her but fought against it. "I swear. I don't know."

"And what do you get out of this mysterious bargain?" she asked, fighting back any pity she might feel for this man. He swallowed hard and looked out the window, seemed to be struggling to find the words. Trace waited. She needed to know everything before she returned home . . . hell, before she moved another inch.

"My parents," he said, looking back at her. She could see the emotion in his eyes, tried to dismiss it. "I told you the truth about them. I help them out when I can but I barely steal enough to keep myself alive. They're old, can't make money anymore. They . . . wouldn't have survived much longer. So when I heard that Chancellor Stewart was looking for volunteers to help save the city . . . when I saw how many credits he was offering . . . I realized it was a chance to save them. I . . . didn't have a choice."

Tracer's mind raced. What would President Bell want with a common thief from Apex City? Even if he was the best thief who had ever lived, Bell had more than enough credits and luxuries to keep her content for the rest of her life. And she had Gunnar and Tracer to deal with any malcontents who made trouble.

It didn't make any sense.

"Why did you approach me at the bar?" she asked, though she already knew the answer.

"I also wasn't lying when I said that everyone was talking about you. And I knew that you were the person who would be transporting me to PH City . . . to whatever my fate is gonna be when I get there. And I didn't want our first meeting to be in front of the chancellor. I wanted to see what you were really like. And for you to see me without any prejudgments." He swallowed again, blinking at her, trying again to formulate words. She hated how beautiful she still thought his eyes were. "I *knew* it was a risk. But I'm glad I did it. I thought we . . . really connected while we were talking."

"You thought wrong," Trace lied, and then threw Goldie back into Drive and sped away, racing toward the next gate, which would take them back to the highway, and then eventually to PH City.

She silently hoped for an uneventful trip home.

PART 4

THE ROAD

23

At the second gate, they didn't even see anyone, not even a guard, but it opened dutifully for them, and Trace barely needed to slow down as she made her way through it.

Soon, they hit open road, and she pushed Goldie hard, the wind whipping through the open windows and cooling the air down slightly. It was hot, much hotter than when she'd made her way to Apex City with Brisby. They passed the spot where he'd been stabbed by the vagrant, and Trace swallowed down her guilt.

Just thinking about the pyro-tech made her angry all over again. She worked her jaw, tried not to focus too much on what might be happening to Frost at this point. For all she knew, they were torturing the man to keep him working on their damn machine. She cursed Bell for getting her involved in any of this in the first place.

"I've never been in a car before," Ezra ventured after several hours of relative silence, his tone strained in an attempt at lightness. She could tell he was trying his best to break the ice with her.

"Good for you," she replied, her eyes on the road.

"Ridiculous," he mumbled.

She told herself not to take the bait, *commanded* herself not to take it.

"*What's* ridiculous?"

Great, she thought. *Nice work, Trace.*

"Do you think I *want* to be a prisoner, Tracer? If it wasn't me, you would've been stuck with some other random Apexer. Do you know how many people volunteered to be considered for this trade-off? There must have been a hundred of us being poked and prodded and interviewed. I don't know why I was chosen, but I was. And I'm sorry that it's inconvenient for you, and I am doubly sorry that your pyro-tech—who seems like a great guy, by the way—is a prisoner now, too. But I am *not* the one to blame here. None of this is your fault, but none of it is mine either. So stop treating me like I'm your enemy." He took a deep breath, and she could feel his eyes on her, even though she refused to look over at him. "Please," he added, his voice quieter, again sounding more like he had back on the roof a day earlier.

She felt some of the fight go out of her, and she sighed angrily—but not at him, she conceded. This was all Bell's fault, and Stewart's.

She and Brisby and, yes, Ezra were just pawns in some dumb game the two city leaders were playing.

Trace realized she had the accelerator pressed to the floor in her anxious state, so she eased up, let Goldie slow down a bit, before she finally glanced over at Ezra. He still had his eyes on her and even allowed that annoying, amazing little smile to play on his face.

"Truce?" he asked.

The sun beat down on the car, and despite the wind blowing in from the open windows, Trace realized she was sweating profusely. She was overcome with anger at President Bell for putting her into this situation. For lying about the details. For putting her in danger yet again. What kind of boss did that?

Boss. Mother. Trace didn't know what Bell was to her. Part of her was desperate to figure it out, more than ever before. But this wasn't the moment to do so.

"It feels weird to be so far out in the desert," Ezra murmured, gazing out the window. "And look how the landscape is changing now. Totally beautiful. But also kind of totally terrifying."

"Enjoy it while you can," Trace responded. "PH City is way less fancy than Apex. You definitely didn't trade up."

Ezra looked over, taking her in. She could see him in her peripheral vision and didn't like the way he was looking at her, but liked it as well. The dichotomy of everything he did and said was driving her insane.

"I don't know about that," he said quietly.

She glanced over at him, and they stared at each other for a moment until she broke off, something that annoyed her further, like she was losing some kind of childish game, even though she knew she had to keep her eyes on the road.

She laughed slightly and then took a deep breath, enjoying the peculiar scent of the desert. Being out here with Ezra reminded her of her trip a couple of days earlier with Brisby, and she lost herself for a moment in the sweet melancholy of that memory. Despite the pyro-tech annoying her so much, she found herself missing him. He was a good man . . . a good friend.

Lost in the memory, Trace thought she heard a distant popping sound, and for a moment, confusion played in her mind. But as Goldie skidded out across the highway and she fought against inertia and tried to control the protesting steering wheel, she knew exactly what had just happened.

"What are you *doing*?" Ezra shouted, looking around, clearly assuming that Trace was doing this on purpose. "You're not gonna shoot me and leave my corpse on the side of the road, are you?"

"Don't tempt me," she responded through gritted teeth as the car came to a halt in a fury of smoke and sand.

Reaching for her SIG Pro and then remembering there were no bullets, Trace swore under her breath and studied the desert, running through options in her head. She heard something to her right and looked over, shocked to see Ezra getting out of the car, stretching his long arms over his head, and staring out at the desert.

"Get back in the fucking car!" she shouted.

As a shocked Ezra complied, Trace took in the surrounding area and realized she recognized it. Her mind quickly ticked through the events that had occurred during their trip from PH City to Apex. Then it all clicked into place, and the hairs on the back of her neck stood up. She'd been too busy chatting with Ezra to notice, a mistake that might cost both of them their lives.

Especially without a loaded gun.

"What the hell is happening?" Ezra asked, now seated next to her again, cocking his head and looking at her like he'd misheard her. "Is something wrong?"

A second popping noise sounded in the distance, and a smoking hole suddenly appeared in the door behind Trace, exiting Goldie through the other side of the car. If the bullet had hit only a few inches farther toward the front, Trace would already be dead.

"God damn it," she whispered.

They were currently parked in almost exactly the same spot where she and Brisby had encountered the Nomad, if that was what he really was. But *whatever* he was, whether he was alone or not, Trace guessed that the man was currently looking for some payback for his two broken limbs.

Ezra blinked rapidly, still confused. "What's happening?" he repeated.

"Raise your hands and get out of the car. Slowly," Trace instructed. "*Now.*"

Hearing the tone of his companion's voice, Ezra complied. Trace did the same and looked across the shrub-pocked hills, hoping to see whoever had just knocked out one of Goldie's tires and had then followed up with a warning shot. She suspected that if the shooter had really wanted her dead, she'd be bleeding out at this very second.

"We mean you no harm!" she shouted. "We're just passing through!"

"*Sure* you are," a voice came back, and Trace knew right away that it wasn't the man whose arm and leg she'd broken. It was deeper, more authoritative. Which wasn't good for her and Ezra.

After a moment, a group of people emerged from a nearby cluster of tall bushes—one moment there was nothing, and the next, there they were. Trace had no idea how they'd managed to keep so many people hidden, so close to the road, but she had to admit it was impressive. A Nomad secret, perhaps.

There were a dozen of them, she noted, including the gray-stubbled man who had attacked her on her way to Apex City. As he limped forward—leaning on another man with his one good arm, the other in a sling, his injured leg wrapped so many times that it looked double its normal size, still wearing that same dirty red hoodie—he stared at her with naked hostility.

The man at the front of the group was clearly the one who had spoken and the apparent leader of this group—perhaps the leader of all the Nomads, based on the confidence in his stride and the way the others looked at him. He was a huge man, bare chested and clean shaven, his dark hair pulled back into a long ponytail. The group was evenly split between men and women, and their ages varied wildly, from teen- to middle-aged, and several were armed with assault rifles.

They stopped about twenty feet away from Trace, on a stretch of packed dirt next to the road. A long moment of silence played out.

"Is there a problem?" Trace asked, even though she knew there was. The man she had broken raised a shaking finger and pointed it directly at her.

"That's her! The bitch who broke my arm and leg!"

"Come on over," Trace called out in a pleasant voice, "and I'll finish the job."

The stubbled Nomad bristled at the comment and opened his mouth, apparently about to retort, but his leader, the massive figure with the ponytail, simply held up his fist, and his subordinate grew instantly still and silent.

Trace took a deep breath and then made a decision. Her arms still raised, she started to walk toward the Nomads. Her heart pounded in her ears. She realized this might be the dumbest, and last, thing she ever did—but Mackie hadn't trained her just to stand around when faced with danger.

With an incredibly fluid motion, one of the women holding an assault rifle took aim and fired, the bullet whizzing right past Tracer's face and embedding itself in Goldie. That was at least three holes in the car and a flat tire. President Bell was going to *murder* Trace when she got back to PH City. *If* she got back.

Tracer stopped walking. The woman with the gun smiled, her long dirty-blonde hair pulled back into a ponytail, not dissimilar to Tracer's.

Another long moment of silence settled over the scene.

"What do you *want*?" Trace shouted, feeling the rage boil

over. She knew she should keep her calm but was unable to do so. She was tired and frustrated and just wanted to get home.

The Nomad leader raised a hand once again, and the shooter lowered her gun, keeping her eyes on Trace. The huge man began walking forward. Compelled to match his movement, Trace moved toward him as well, arms still in the air. She could hear Ezra behind her and just hoped that his hands were up, too.

Trace faced off with the bare-chested man at the edge of the road, his small Nomad army spread out behind him in a semicircle.

"What do *I* want?" the man scoffed. "I simply wish to look my enemies in the eye before I kill them for their crimes."

"And what are my crimes?" she countered, fear building deep in her stomach despite her bluster. She'd gotten herself out of many dangerous situations over the years, but she had no options at this point. She was outnumbered, and her gun was out of ammo. There was no way out, no miracle on its way.

"Do you deny crippling my soldier?" the man spat, indicating the older Nomad behind him.

"He attacked me first, unprovoked," Trace answered. "So I defended myself."

"You were on *our* road. Without permission. And you destroyed this man's body. And for that, your life is forfeit. Your complaints are heard, and rejected."

He glanced over, and the Nomads with guns trained their weapons on Trace and Ezra. The stubble-faced man broke into a huge grin, and Tracer shut her eyes. Maybe this was the way her end was supposed to go down. In the middle of nowhere on a desert road. On some level, it made sense. She just wished she could have somehow saved Brisby before dying.

"I challenge you!" Ezra's voice suddenly rang out.

Trace quickly glanced over at him, completely confused. "What the *fuck* are you doing?" she whispered.

"It's okay," he said, even though the fear in his eyes indicated that it was most certainly not okay.

"What did you just say, little boy?" the Nomad leader asked, amusement playing on his face.

"I know the rules of the Nomads," Ezra responded, face pale, truly looking like the little boy he had just been accused of being. "You became their leader by killing your predecessor. Because you challenged him. And won. So, I, Ezra Jenkins, officially challenge you . . ."

The huge Nomad just stared, increasingly annoyed by what was happening. His followers seemed to be holding their collective breath.

"Korath," the man said, contempt soaking through the word.

"I, Ezra Jenkins, challenge you, Korath, to battle. The winner shall be named the leader of the Nomads. So it has been written, and so shall it be done."

All the Nomads looked at each other in unfettered surprise. Their expressions all said the same thing: *How had this pathetic Apex City weakling learned the correct way to challenge their leader to a duel?*

Even Korath seemed shocked but quickly wiped any emotion from his face. Instead, a cruel smile appeared there.

"Fine," he growled, stepping to the center of the road, telling his followers without uttering a word to give him space. The Nomads fanned out, creating a circle around the concrete and the combatants.

"What the *hell* are you doing?" Trace repeated in a harsh whisper, turning to face Ezra.

"Saving your life," Ezra replied, forcing a painful-looking smile onto his face. "Like I told you, I spent a *lot* of time out here as a kid. And I met some people, learned a few things. He can't say no to my challenge. And when he kills me, he'll be forced to let you go. It's part of their stupid rules."

"Ezra," she said, stepping even closer, knowing that Korath was behind them, ready to fight. "I can't let you do this."

"Sorry, Ms. Tracer," he responded, his eyes watery but locked on hers. It seemed like there was so much more that he wanted to say. "But it isn't up to you."

Fuck. That, Tracer thought, then turned to face the massive Nomad leader, who looked ready to kill, and to enjoy doing it.

"Korath!" she shouted.

"What now?!" he yelled back. "I desire *blood*, little girl!"

"I'm taking his place!" she responded, shrugging off her trench coat and shoving it into Ezra's arms, reveling in the feeling of the slight wind against her now-bare forearms despite everything that was about to happen. Glancing down, she saw the splatters of blood on the white T-shirt, which was even dirtier than the last time she'd looked at it. And she knew that it was about to get a *lot* dirtier.

"Okay, what are *you* doing?" Ezra demanded from behind her, putting a hand on her shoulder, which she batted away. "You're not using the correct language for the duel."

The look in Korath's eyes seemed to back up Ezra's concerns about Tracer's breach of protocol.

"Unless you're afraid," she added, eyes locked on the Nomad's.

Screaming in rage, Korath bolted forward, slamming into Tracer's midsection, and they both went to the ground, hard, skin scraping off onto the concrete, blood flowing instantaneously.

Despite her words, Trace suddenly found herself to be the one who was very, very afraid.

24

Trace rolled, freeing herself from the Nomad's violent grasp, and quickly got back to her feet.

Korath was already standing, too, faster than Trace would have expected possible for a man his size. They circled each other as the other Nomads spread out, chattering excitedly among themselves. Part of Trace wanted to look over at Ezra, to make sure he was okay, but to do so could be a death knell. She had to keep entirely focused on the hulking figure in front of her, who seemed pretty damn determined to end her life.

As Tracer watched his movements, studied his style, she thought back to her fight with Jevon—which was only a couple of days ago but felt like years. She'd thought the Nix brother was a monster, but this Nomad leader made Jevon look like a child. Trace wasn't sure she'd ever seen such a large human being in her entire life.

Then again, it shouldn't have surprised her. To survive out in this desert, without any plastic or water as far as the eye could see—it seemed like nothing short of a miracle. It was clear that only the strong—the very strong—would survive.

Korath shot out with a clumsy, powerful punch, but Trace ducked under it and got in close, which she recognized might be a mistake. But she also knew there was no way that this man, clearly overconfident, would be expecting it. She threw a quick uppercut—like the one she'd used against Captain Janus—and then quickly moved out of his reach as his head snapped back and a pained grunt shot from the back of his throat.

"I'll *kill* you for that!" he shouted, spitting blood onto the concrete.

"What are you waiting for?" Trace responded, smiling despite her fear. She knew her response would enrage him further, cause him to lose control, and she wasn't wrong.

But she *was* wrong about being outside his reach. Before she knew what was happening, Trace watched in disbelief as Korath suddenly shot forward and wrapped his fingers around her neck, his crimson smile inches away from her face.

"What was that . . . ?" he asked, squeezing slowly, clearly enjoying the moment. Trace felt the breath being choked from her body. The man was incredibly strong, and stars already began dancing on the edge of her vision.

"Trace!" she thought she heard Ezra scream. Or maybe she'd imagined it.

As darkness closed in, her mind reached back and a memory rose, unbidden. She was standing in the training room in PH City. On this particular day, Mackie watched as Trace took on four men in unarmed combat. She was sixteen, smaller than all of them, but her mentor had been preparing her for this test for months.

Still, she found herself overwhelmed by the multiple attackers, even though she was far more skilled in violence than any of them. As she was beaten back, the four men not pulling their punches, blood running down her face, Trace heard Mackie's words echo throughout the large room.

"Whatever it takes, Tracer. Whatever it takes."

She'd won then. Somehow. She wasn't proud of what she'd done that day, the things she had been forced to do, but she'd won.

Blinking against the encroaching darkness, her mentor's words echoing in her mind all these years later, Trace suddenly lunged forward and locked her teeth on the Nomad leader's left cheek—then twisted her head, and pulled away. She spit the huge chunk of flesh onto the concrete, an insane smile spreading on her face, her enemy's blood splattered all over her like an impressionist painting from the old world.

A red geyser exploded from Korath's face, and the man screamed, his hands falling away from Tracer's throat, and they both collapsed to the ground, heat vapors rising up around both of their writhing forms.

"I'll kill you," he repeated, but with less conviction now, holding his hand against his shredded face. "I'll fucking kill you."

But Trace was on him before the man seemed to realize what was even happening. She began punching the exact spot she had bit, each word that she shouted punctuating the more and more violent blows.

"So! You! Keep! Saying!"

She pulled back for another punch but realized the man was barely conscious, eyes fluttering and mouth wide open as if shocked at what had just occurred. Silence settled once again, and Tracer shakily got to her feet, gore dripping from her right fist, both his and her own from the gouges in her now-rent knuckles. She stared down at Korath, whose head was lolling back and forth. After a moment, he started to make an attempt to get back onto his feet, eyes rolling in their sockets, but Trace raised her foot and planted a boot directly into his nose, and the man went down again, head bouncing off the concrete, unconscious.

Trace stumbled back a step, realizing that her throat was

throbbing, that she still might pass out based on how much her mind was swimming. The desert seemed to spin around her, and suddenly Ezra was there, helping her stay upright.

"You did it," he said, disbelief in his voice.

"Just another day at the office," Trace mumbled, parroting something that Brisby used to say now and then back when he'd process plastic for her.

"I'm sorry," Ezra continued. "But it's not over."

His words sobered her instantly, and she fought against the pain, the dizziness, the nausea. "What are you talking about?" she asked, annoyed, even though he hadn't done anything wrong.

"You have to . . . you have to *kill* him, Trace. It's their law."

Tracer glanced over, and sure enough, the Nomads had tightened the circle around them, their faces solemn. The older Nomad with the broken limbs looked shocked, maybe even terrified. Trace looked down at Korath, his body completely still except for the rise and fall of his bare chest. Despite the blood gushing from his face, he looked almost peaceful now, a strange contrast after his earnest attempts to murder her. She thought about how easy it would be to kill him. And it wasn't like she'd never killed before. She had. Many times. Far too many times.

"No," was all she said, then turned away, shoving her way through a pair of startled Nomads, and started walking back toward Goldie.

After about three steps, there was a loud report, and a bullet shattered the ground next to her. She stopped walking and slowly turned. The woman with the ponytail had her weapon aimed directly at Tracer's chest.

"You don't have a choice," the Nomad said, her voice low. "Our law is binding. You won. You *have* to kill him. And then you lead us."

Trace stared at her for a long moment and then walked

forward, keeping her eyes locked on the Nomad's. In her peripheral vision, she could see everyone tensing up, even Ezra, but she didn't give a damn.

Tracer stopped moving when the barrel of the gun was pressing against her chest. But still she kept her eyes on the woman's.

"What's your name?"

The Nomad blinked, surprised.

"Therese," she said, her tone softening slightly.

"Therese. I'm Tracer. I respect what you've all been able to do out here. I'm sure it hasn't been easy. But I'm sorry, I have no interest in following along with your arbitrary law. You can shoot me if you want . . . but I am *not* going to kill him."

Therese's eyes twitched, and the older Nomad, the one Tracer had crippled, screamed, "Fucking kill her!" but no one else moved or spoke.

The wind whipped around them, sand flew against their faces, the sun beat down. Therese blinked again, clenched her jaw. Tightened her finger against the trigger.

"I . . . I might have an idea," Ezra said, stepping closer to the two women, raising his hands slightly as he approached.

"Maybe I'll shoot him and then I'll shoot you, too," Therese said to Tracer, raising an eyebrow.

"I don't think so," Trace responded. "If you wanted to kill me, you would've done it already."

Therese considered this and then flicked her eyes toward Ezra.

"*What?*" she barked, turning the weapon on him.

"I . . ." he started to say, and then faltered, staring at the gun barrel pointing directly at his face.

"Spit it out, Ezra," Trace said, trying to keep her voice calm. She recognized that they were running out of time. "It's now or never."

"When I was young . . . when I spent a bunch of time out

here in the desert . . . I met some Nomads once. Young ones. For whatever reason, they decided not to kill me on the spot. We talked for a while . . . they even answered my questions. And I had a *lot* of questions."

"Shocking," Trace mumbled.

"Get to the point!" Therese shouted, tightening her grip on the gun. The other Nomads were getting restless, staring at Trace and Ezra with barely contained violence in their eyes.

"I don't remember all the details . . . but they did tell me a little bit about how their . . . about how your leadership structure works. It's death by combat . . . or if the leader willingly submits."

"What?" Tracer said, feeling the slightest glimmer of hope.

"Something that has never happened, apparently," he added.

Trace glanced over at Therese, who stared back, stone-faced, for a long moment. Finally, after what felt like hours, the Nomad nodded imperceptibly.

"Fine," Trace said, then walked back over to Korath, who moaned and twitched on the road. Slowly, knowing it might be a mistake, she reached down and unholstered her SIG Pro. Feeling the crowd's eyes locked on her and without saying a word, Trace carefully placed the gun in the Nomad leader's mouth. His eyes popped open instantly, and he blinked up at her, comprehension slowly registering.

"*Submit*," she demanded, despite the fact that there were no bullets in her weapon. No one else needed to know that.

The man shouted something through the metal that sounded very similar to "Fuck you!"—but Trace ignored the words and instead cocked the gun. Then leaned in close.

"I'll kill you right here, right now," she whispered. "I've killed more people than I can remember. And if you force me, I'll blow your brains all over this road, then take over your stupid fucking tribe. And then I'll kill every single one of them, too, one by one. Is that what you want, Korath? The end of your tribe?" His eyes went wide at her words and then narrowed with what seemed like hard-headed determination. "Think very carefully about the next thing you say," she said. "I won't ask again. This is your final warning."

The Nomad's entire face shuddered with rage, and Trace thought for a second that he would call her bluff and she would be forced to either beat him to death with her gun or die herself—until his face softened and water filled his eyes. She'd seen more dangerous men than him cry, so the sight didn't surprise her. But she still felt relief. She didn't want another soul on her conscience and wasn't ready for her own life to end.

Or Ezra's, a distant part of her mind said.

Ignoring that annoying inner voice, Tracer removed the gun from the man's mouth and stood up, keeping the weapon aimed at his face.

"Say it," she commanded.

"I . . ." he started, struggled to finish, and then shouted, "I submit!"

There were audible gasps from the Nomads, but they lowered their weapons. Ezra appeared next to her and whispered, "Ho. Lee. Shit, Tracer."

She ignored him. The Nomads approached her cautiously. The hatred was still naked in their eyes, but their postures indicated they were waiting for her to speak. She tried to push away her irritation at this entire situation—she just wanted to get home to PH City and see why the hell she was toting around this guy from Apex City, and then figure out how to get Brisby back. She was still racked with nearly overwhelming guilt over leaving the pyro-tech behind.

"What next?" she asked.

"You're our leader," Therese said. "That's up to you. Do you

want me to kill him?" She pointed her assault rifle at Korath, who blinked up, still in seeming surprise at the chain of events that had led to him being splayed out on his back in the middle of the highway.

"No," Trace said quickly. "Korath was an honorable opponent. He doesn't deserve to die. Any more than Ezra or I did for being out here in the first place."

"Steve," Therese said. "His name is Steve. He made us start calling him Korath when he killed our last leader."

Ezra attempted to fight back a snort and failed, but Trace kept her face blank.

"I don't care what his name is," she said. "And I have no interest in being your leader." An angry murmur rose up from the Nomads, and fingers tightened once again on weapons. Trace ignored this and continued, pointing at their former leader. "If he had died of natural causes, who would have been your next leader?"

"Me!" the older Nomad suddenly shouted—the man Trace had broken during her trip to Apex City. "I am the rightful leader of the Nomads!"

Trace glanced at Therese and raised an eyebrow. "It's true," the woman confirmed. "Finn is next in line. But it doesn't matter. *You're* our leader now. And we are all sworn by blood to follow you. That, or kill you."

Trace looked over the Nomads, waiting to see if anyone would challenge her, but they averted their eyes. They'd seen the results of what she'd done to Finn, and had witnessed with their own eyes her battle with Korath, or Steve, or whatever the fuck his name was.

"And what if I willingly give up my position of leadership?" Trace asked.

Therese laughed, and Trace saw the dark and violent

experience etched in the skin around the younger woman's eyes. She had clearly seen—and been through—a lot.

"It isn't something that has *ever* been brought up," she said after a moment. She glanced at her fellow Nomads. "I suppose it isn't against our laws—but simply because it was never contemplated. Only a fool would give up such power."

"Well, I guess I'm a fool then. I am officially giving up my leadership . . ."

Finn's eyes went wide with excitement.

"To you, Therese," Tracer finished.

The younger woman's mouth dropped open, and shouts rang out from the other Nomads. Trace eyeballed them, shocked at the outrage, and wondered if she had played her hand wrong. Ezra stepped even closer to her, and she could practically feel the fear radiating off him.

"Is it not within my power to make you their leader?" Trace asked, genuinely confused.

"Of course!" Finn shouted, indignant. "But she is a child! And a *female*!"

Therese raised and fired her gun before anyone even realized what was happening. It caught the edge of Finn's ear and a burst of blood exploded out. The man screamed, falling to the ground and holding his head. The Nomads looked to their fallen companion and then back up to Therese.

"Anyone else have a problem with a *female* leader?" she yelled.

No one said anything. But another Nomad stepped in close, an older woman, worry wrinkling her forehead.

"It's never been done," she said quietly.

"Exactly why it should then," Therese replied. "The laws of our people, handed down since the Before Time, have been followed. This conversation is over, and I am now your leader. Return to the Yard. I'll join you shortly."

After a tense moment, the Nomads nodded and grunted their assent, heading off into the desert. A few of them helped Korath get to his feet and followed the others.

Therese hung back, the gun resting against her forearm. She looked at Trace, then smiled.

"Thank you," she said quietly.

"It was literally my pleasure," Trace responded, then rubbed her tender neck. "For the most part."

Therese smiled and then turned, but Trace clearing her throat caused the new Nomad leader to stop in her tracks.

"Is there something else?" she asked.

"In return for what just happened, I'd like to ask a small favor," Trace responded.

"Anything," Therese said.

Tracer pointed at Goldie, which glinted in the bludgeoning sunlight.

"One of you Nomads took out one of our tires. I don't feel like driving back on a rim and having to explain the damage to my boss. She's already going to freak out as it is."

"That was me," Therese admitted. "Sorry about that."

"We'll call it even if you rustle up a replacement," Trace said.

The Nomad leader nodded, considering. "Okay. I know where I can find one. It's going to take me a minute to get there, get it off, and get back to you. So, you two stay put, find some shade, and I'll come back as soon as possible. Fair?"

"Very," Trace answered. "Thank you."

Without another word, Therese turned around and hustled off toward her fellow Nomads, who were now a series of dots in the distance.

Ezra stepped next to Trace, wiping sweat from his forehead. "What now?" he asked, staring after Therese's receding form.

"Now?" Trace replied. "Now . . . we wait."

25

It took Therese longer than expected to return with a tire, but eventually she appeared out of the desert as the sun dipped behind the hills in the distance.

Trace and Ezra watched as the Nomad single-handedly replaced the tire—which wasn't the same exact type as the other three, but it was fully functional, and that would have to be good enough. The Nomad said a quick goodbye, and then headed back the way she'd come, the shattered, shredded old tire under her arm.

Smart, Trace thought. *Never waste resources.*

It was dark by the time they pulled back onto the highway, but Trace almost immediately felt herself nodding off. She was tired—exhausted, really—and her throat was throbbing with pain. Korath—Steve—had done more damage to her than she'd been willing to admit, even to herself.

They saw a pockmarked, fading sign that indicated an old town not too far off the highway. Without saying a word, Trace pulled off at the next exit. When they arrived, they discovered a small town dotted with multiple deteriorating buildings at its center. The middle of the ancient town square had an open layout, which made Trace feel more comfortable. It was unlikely that anyone—or anything—could sneak up on them without her seeing them coming.

She managed to find a large piece of shattered porcelain next to one of the collapsed buildings that held a fair amount of old rainwater, so she took the opportunity to kneel down and wash the blood off her hands and face. It was a far cry from the shower back at Apex City, but it still felt amazing to get the gore off her skin.

When she was done, she headed back toward the center of town and saw that Ezra had collected wood from the decaying edifices and was now expertly building a fire, the buildings surrounding them like oversized coffins reaching up to the dark sky. Soon, embers climbed from the growing fire and into the night.

Trace, sitting on her folded-up trench coat, watched the firelight playing off the collapsing wood and metal and concrete that surrounded them, amazed at the sight. She had never seen anything like it during her time in either Puente Hills or PH City. It was stark, and primal, and beautiful.

"Sorry I couldn't find any food," Ezra said, pushing a piece of half-burning wood around in the makeshift campsite. Behind him, Goldie shimmered in the uneven light from the blaze.

"It's not your job to feed me," Trace responded, her eyes heavy, staring at the flames. "Besides, I sometimes go days without eating when I'm on a mission for President Bell."

"*Days . . . ?*" Ezra said, looking up at her, his face a mask of bewilderment. "You don't eat for days at a time? Regularly?"

She pulled her focus from the fire and matched his gaze. "I wouldn't say *regularly*. But when a job needs to be done . . . I do it. Whatever it takes."

Ezra didn't say anything for a long moment, then seemed like he was going to speak, then stopped himself.

"What?" she asked.

"Nothing," came the quiet response.

"No. Say it."

"You don't always have to be . . . *on*, you know? Don't always have to act so tough."

She felt her face flush with anger. "I'm not acting *anything*. This is how I am. I'm sorry it's not good enough for you, Ezra."

"I'm not—" he started to say, his own anger rising, but stopped himself again, then inhaled slowly and swore under his breath. "I'm not telling you how to be. Or not be. I'm just saying . . . if you *want* to talk to me, you can. Like you did back on the roof." She narrowed her eyes at him. "And I know I lied, or didn't tell you the whole truth right away, so I understand that I may have lost my privileges with you."

"You're not wrong," she muttered.

"Totally fair," he replied. "And I get it. Trust me. It's been like this my whole life—scraping for everything, lying and stealing when I have to, to survive. I mean . . . I'm a street rat from Apex City and now I've been . . . what? . . . Bartered off to your president for god knows what reason . . . maybe to toil out in the garbage and find plastic for her? Regardless, I'm the lowest of the low. And I betrayed your trust once. But right now? In this moment? It's just you and me. In the middle of nowhere. Anything we talk about can stay between us . . . you, me, and the desert. And the fire. And . . . this ghost town." He cleared his throat. "And the ghosts."

Trace laughed and hated herself for doing so. But damn it, there was something about this man that got through her carefully curated defenses.

"You're *very* annoying," she said.

"I know," he replied sheepishly.

Trace stared into the fire, which was dying down a little. She had seen fires in her life, certainly, but never like this, had never sat in front of one for pleasure and just watched it burn for no reason at all. The colors were amazing, the heat, the smell. It felt almost intoxicating. She absently rubbed at her aching neck and felt the words tumble out of her, almost as if they were coming from somewhere far away.

"You're not the only who feels . . . bartered away," she said quietly. "My whole life has been one big trade. The couple who found me in the garbage heaps—people I thought loved me, people I thought of as my parents—traded me to President Bell for credits, and I've been living off that swap my entire life. I've deluded myself into thinking that she . . ." Trace was surprised at the sudden rush of emotion but forced herself to continue talking. "That *she* was my mother. But deep down, I know she never saw herself that way . . . *doesn't* see herself that way . . . no matter what she says. I'm a slave, and I've always done exactly what she's told me. Including walking away from Brisby Frost. Who's a slave now, too."

"I'm sorry about your friend," Ezra said after a long moment, the crackling of the fire filling the space between them.

"Yeah. Same," she murmured.

Several minutes passed and neither of them spoke. The flames began to dwindle.

"Shit," Ezra said suddenly, and scrambled to his feet, grabbing a few sticks from the nearby pile that he'd collected and throwing them on the ebbing blaze. After a moment, the small pyre roared back to life.

"Definitely don't want to have to get that started from scratch again," he mumbled, wiping his hands off on his pants, and sat back down, closer to Trace now. She noticed and was surprised that his proximity didn't bother her. Generally, she preferred her space—had once knocked someone unconscious at Old Joe's bar when they felt at liberty to put their hands where they didn't belong after getting a bit too up close and personal.

She tried to think of something to say but was having trouble collecting her thoughts. She glanced over at Ezra. He was staring at the fire, lost in his own moment, and she realized how clean his clothes were—at least compared to hers.

She looked down. The once-white shirt was a collage of blood and dirt, and she abruptly grew self-conscious about her appearance, something she couldn't ever remember feeling before.

"I'm a bit of a mess," she said, hating the words as she spoke them.

"Huh?" Ezra said, and then looked at her, confusion registering on his face. "Not at all. I mean, you did just fight the leader of the Nomads to the almost death. You look pretty amazing, all things considered. I mean, you look pretty amazing, period."

Trace's mind swam. She wanted to say something, wanted to get up, wanted to punch him in the face, wanted to thank him. She had no idea what to do.

"Sorry," he continued, "I just meant . . . you're not a mess. At all."

"You don't have to apologize," she said, wondering if she was leaning toward him or if it just felt *like* she was. The fire seemed hotter all of a sudden, the light playing across his face.

And he was leaning forward, too, his eyes locked on hers.

"Okay, I'm not sorry," he said quietly.

Tracer's heart was pounding in her ears as all the other sounds fell away. She loved his eyes, loved the way he looked at her. The way his hair fell across his forehead. His nose. His lips.

"Tell me to stop," Ezra whispered, moving even closer.

Trace kissed him, and though she had seen people do it, had heard people talk about it, the sensation was unlike anything she had ever experienced. After a long moment, he pulled away, seemed to be struggling for words.

"Are you okay?" he finally managed.

In response, she grabbed him and kissed him again, wrapping her arms around his body. He did the same, the stars blinking down silently overhead, the desert wind moving in the distance, the fire popping and throwing its smoke deep into the night.

The morning was cool.

Trace blinked against the light and then quickly got to her feet, turning in a semicircle as if under attack. Then she remembered where she was and what had transpired the previous night. She looked over her shoulder and saw that Ezra was already awake, tending a small fire. She wasn't sure if it was the same one as the previous night or if he'd gotten up early and made a new one.

He looked up, a smile spreading on his face. "Good morning," he said, standing up.

"Morning," she replied, then decided *Fuck it*, and kissed him gently. His smile got even bigger.

She smelled something delicious and glanced over at the fire. Something on a stick was splayed out across the flames, bubbling and dripping juice down into the heat.

"What is *that*?" she asked, raising an eyebrow.

"Breakfast," he replied, squatting back down and turning the makeshift spit.

"Yeah, but what is it?"

"You sure you really wanna know?" he asked.

"You should see some of the things I've had to eat to keep myself going on a mission. Spill it, Jenkins."

He barked a laugh, looked at her appreciatively. "Okay, you

asked for it. Literally. It's lizard. Not sure which kind. It was green. And now . . . it's not."

"Good enough for me," she said. "Let's eat."

Goldie roared down the highway.

By Tracer's estimation, they were less than an hour from PH City. Despite her excitement at almost being home, an uneasiness had settled somewhere under her ribs. She and Ezra hadn't spoken a lot during this last leg of their journey, but they'd looked at each other often, and he was the first person in her entire life that made it feel like she could have a conversation without even speaking. It was unnerving, and amazing.

She worried about what task he'd be assigned once they reached President Bell. He was probably right—it was most likely plastic scavenging, or maybe even Bell had somehow heard from Chancellor Stewart how good a thief Ezra was. While the president didn't need more plastic or credits, she always *wanted* more. And she utilized the talents of the people in her employ however she could in order to attain that singular goal.

There was no reason Trace and Ezra couldn't be in a relationship despite whatever job he was given—even if they had to keep it quiet at first. She was worrying over nothing, but that had been part of her training, too. Always overanalyze. Underanalyzing a situation could lead to serious pain or death.

"We're close," she said, the wind from the open windows pushing against her face. The coolness of the morning was starting to burn off as the sun got higher in the sky, and she could feel the temperature increasing quickly. The wind made it bearable, though, and the scent of the desert was one she'd come to truly enjoy.

"Okay," Ezra said, and she heard the nerves on the edge of his voice. She wanted to tell him that everything would be fine, that she'd make sure he was okay, but she also knew how unpredictable Bell was. Still, she was confident that she could shield Ezra from anything too terrible, could show him the ropes as he took on whatever job the president was going to thrust on him—perhaps they would even be teamed up to retrieve plastic from criminals.

The thought of it filled her with emotions unlike anything she'd felt before. She had always balked at even the vaguest concept of working with someone when sent on a mission—and luckily had never been asked to team with Gunnar—but she could envision her and Ezra's talents complementing each other. And while she was cautious about these new feelings, she was eager to explore them—at her own pace.

"I'm excited to show you my city," she said, glancing over at him as she pushed down slightly harder on the accelerator. She was ready to be home. With him.

"Me too," he responded, but didn't match her gaze. Instead, he stared out the open window at the burnt-out buildings and cars, apparently lost in thought.

Respecting his current state of mind, Trace turned back and focused on the road ahead. In the distance, she could see the barest outline of a structure, a thin line etched into the oncoming haze.

PH City.

She steeled her nerves, remembered who she was, who she'd been trained to be.

Tracer was going home.

PART 5

PH CITY

26

The gate opened slowly, the metal shrieking loudly as it did so.

Trace was painfully aware of how rudimentary it all looked—the pockmarked wall surrounding Puente Hills, the rusted metal gate. Even PH City itself, which had always felt like a technological marvel to her—especially as a Garbage Dweller looking up at it—seemed shabby and embarrassing now that she'd been to Apex.

"It's . . . not much," she said absently, aware of Ezra next to her, aware of him staring out the passenger-side window as they drove through the gate and along the winding, trash-lined road toward the spire at its center.

"Are you kidding me?" he responded. "It's awesome."

To her surprise, she didn't hear any sarcasm in his voice, and she glanced over at him again, scrutinizing his words. "Seriously?"

Ezra looked at her, and that disarming smile appeared on his face, making her stomach flip.

"Yes, Trace. Seriously. Apex tries too hard. It's exhausting. This just feels more . . . *real*, you know? Like you. You're the most real person I've ever met."

Trace tried to answer but couldn't find the words. He reached over and took hold of her right hand, held it while she drove with her left. No one had held her hand before. Ever.

And it felt amazing.

She focused on the road, and as the tall, single-story city emerged ahead of them, she subconsciously withdrew her hand from his, gripped the steering wheel more tightly. She felt all her walls creeping back up, and part of her welcomed it, while the other part hated the reversion to her fundamental self.

"You okay?" Ezra asked, and she could hear the concern in his voice.

"Fine," was all she gave back.

As she pulled up close to the main elevator bank, and the hidden garage door just beyond that, Gunnar appeared out of nearby shadows and raised his hand, ordering her wordlessly to stop. For a moment, Trace entertained the idea of flattening him with the car, but she was already nervous enough about the three bullet holes in the car and the beat-up replacement tire—Bell was going to murder her. Maybe literally. She didn't want to add to her problems by denting the front of the car on Gunnar's corpse.

She chuckled at the thought, even though it was just a fantasy. Despite the tension that had existed between them for almost their entire lives, the two of them had never come to blows—probably far too afraid what their adoptive mother would do to them if they did. Still, Trace wondered who would win. She hated Gunnar with a passion, but she'd seen him fight. Knew he was a dangerous opponent. He'd been trained by Mackie, too, after all. The thought of her mentor, with Gunnar standing in her vision, filled her chest with a sudden heaviness—but she pushed it away. There wasn't time to get lost in emotion and memory.

Goldie came to a halt in a cloud of dust. Trace waited a moment, stared at Gunnar through the dirty windshield. He stared back with an equal amount of distaste.

"Umm . . ." Ezra interjected. "He looks nice."

Trace shut the car off. "Just stay close to me. And don't say anything."

She got out of the car, slowly put on her trench coat while eyeballing Gunnar, and then walked directly at him, stopping a foot away from his waiting form, and gazed into his heavy-browed face.

"The gate radioed ahead that you'd arrived," he said, his tone as clipped as usual.

"No shit," she responded, and the man visibly bristled. Trace loved it.

"Hi," Ezra said, suddenly appearing next to Trace. "I'm Ezra. From Apex City. And you are . . . ?"

Trace bit down, ground her teeth together. Did everything in her power not to yell at him. She cared about Ezra, more than she thought possible, but he needed to listen to her if he was going to survive a single night in PH City, let alone the rest of his life here.

Gunnar looked at the newcomer like he was a bug he needed to wipe off the bottom of his boot. He let a little laugh out of his nose and then turned his attention back to Tracer.

"President Bell is waiting for you. Impatiently, I might add. She thought you'd be back sooner."

"That's between me and her," Trace responded, shoving past Gunnar, who threw an extra bit of shoulder into the contact. She looked back at Ezra, who was hesitating, confused about the unspoken aggression he'd just witnessed.

"Let's go, Jenkins!"

That was all the encouragement Ezra needed. He was back

at her side instantly, and the two of them headed toward the elevator.

"Nice to have you back," Gunnar shouted after them. "I can't wait for the president to see what you've done to Goldie!"

"Ignore him," Trace instructed, and this time, Ezra listened.

Mercifully, the elevator doors opened as soon as Trace pushed the button. She stepped in, reached back for a distracted Ezra, grabbed his shirt roughly, and pulled him inside.

As the doors shut behind them, Ezra looked up at her with big eyes and raised his hands up, palms out. "I'm sorry. When I get nervous, I—"

But Trace didn't let him finish. She shoved him against the elevator wall, hard, and pushed her mouth against his. He resisted for a moment, caught off guard, and then gave in, wrapping his arms around her.

All was quiet for a few moments.

At length, Tracer pulled away and pointed a finger in his face.

"When I tell you to do something, I need you to do it. Okay?"

Ezra blinked at the shifting of her emotions. "Yes. Of course. I talk when I get nervous. It's a survival thing. My big mouth has gotten me out of more than one scrape back in Apex."

"I'm sure," she said, taking her hair out of the ponytail, then pulling it back into a neater version of her signature look. "But I don't know what the hell is going on here, and I need you to shut up and let me figure it out. It's weird that she sent Gunnar out to meet us, and not just some random guard."

"Gunnar," Ezra responded. "I'm assuming he's that super friendly guy that you were about to kill down there?"

"Exactly," Trace said. "My brother, for lack of a better term. He was raised by Bell, too, and he's dangerous as fuck. I need you to stay away from him as much as humanly possible."

Ezra clearly heard the severity of her tone because he just nodded, kept his mouth shut. Trace nodded, glad that he understood. They rode the rest of the way in silence. She fought an urge to kiss him again. There would be time for that later. After he got his job assignment from the president.

The elevator dinged, and the doors opened on the top floor, revealing the short hallway that led to Bell's office. "Stay close," she ordered, and then moved forward, Ezra right on her heels. She knocked on her boss's door, waited a moment, and then heard Bell's voice call out, "Come in!" on the other side.

"Okay," Trace said, mostly to herself, then turned the handle, and entered the office.

The president was sitting at her desk, and she watched them enter, a big closed-lipped smile on her face. Trace felt like her every nerve was on fire. The last time she'd been in this office, she'd been a totally different person—it felt like a lifetime of experience had occurred since then, and maybe it had. Still, being in Bell's presence again made her feel like a child—weak and needy and dependent. And she absolutely hated it.

"Well, well, well," Bell said, standing up. "Look what the fucking cat dragged in."

As was her habit, and as a result of her extensive training, Trace quickly took in all the details of the room and of the person in front of her. The office seemed cleaner than usual, the normal mess of papers on the desk tidied up and organized in careful piles. The couch cushions were more ordered, spaced out evenly, and faint music tinkled from some unseen speakers. Trace couldn't remember hearing music in here—or *ever* in the presence of her boss.

And the president herself looked different, too. The contrasts were subtle, but Trace had been in the presence of the older woman for the majority of her life. Bell was wearing a crisp new business suit, her hair combed and shiny. Her shoes were new, too, and she wore earrings that caught the light and sparkled.

And unless Trace was mistaken, Bell was wearing the slightest hint of makeup, something Trace had never seen on the president before.

What the hell is going on? Trace wondered as Bell worked her way around the desk and approached them.

"Ma'am," was all Tracer said, keeping her eyes low just like she'd been trained to do.

"Lemme look at you," Bell said, grabbing her XN's face roughly—though that itself wasn't unusual—and forcing the younger woman to make eye contact. "A little worse for the wear but nothing out of the ordinary for my absolute ass kicker." She poked a finger at the bruises on her subordinate's neck. Trace almost flinched but used all her willpower to ignore the pain, to focus on the moment, on the job she was expected to do, that she had always done. "Ouch. The chancellor sent a telegram, told me you made quite an impression on everyone. But he didn't mention anything about you getting choked the fuck out, Trace. Those *are* finger marks, are they not?"

"They are," Trace admitted. "We ran into a little trouble on the way back. Nothing I couldn't handle."

Bell patted her on the face a couple of times, gently, but enough that the contact made a slapping noise. Trace could feel Ezra shifting uncomfortably next to her, begged him silently to keep his goddamn mouth shut. He must have sensed the command, or had wised up since their encounter with Gunnar, because he kept silent.

As if on cue, the president turned her attention to the new arrival from Apex City. Her eyes went slightly wide as she got a good look at him, the sly smile returning.

"And what do we have here?" she said, her tone gentler

than Trace could ever remember hearing from her boss before.

"Ezra Jenkins, ma'am," he said, matching her smile. Trace saw it out of the corner of her eye, and even in the middle of this awkward, tense moment, it made her stomach flip. She was excited to get him alone after this meeting. To continue getting to know him. To kiss him again.

Bell barked a laugh. "Ma'am!" she shouted, elbowing her XN as if they were in on some secret joke. Trace kept her composure—didn't move, didn't say a word. "Ezra, you don't have to call me ma'am. You don't even have to call me President Bell. Please. My name is Katherine."

Trace inhaled audibly, and based on the way Bell side-eyed her, she was confident she was about to get a backhand from her boss—and it wouldn't have been the first time. But the president just chuckled, stepped even closer to Ezra, eyed him as if she were appraising a piece of art. Or meat.

"Tracer is just a little surprised. I don't usually share my first name with people. But you . . . Ezra Jenkins . . . you're special."

"Um . . . thank you?"

"You are very welcome, young man," Bell said, then let out a breath, and turned her attention back to her XN. "I heard about Goldie." All the air in the room seemed to vanish, and Trace's mind raced as she tried to think of something to say. The bullet holes and the tire hadn't been her fault, obviously, but that didn't matter. She had seen Bell torture and murder people for smaller offenses. Much smaller.

"I-I'm sorry," she stuttered. "We were attacked. If I could have kept Goldie completely safe, I would have. I would have died for her if that would have kept her unharmed." She could see Ezra goggling at her, felt like she was going to throw up.

Bell laughed again, shaking her head in what seemed like genuine amazement. "I know you would, Tracer. That's why you're my best soldier. And that's why I forgive you. After all, you brought my fiancé home to me. It's a fair trade for a little bit of damage to one of my prized possessions."

Bell continued talking, about Goldie and about the chancellor's message, and about how she had single-handedly saved Apex City with her brave executive decisions, but all Trace could hear was a single word, which echoed painfully over and over and over again in her mind.

Fiancé.

She risked a glance at Ezra, who looked just as shocked as Tracer—if not more. His face had drained of color, but he stared at the president like he was taking in every word she was saying. Trace forced her brain to focus and watched as Bell walked over to a small table and poured two glasses of a golden liquid. She brought them over and handed one to Ezra. He took it with trembling fingers.

"To us," Bell said, and drank deeply, her eyes locked on the man who was apparently about to become her husband.

Ezra opened his mouth but seemed unable to speak, so he just drank and nodded as if he enjoyed the taste.

"Good, right?" the president said, taking the glass from him and placing both back on the table. "Alcohol is illegal in PH City—unlike the debauchery in Apex—but I had my team make a special drink for the occasion. Apple juice. A little bitter, maybe, but we're still working on it."

"Thank you," Ezra said, his voice slightly choked. He looked over at Tracer, eyes searching, and Bell must have noticed because her voice changed, back to its normal timbre.

"And with that, Trace, you are relieved of duty. You have more than done your job, and I can't thank you enough. Why don't you take the rest of the week off? Gunnar can run some missions for you. Kick some ass and take some plastic." Bell laughed at the joke as if it were the first time she'd ever made it, and looked at Ezra. He laughed, too, and Trace knew it was forced, wanted to tell him he didn't have to do that, that he could leave with her, but she also knew he was trapped, and so was she, and it was even possible she might never see him again. Or if she did, it might be nothing more than fleeting glimpses. If Bell caught even the slightest whiff that Trace had fallen for her fiancé, the president wouldn't hesitate to have her XN killed on the spot. Trace knew that beyond a shadow of a doubt.

Further confusing her was the fact that she had never, since meeting Bell, been offered more than a day or two off. The idea of a week without a mission for the president was nearly impossible for her to conceive. And to spend that week away from Ezra while he was whisked off and forced to marry Bell—she felt rage building up from the pit of her stomach, and her fingers slowly clenched into fists without her even being aware of what was happening.

"Tracer," Bell hissed. "I said you are *relieved*."

The XN snapped out of it. Her training reasserted itself, and she shunted her emotions down into that unseen pit somewhere deep in her being, the same place the memories of herself as a young girl out in the garbage heaps went.

"Of course," she said, nodding at Bell. "I'm sorry. I must be tired. I appreciate the time off."

"You're god damn right you do," the president snapped. "Now get the fuck out of here so I can get to know Ezra a little better."

Trace nodded once more, then turned and headed toward the door. As she took hold of the handle, a thought crossed her mind, and she paused. She knew she shouldn't say anything, that she should take the advice she'd given to Ezra, but she was unable to stop herself.

"One more thing, ma'am," she said, her back to Bell and Ezra.

"*What?*" Bell said, not loudly, but the rage in the single word made Trace's blood run cold. Still, she had to ask.

"What's going to happen to Brisby Frost?"

The silence that blanketed the room over the next five seconds was oppressive. She heard someone approaching, so she turned and saw that Bell was only a few feet away from her. The anger on the president's face was unlike anything Trace had ever seen there, and it was terrifying.

"That is *none* of your fucking business. Do you understand me, Tracer?"

Trace tried to say yes but couldn't seem to get the word out.

Bell took a step closer, her voice lowering to a strained whisper. "I don't know what the hell is going on with you, but I'm going to chalk it up to pain and fatigue. You are one word away from having the worst day of your life. Maybe the *last* day. Now, tell me that you understand what I'm saying to you, and then turn around and get the fuck out of my office."

Trace's gaze flicked to Ezra, just for the slightest moment, and the look on his face broke her heart. His eyes said so much, things she understood and things she didn't, but mostly he was telling her that it was okay. That she should go.

She looked back at her boss. Her mother. Whatever the hell she was.

"I understand," Trace whispered.

Bell winked, her face slackening, that infuriating smile returning. "Fantastic. Have a nice vacation, Trace. See you in a week."

And with that, President Bell reached around her XN, opened the door, gently shoved the younger woman out into the hallway, and slammed the door shut.

Trace took a deep breath, tried her best to calm her rattled nerves, and then headed toward the elevator, trying to forget the desperate look in Ezra's eyes. And failing.

27

Trace sat in her apartment, staring at the wall.

It had been hours since she left Bell's office, and she'd come straight home, hoping to get some sleep, maybe even wake up and feel completely different about the events in Apex City, and about Ezra. After all, it had only been a couple days of her life, and she barely knew the man. He was a stranger.

But the opposite had occurred. She couldn't stop thinking about him, about the look on his face when she'd left him. Couldn't stop thinking about that first kiss in the desert, about the words he'd spoken to her that night, about how she'd felt long-abandoned parts of herself opening up to him.

He was more than a stranger, and every fiber of her being knew it.

"Fuck," she muttered, standing and pacing the room. Her place was bigger than the quarters she'd been given, however briefly, in Apex, but she felt the walls closing in and realized that even though she'd been living here since she was young, it had never felt like home, not really. Bell constantly mentioned how she paid for Trace's apartment and everything in it, the underlying message being one of obligation. Every aspect of Tracer's life was about debt—debt to Bell.

And she was sick of it.

Her stomach roiled. She knew she should be hungry, that the little bit of lizard meat wasn't nearly enough, but food was the last thing she wanted. If anything, she wanted a drink—as strong as possible—but then remembered her last conversation with Old Joe. How she'd told him to close down for a little while, to lay low.

She walked over to her small desk, opened the lowest drawer, and removed a box of ammo. Reloading her SIG Pro always made her feel better, safer, and this was the longest she'd ever gone with it being completely empty. She placed it back in its holster, then moved to the door and grabbed her trench coat off the rusted hook. She'd changed her shirt—putting the one from Apex City in a small container of water—but hadn't even bothered taking off her boots. Some integral part of her knew she wasn't going to be able to sleep, or even sit still, for that matter.

Tracer slipped quietly out of her apartment with a very specific destination in mind.

PH City was quiet.

Trace knew the structure like the back of her hand, had spent most of her life traversing its halls, and she stalked along the ninth floor, surprised at how little activity there was. It was true that she hadn't spent much time in this particular section, where people with some—but not much—money lived. Despite their somewhat limited means, the residents of Nine were generally well behaved, which meant Trace was rarely dispatched here to employ her gifts on her boss's behalf. Or on the behalf of any of her boss's many benefactors. Thinking back to all the violence she had enacted for

Bell and her sycophants, Trace felt physically ill. The only thing worse was the fact that it hadn't bothered her before now.

She pushed those thoughts away, took small comfort in the fact that she'd been raised to never question her actions, her spectacular violence. It had taken a trip to Apex City to open her eyes, and then to turn that gaze back on herself.

And she fucking hated what she saw.

She finally reached the door she'd been searching for and pounded a fist against it. There was a long pause, and then she knocked again, gentler this time. She needed to control her anger—there was nothing she could do about Ezra, but she didn't need to scare the only friend she had left in this damn city.

"Joe, I know you're in there," she lied. "It's me."

There was another moment of interminable silence, and then she heard a shuffling noise. The door opened, only about an inch, and she saw a scarred eye and a mess of hair appear in the shadows on the other side.

"Trace? What . . . what the hell are you doing here?"

"I missed you," she said, smiling slightly.

"And you need a drink," he added.

"And I need a drink," she confirmed.

Joe laughed and then opened the door a few more inches, turning away into the darkness of his apartment. "Come on in," he said. "And make sure you lock the door behind you."

Trace did as she was instructed and blinked against the light as Joe turned on a lamp on the other side of the room. He pointed to a cushioned chair, and she sat down, watching him move to a recessed, makeshift bar set into the wall opposite her. He was wearing shorts and a T-shirt, and his usually styled hair was a mess—a very different look than she was used to from him.

"Not gonna lie," he said, "I wasn't expecting you to show up at my front door. Didn't even realize you know where I live."

Trace allowed another small smile to play on her face. "I know where everyone lives, Joe." It was an exaggeration—but not by much.

Joe chuckled, then nodded his head as if the statement made all the sense in the world. "Well, I'm glad you're here, even if that is completely creepy. I have something I think you're going to love. I've been saving it for a special occasion."

He reached up and opened a cabinet above the bar area, pushing past a cluster of glasses and taking hold of something that was clearly as far back in the small hideaway as possible—either on purpose or by dint of time.

Joe walked back over to Trace and presented a bottle, which he cupped in both hands as if holding a religious artifact.

"Looks dusty," she quipped.

He scowled at her, then cleaned the bottle off on the bottom of his shirt. "Don't be a jerk. This is Glaswegian whisky. One of the last batches they made before the Jar Flu hit. Do you have any idea how much plastic this cost me?" Trace didn't even attempt to answer. "Hold this." Joe handed her the bottle and headed back to the bar, where he grabbed two small glasses. Tracer stared at the faded label—at the blurred image of a castle and faint writing she couldn't quite make out.

"Here you go," Joe said, handing her one of the glasses, then took the bottle from her, gently opened it, and poured a couple fingers for each of them. He placed the bottle on a small table next to her, sat down on another cushioned chair, and held the shot up in front of himself.

"What are we toasting to?" he asked.

"I . . . don't know," Trace answered, and she realized she truly didn't. She felt the same as she had as a young child, when she took a wrong turn at night in the garbage heaps and had no idea how to get home. It wasn't a specific memory, but it had happened enough times that it had coalesced into a singular feeling.

"Well, what do you *want* to toast to?" Joe asked after a moment, scrutinizing her. She realized that he had never seen her like this before either. Vulnerable. Unsure of herself. She let out a long breath, then nodded as the answer came to her. Obvious in its simplicity.

"To change," she said.

Joe's face scrunched up in admiration as he considered her words. "I can live with that," he conceded, clinking his glass against hers. "To change."

Trace took a small sip of the alcohol, though part of her wanted to shoot it. But she could tell, based on Joe's reverence, that this was a drink worth savoring. And she wasn't wrong. Even though it burned, the liquor was full of flavor: aromatic and layered and complex. She laughed slightly as the taste radiated out across her palate.

"Wow."

"Yeah," Joe agreed. "Change is good. And so is this whisky."

Trace took another sip. Not quite as good as the first one but still better than any liquor she'd ever tasted before this visit. "Hard to argue," she murmured, and they sipped in silence for a few minutes. When they both finished, he poured himself another and went to refill her glass, too, but she held up a hand. "No, thanks."

His face wrinkled in surprise, but he didn't say anything. She'd always appreciated that about him. He never pushed more alcohol than she wanted, even when he admitted he was low on credits. Considering how desperate so many PH City citizens were, it was a refreshing change of pace.

Joe took another sip and fixed his gaze on her, unspoken words dancing behind his eyes. It was clear that he wanted to broach some taboo subject, seemed to be waiting for permission to do so.

"What?" Trace finally said.

"Well . . ." he started, then shrugged and dove in. "I heard through the grapevine that you went to Apex City."

It was Trace's turn to be surprised. She had assumed her trip was classified information, especially given the delicate nature of the situation. She had clearly assumed wrong. She thought about lying and then decided against it. Besides, the whisky was making her brain buzz pleasantly—a relief after stewing in her apartment for the last few hours.

"How the hell do you know that?" she asked, though there was no fire in her voice. She was genuinely curious.

Joe laughed. "You're not the only one with access to information, Trace."

She considered his words, then cocked her head slightly, enjoying the fact that there was more to Joe than she had guessed. "Fair."

"So, how was it? I've only heard rumors about that place."

"It was . . . pretty crazy," she admitted. "*So* many lights. And so many people. But also, kind of completely beautiful, you know? There was a much stronger sense of . . . community, I guess. At least on the surface. More freedom or something. More people out and about, not looking totally miserable, for the most part. More nightlife."

"Well," Joe said, eyes wide, "*that* sounds fantastic."

"Yeah, it was, but there was something below the surface. A darkness. A violence. I mean, obviously Bell runs PH City with an iron fist, and I . . . well, I'm no stranger to violence. But Apex City has this veneer. And when you push through it, in some ways it's way more terrifying than what we have going on here. *Because* of that veneer, you know? I don't know. I don't think either place is perfect. I guess nowhere is perfect. Not anymore."

"Based on what I've heard and what I've read," Joe interjected, "I don't think anywhere was perfect *ever.*"

"Maybe," Trace mused. Her mind went back to Brisby, a prisoner in Apex. And Ezra, a prisoner in PH City. She winced at the thought of them.

"You okay?" Joe asked, leaning forward and putting his half-finished glass of whisky on the table. He wasn't just being curious—she could see the concern in his eyes.

"I'm fine, Joe. Thanks."

"Okay. But if you ever want to talk about it, I've been told I'm a good listener."

And Trace knew this was true. During her many visits to Joe's bar, while she may have been guarded about her own life, she had seen more than one person pour their soul out and watched as Joe talked them through their pain, or heartbreak, or loss. It was always something she admired, even if she hadn't fully realized that until now. She realized, also, that she trusted him.

"I . . . met someone."

"Oh yeah?" Joe responded, sitting back and grabbing his drink. He was curious now, there was no doubt about that, but he was doing an admirable job of keeping it casual. "In Apex City, I'm assuming."

"Yes," she confirmed.

Joe waited. Didn't push. And after a moment, Trace continued.

"It's a long story. And I can't . . . I don't want to talk about it. Not really. But he wasn't like anyone I've ever met. And we shared something. Something I didn't know I could have." She pictured Ezra's face the last time she saw him. And Bell's face, too, that stupid shit-eating grin. "That I *can't* have. And I need to get over it. But I don't know how. Don't know if I . . . if I *can*. Anyway. It doesn't matter. It's over."

"I'm sorry, Trace," Joe said after a long moment. "I don't

know exactly what you're talking about, obviously, but I've been in love before. And I lost it. I know it can be devastating."

"I didn't say I was in love," she snapped.

Joe stared at her, and she felt the weight of his gaze, and more so the weight of the untruth she had just told.

"Okay," was all he said in return. Then, after a long pause: "I know we're basically the same age, Trace, but in my line of work, I see a lot of human nature, good and especially bad. Which is how I got this." He tapped his scarred eye. "I also see a lot of relationships play out in real time. And I still owe you a favor from when you saved me from those thugs who tried to rob the bar last month, so can I give you some free advice?"

Trace bristled at the suggestion and then forced herself to calm down. She took a breath, thought about the emptiness she felt deep inside. Despite the walls that threatened to rise back up, to cut off this conversation and turn Trace back into the person she'd been before her trip, she decided that hearing some advice from the closest thing she had to an actual friend couldn't be the worst thing in the world.

"Okay," she said.

Joe grabbed his drink again, took a bigger sip than he'd been taking until now, then gazed down at the dark liquid in the glass, as if trying to figure out the perfect words to impart.

He looked up, directly into her eyes.

"You're a fighter, Trace. I've seen the bruises, even when you try to hide them or refuse to talk about them—which is pretty much always. Including right now. But you work for President Bell, and you're always fighting her battles. This one . . ." He smiled sadly at her. "This one is *yours*. And sometimes it's worth fighting for the people you care about."

Trace didn't move, didn't betray any emotion on her face, but the words struck her like an open-handed slap. She thought about Ezra. Then about Brisby. And finally, her mind conjured up an image of the pyro-tech's daughter, Rachel, even though she'd never met the girl before.

"Please take care of Rachel."

Brisby's final words to her echoed painfully in Tracer's mind. She thought of her own girlhood, how she'd been sold to Bell like a piece of plastic. How so many people in her life were bought and sold at the whims of those in power.

Enough.

Trace abruptly stood and stepped toward Joe, gently taking the glass out of his hand and downing the rest of the shot in a smooth motion. He looked surprised for a second but then smiled again as she handed the glass back to him.

"You're a good guy, Old Joe."

"With age comes experience," he responded, winking.

"Now I owe *you* one," Trace said, and then headed for the door. She knew exactly what she needed to do.

28

The water felt like bullets against her skin.

Every cut, every wound, which felt like her entire body, screamed in pain at the harsh jet of PH City's public shower system. Even though she was Bell's executive enforcer and enjoyed many privileges, hot water wasn't one of them—except on the few occasions she had been allowed to use Bell's private washroom in her office, usually after a longer-than-expected mission, where she would relieve herself and then run her hands under Bell's hot water tap for much longer than required. Those seconds had felt like a miracle at the time—until Trace experienced the seemingly unlimited hot water in Apex City. And now, this lukewarm shower felt especially torturous.

One of many tortures implemented by President Bell.

Trace cranked the water off, let the water drip off her body, ran through the plan in her mind again. Not that it was much of a plan.

Clenching her jaw, clearing her mind, Trace exited the stall, dried off, and stepped over to the mirror above the small sink. Wiping away the steam, she took a long look at herself, took stock of the injuries she'd received in the last few days.

The bruises on her face were almost entirely gone now, and the sewn-up cut on her arm looked to be healing well. The scabs on her right palm were smaller, barely visible, and even the newer ones on her knuckles weren't all that bad, all things considered. The bruising on her neck was the worst—dark and noticeable—and ached like a motherfucker. Still, things could have been much, much worse.

Maybe it was the tough environment growing up out in the garbage heaps, maybe it was because of her unknown genetics, but she tended to heal quickly—her many, many cuts and bruises over the years fading faster than the ones Gunnar often showed up with after his missions.

As the mirror slowly fogged back over, Trace got dressed. Though she appreciated the new clothes that Apex had provided her, they ultimately weren't her—particularly that white shirt, despite any emotional attachment she now felt toward it.

Which is ridiculous, she berated herself.

She shrugged into her own outfit—all black, like usual—then put her hair up into a ponytail and headed down the hallway, back to her apartment, where her boots and trench coat were waiting. And her SIG Pro.

She readied herself slowly for what was coming next, lacing the combat boots methodically and checking over her gun, which she had cleaned right after returning from Joe's apartment. It was late now, and people in PH City tended to turn in early.

Including President Bell.

Fully dressed, gun at her hip, Trace headed for the door but stopped and turned around, taking in her apartment. She'd been living here since she was young—far too young to be living by herself—but looking at it now, through fresh post-Apex eyes, she realized how dismal her quarters were.

The apartment was fairly spacious, but she'd never taken the time or effort to make it her own. Nothing on the bare walls, no small Trace-specific touches. Everything just gray and white and black. The sight of it now, as she realized it might be the last time she ever saw it, made her insides ache. It represented so much—so many things she had lost, or had never even had in the first place.

She stepped out into the hallway and closed the door behind her quietly, shoving those feelings aside and focusing on her mission. Then she stalked down the hallway toward her destination.

President Bell lived on the second-highest floor in PH City.

She had the whole floor to herself, and there were two elevators that serviced it. One was the same bank that serviced the entire city, but only a few people had the elevator code to get there. Trace was one of them.

The other was a special private elevator that ran from her office on the top floor directly down to her apartment. Trace had never been in that particular elevator but had been outside Bell's apartment a few times via the regular one when she'd been asked to deliver something important after "office hours." She'd never been invited in, had barely been able to get a peek inside.

What she did see was lavish. And now, in hindsight, infuriating.

Trace knew a lot more about her boss than she'd ever let on. Not that Bell revealed much directly. But Trace had been around the president nearly her entire life and knew that the older woman often forgot her XN was even in the room. Trace listened to every single word. Absorbed information like a sponge because that's what Mackie had trained her to do—but also because she didn't have anything else going on in her life, other than her seemingly endless missions and an occasional drink at Joe's. And all that knowledge boiled down to one indisputable fact.

Bell was incredibly dangerous.

Trace knew she was insane for what she was about to do, knew that she should just sink back into her old life, her by-the-numbers existence before the trip to Apex City. But the thought of that was worse than whatever might happen next. She would rather die than go back to that version of herself.

And maybe you're about to, she thought.

Trace took a deep breath, feeling her entire body relax just like it did in the moments before any mission.

Just another job.

Which she knew was a total lie.

Tracer knocked on the door and was surprised when it opened farther at her touch. It had been slightly ajar, and she somehow hadn't noticed. Proof that she was already off her game on this so-called mission. Back before Apex, she would have immediately noticed a detail like that.

Her usually decisive mind waffled. The deepest, most instinctual part of her knew that she should walk away, go back home, get a good night's sleep. She could come up with a new plan in the morning—or maybe she'd wake up and realize she was being ridiculous.

This whole insane idea might all just be a result of that—admittedly delicious—whisky that Joe had given her. Maybe she wasn't thinking straight. She could just sleep it off and then settle back into the relatively safe and comfortable life she'd been enjoying for decades.

But the other, much louder part of her brain was telling that other part to *shut the fuck up.*

Trace withdrew her SIG Pro and gently nudged the door the rest of the way open.

"President Bell?" she said cautiously, taking a step inside. It was dim, the foyer dark except for a small amount of ambient light that bled in from other rooms she couldn't see. Despite the feeling that something was very wrong, she fell back onto her training and forced herself to breathe calmly through her nose. Then she took another silent step forward, listening intently.

Nothing.

"I'm sorry to barge in," she said, forcing her voice to remain calm. "But there's something important I wanted to discuss with you."

It was still completely quiet in the apartment, and she took another couple of steps forward, her movement blunted by the thick carpet beneath her boots. As her eyes adjusted to the gloom, terrible images rose unbidden to her mind.

President Bell, dead, lying in a pool of her own blood, killed by a rampaging Garbage Dweller who had somehow made it inside. Or perhaps murdered by a terrified Ezra.

Ezra. It was so much more likely that Tracer would find his corpse inside. Maybe he'd refused the president's demands, declined her advances. Trace had seen Bell kill people, horribly, for all manner of slights. Trace's stomach churned as she imagined Ezra in a pile of his own gore lurking just around the next corner.

Remembering her training, feeling her old safeguards clicking back into place, her thoughts receding and instinct taking over, Trace crouched lower and then slowly made her way into the next room.

A tall, ornate lamp on a long table lit the spacious room, which had two large couches pushed against the walls to Tracer's left and right. The center of the room would normally have been a wide-open space, but someone had placed a big—and expensive—piece of plastic onto the carpet, upon which sat a wooden chair. And much like Tracer's fears, there was indeed a corpse tied to it. Visions of Mackie's final moments rose up, and she had to force them away as tears filled her eyes.

The body in front of her had suffered countless cuts, all over its naked body, and blood pooled on the plastic below. The smell hit Tracer's nose, and it was unfortunately a scent she was used to. But the sight of the dead body nearly made her vomit, or scream, or both.

It wasn't Bell, wasn't Ezra.

Old Joe had died in this room, painfully, and had done so recently.

"*No*," Trace whispered and began to move forward, but stopped when she felt a piece of metal placed gently against the back of her head.

"Drop. Your fucking. Weapon," President Bell said, her voice right next to Tracer's ear.

Trace complied. The SIG Pro thumped to the ground, almost noiseless against the thickness of the lush carpet. She thought about her own apartment, its wooden floor. Her rage built, and she struggled to push it down. She realized she was mostly mad at herself.

The president picked up the gun and moved around Trace, keeping both weapons trained on her XN. The other gun was Bell's pistol, the one she almost always had on her, hidden somewhere but within reach. It was smaller than the SIG Pro, housing a smaller-caliber ammunition, but just as deadly if used right.

The president stared up into her subordinate's eyes, then shook her head in disappointment.

"Just how fucking dumb do you think I am?" she said, her voice low and full of the promise of violence.

Trace didn't answer the way she wanted, didn't say anything.

"You think you can just run around *my* city, whine about

my property to your dead friend here, and then come waltzing into *my* house with your goddamn weapon drawn?!"

Bell suddenly lashed out and clipped Trace in the jaw with her pistol, and Tracer went down to a knee, blood immediately gushing out of her mouth. She didn't yell, didn't grunt, didn't make a sound. Just took it. Knew she deserved it. She'd gotten Joe killed.

Trace looked up as Bell leaned down, both guns held out in front of her. "And yeah, Tracer, when I say 'property,' I mean Ezra. Cuz I fucking *bought* him. And all it cost me was that stupid little pyro-tech that you're so in love with. And you know what? You know what I'm thinking? After the mess that *you* made? Maybe I'll cut up his pathetic little wife and daughter next."

Trace moved faster than she even thought possible. To her credit, Bell moved quickly, too, firing both guns simultaneously. The bullet from the SIG Pro missed, sailing right past Tracer's ear, but the pistol in the president's right hand found its mark, blowing a small hole through the younger woman's left shoulder.

Now Trace screamed, the pain nearly overwhelming, but the momentum took her body directly into Bell's, and the two women went down onto the ground in a discombobulated jumble.

The president lost her grip on the SIG Pro but held on to her own weapon and fired it again, indiscriminately. She didn't hit Trace, but the sound, following the first two concussive bursts, was deafening, and as Tracer rolled along the floor with her adoptive mother and boss, she realized she couldn't hear anything. And could barely feel her left arm.

Blood sprayed across the white carpet while the two women grappled, Bell pulling the trigger several more times when she thought she had Trace in her sights—but the younger woman was fast, trained to react instantaneously in life-and-death situations like this. She kept violently nudging Bell's arm when she saw the president's finger tightening on the trigger.

Much to Trace's surprise, Bell was stronger than she looked. The president had always terrified her, but it had nothing to do with her physical presence and everything to do with her cruelty, her predilection for over-the-top retribution. Trace had been punished by her adoptive mother before, but the woman had never actually tried to kill her. Until now.

As if in response to these fleeting thoughts in the back of Tracer's mind, Bell threw a punch with her right hand—which still held the gun—and landed it on the wound in her XN's shoulder. Trace screamed, the pain racing down her mostly numb arm and across her chest. Her hearing was starting to return—a small comfort in an otherwise dire situation.

"You like that, you ungrateful bitch?" Bell yelled gleefully, and pulled her bloody fist back to land another blow in the exact same spot.

Despite her brain swimming, Trace tapped into a deep well of calm that she'd cultivated over years of training and missions. She allowed Bell to think she was about to connect with the punch, but rolled at the last second, both women toppling over, smashing into the long table, the tall lamp crashing to the floor. While the base of the lamp didn't break, its new position on the floor, with the shade broken and bent in many places, cast surreal bands of light across the room.

Trace tried to stand up, intending to race across the room and pick up her SIG Pro, but her head continued to spin, and she slipped slightly on her own blood, and that was all the advantage the president needed. Bell landed another right-handed blow to Tracer's face, and the XN went down to her one good hand and knees, more blood gushing from her nose and mouth. She tried to move her left arm to help in her efforts to stand up and was relieved to find she still had some control over it. Despite that, realizing she didn't have any clever ways out of her current situation, no backup plan, no one coming to save her, she glanced up and saw that Bell was now standing, her gun pointed directly at Tracer's forehead. Her hearing was starting to come back, but listening to the president's words, she wished it hadn't.

"I should have known," the president said, shaking her head. "I convinced myself you were so single-minded, so loyal. But you're just like the rest of them. All the ones who betrayed me over the years. Like my husband. Like Mackie. And now you're gonna die, Tracer. And for what? Some piece of meat from Apex City? Ridiculous." Bell cocked the gun. "And just so you know . . . I think it's important you hear this before I blow your stupid brains out the back of your head . . . I always told you what you needed to hear to do your job, to get me what I wanted. You were *never* a daughter to me."

Tears formed in Tracer's eyes at Bell's words. On some level, she'd always known this was true, but it still broke her heart. She blinked, felt the water run down her cheeks. Maybe she deserved to die after all. Maybe she'd lived a life of complete disillusionment, and this was the obvious conclusion. Maybe it would be a relief.

But then she thought about Brisby. About Ezra. And her heart broke all over again. She desperately wished she could somehow save both of them before she died—but she had failed. It was over.

Bell pulled the trigger. And the gun clicked.

"What the *fuck*?" the president said, staring at the weapon.

Trace didn't hesitate. She lunged up at Bell, forcing her injured arm to work, ignoring the insane amount of pain that radiated from the still-bleeding wound. She took the president to the ground using one of the first moves Mackie had taught her when they first started working together. It was an inelegant takedown, one Trace hadn't used in years, but it was effective—and the XN slammed her boss onto the ground, face-first, with an incredible amount of force. The breath exploded out of the president's lungs, and her spent gun went tumbling across the blood-soaked carpet.

Trace instantly looked around for a weapon as Bell struggled to get her bearings. The SIG Pro was too far away, would require Trace to get up and cross to it—and there was no guarantee that Trace's continued blood loss wouldn't catch up to her while she did so.

No, it was too risky.

But there was nothing else, no obvious weapons within grasp, or even in sight. And then her eyes landed on the perfect choice. The *only* choice at this point.

Part of her didn't want to do it, was tired of killing, but she realized that only one of them was going to walk out of this room, and she was determined to save Ezra and Brisby—if either of them were even still alive.

Trace grabbed the lamp and pulled it close, digging her knees deeper into Bell's protesting form.

"I'm gonna fucking *murder* you, Trace! And then feed your corpse to the Garbage Dwellers! You hear me?!"

Tracer ignored Bell, focused on her mission. She yanked the cord as hard as she could with her good hand, and the wire disengaged from the lamp, the room falling further into darkness. Another room deeper in the spacious apartment threw off a sufficient amount of light, so Trace could still see what she was doing.

The cord was long enough that she was able to wrap it around Bell's neck, and she pulled it tight, simultaneously looping it around both of her hands. Her left shoulder screamed in protest. She ignored it.

"What . . . ?" Bell sputtered, realizing what was happening. "No. Tracer. No."

Trace disregarded the words. Pulled tighter. Felt the wire cutting into Bell's neck. Realized tears were still falling down her face. More and more of them.

"Please . . ." Bell said, voice barely more than a raspy whisper. "You were always the one. Not Gunnar. I saw . . . saw myself in you. I love you, Tracer. I . . . I *love* you."

Hearing this made Trace cry harder. It was the only time she'd ever heard the words spoken by Bell. She realized she was sobbing.

Soon the president couldn't speak at all, but Trace didn't let up. She'd been fooled before in this kind of situation. And Bell was dangerous. Maybe the most dangerous mission ever. And hopefully the second to last. Trace was in so much pain, so sick of the constant cycle, of the life that had been forced on her.

Eventually, perhaps after more time than was needed, Trace let go, and President Bell's body slumped to the floor a final time. Tracer fell next to her adoptive mother, the tears still falling, and held her wounded shoulder, the pain a distant roar now. She looked at Bell's face.

Pale. Surprised.

Trace closed the president's eyes.

Then, after what felt like a very long time, she shakily got to her feet, using one of the blood-splattered couches as support. She picked up her SIG Pro, holstered it, and stumbled through the rest of the apartment, shocked at how huge it was, until she found a washroom—approximately the same size as Tracer's living quarters. Clean. Indulgent. And when compared to the life of the Garbage Dwellers, to those people who had raised Tracer and then sold her out of desperation for a handful of credits . . .

Sickening.

Trace grabbed one of the smaller towels hanging from a rack

and carefully peeled her coat back, folding the white material gently over her shoulder and against the bullet wounds in her shoulder, the front and the back. If Bell had hit her with the SIG Pro, this would be a very different situation. While the wound was bad, the pistol was less deadly, especially when handled by someone like Bell—a relative amateur who usually had other people do the shooting for her.

Luckily, the bleeding had slowed a little, and Trace surmised that the bullet had mercifully missed anything vital and had gone clean through the other side. She was lucky. But it pulsed in time with her heartbeat, a constant reminder that she couldn't leave it untended forever.

But there were other things to handle first.

Ezra.

She racked her brain, trying to think where Bell would have stashed him. He wasn't anywhere in this apartment, and Trace knew there was a prison level underground—where Trace had seen horrible atrocities committed by the president in the name of justice.

No. Bell wouldn't have subjected her future husband to that, even if she was enraged with her XN. Ezra had nothing to do with Tracer visiting Joe. He was blameless, just another tool for the president to use.

Trace settled on the next logical place to look and headed back through the apartment, her trench coat hanging from her right forearm. It would be too painful to put it back on right now.

She stopped when she came across Joe's body, still strapped to the wooden chair. In a perfect world, Trace would cut him free, figure out a way to bury him out in the short expanse between PH City and the Puente Hills garbage mounds. But this world was far from perfect, and she knew she was still in danger as long as she stayed in this city. There were many, many people who were loyal to the president and who would stop at nothing to take Trace out once they found out what she'd done.

"I'm sorry, Joe," she whispered, then headed over to the private elevator, which she'd spied during her quick tour of the apartment.

Entering it, Trace discovered there were two buttons: up and down. She pushed the up button, and the doors smoothly slid shut. As the car moved slowly up to the top floor of the city, music began to play from unseen speakers—just like in Apex City.

"You gotta be fucking kidding me," Trace muttered, pressing her palm against her shoulder, which was starting to hurt more, the initial shock to her system wearing off.

After what seemed like hours but was actually seconds, the doors slid open, and Trace stumbled out of the elevator and into Bell's office. She'd never entered it from this direction and found herself momentarily disoriented, partly due to the blood loss and blows to the head, she guessed.

"Ezra!" she yelled, suddenly convinced that she'd picked the wrong place to look, that she would be forced to head down to the prison level—where Bell's guards would be waiting. She wasn't sure if she had it in her to face off against anyone else.

"Tracer!"

His voice made her stomach flip, and she turned, and Ezra was wrapping his arms around her.

"Ow," she said. His arrival certainly hurt, but she didn't care, just took the moment to inhale his scent, a smell she already knew and loved.

"Sorry, sorry," he said, and pulled away, then saw her gore-soaked shoulder, her battered and bloody face. "Holy *shit*. What happened?"

"It's a long story," she said, too exhausted to go into details.

"Come on. We're making one more stop. And then we're getting the fuck out of here."

"What about . . ." he said, looking around nervously. Trace looked closer and saw that Ezra had a slight black eye and a bruise on his cheek. "What about Bell? She said she was coming back as soon as she took care of some business."

Tracer worked her jaw, then let out a slow breath through her nose. Felt her nerves calm as her training once again asserted itself.

"Bell won't bother anyone ever again."

Ezra scrutinized her words, and then his eyes widened slightly.

"Oh. Okay."

Despite everything, Trace smiled. She'd convinced herself only minutes earlier that she would never see this man again. And now here he was, right in front of her. A little worse for wear, but alive. Trace leaned in closer.

"Tell me to stop."

He didn't, and their lips touched, an electric charge racing across Tracer's body.

After a moment, her knees buckled, and Ezra helped her stay on her feet.

"You're hurt," he said. "Bad. We gotta get you help before we go anywhere. I met that doctor. The nervous little guy. Dr. Webb. We can go to him."

"No," Trace said, blinking against the dizziness. Ezra wasn't wrong, but Webb couldn't be trusted. He was scared of Bell, just like everyone else—terrified, really—but even in death, the president might hold sway over the doctor. "I just need to get this wound cleaned up before we make our last stop in this damn city." She swallowed down a wave of regret about their next destination. "And I know exactly where we can go."

29

The hallways of PH City were still empty—thankfully.

Tracer stalked through them, grim-faced and in pain, Ezra staying close by and keeping her steady when she occasionally lost her balance due to blood loss and exhaustion. He hadn't asked her where they were going, which she appreciated. She didn't want to talk about it, was too racked with guilt.

"It's just up here," she said quietly, and then slowed down when Old Joe's apartment door came into view.

Reaching it, Trace tried the doorknob, knew it would be locked—and swore under her breath when she discovered she was correct. She took a deep breath, tried to ignore the throbbing in her shoulder, the continued numbness in her arm, and prepared to kick the door open.

"Wait, what the hell are you doing?" Ezra said, gently grabbing her hand.

"What I need is on the other side of this door. Which is locked. So I'm gonna kick it in," she replied as if it were the most obvious thing in the world.

"No. You're not," Ezra replied, taking a breath. "I am."

Before she could respond, Ezra leaned slightly back and kicked the center of the door. There was a loud thudding noise, but the door didn't budge.

"Ow," Ezra said, frowning.

Despite the situation, Trace laughed slightly. "Yeah. You don't kick the center of the door, you idiot. Line up on opposite side of the hinges and kick it right below the doorknob. And the way you leaned back was very cute, but you need to center yourself and really put all your weight into the kick—one single smooth motion. Okay?"

"I figured when I got a girlfriend, she would call me a cute nickname. Didn't think it would be *idiot*."

Trace raised an eyebrow at him. "Girlfriend?"

"Never mind," he mumbled, then squared up in front of the door, slowing his breathing down. Based on what he'd told her that night in the desert—her favorite night of her entire life, which felt like years ago—he was easily the fastest and most agile thief in Apex City, but brute strength had never been his defining characteristic.

In a sudden burst of movement, Ezra kicked out and landed a thundering kick just below the doorknob. The wood instantly splintered and cracked open, the door swinging forward several inches, shards falling to the ground at their feet.

"Nice work," Trace admitted, then moved forward, pushing through the half-open door, Ezra following. She flicked a light switch, and her stomach dropped when she saw the state of the apartment. Furniture was overturned, objects had been destroyed, and there were streaks of blood across one of the walls. Joe clearly hadn't been taken peacefully.

I'm sorry, Trace thought, and not for the first time.

Ezra looked at her, confused, but she shook her head. She couldn't talk about it. Not yet.

"Go find the bathroom and see if you can find anything that resembles bandages or tape. I need to get this wound properly dressed as soon as possible. The bleeding has slowed but it's not gonna stop on its own. And I don't know how much longer I can last."

"On it," he said, his face serious, and he headed deeper into the apartment.

Swallowing down her guilt, Trace headed toward the inset bar. All the bottles of alcohol had been smashed, glass littering the ground like the stars she had seen above the desert only the night before. Swearing, she reached up with her right arm and opened the small cabinet that Joe had accessed earlier, pushing past the undisturbed glasses. She just hoped that Bell hadn't found the secret stash and destroyed it.

Just as her hope began to dim, her hands wrapped around the bottle, and she withdrew it. Seeing the old Glaswegian whisky now, she felt a hollow ache in her stomach, then shoved the feeling aside. She could mourn her friend later.

After a moment, Ezra returned and held up two handfuls of materials.

"Whoever lived here, they were clearly prepared for the worst."

"That tracks," Trace said appreciatively. "Joe was a thoughtful guy."

If Ezra was curious about the mention of another man, he made no indication and instead moved closer to Tracer. "Okay, so . . . what's the plan?"

"I need you to help me get my shirt off, and then we're gonna sterilize this wound and dress it. I got lucky—it's fairly clean—but this is still going to hurt like a motherfucker."

"I'll be gentle," Ezra offered.

"Thanks," she replied, uncorking the bottle and taking a

swig. It tasted even more delicious than it had earlier. "But it's not gonna matter."

It was even more painful than Trace had expected.

Despite how delicious it was, the whisky felt like a heated iron being applied directly to her shoulder. But it did its job. Ezra carefully wrapped the wound as Trace grimaced against the almost overwhelming agony, and then he helped her get her coat back on.

As they made their way through the seventh floor, she knew that the stop had been worth it. Despite having lost some of the mobility in her left arm, she was in less pain, which allowed her mind to focus on the mission at hand—something she had to do before they escaped PH City. Eventually, she'd figure out how to sew the wound up before it got infected, but the hasty bandaging would have to do for now.

"Where are we going?" Ezra wondered out loud, clearly confused. She didn't know how to explain the entire situation to him—didn't have the energy or time—so she just glanced back at him and smiled briefly at his bruised face.

"Trust me."

He nodded. "Okay. I do."

She continued moving forward until she reached the apartment number she'd been looking for—a door that looked like every other one in this dim, dirty corridor. The lower the level in PH City, the less the maintenance crews visited, resulting in smudged walls, cracks in the concrete, and blinking or dead light bulbs overhead.

"Let me do the talking," Trace instructed, then knocked on the door gently.

After a moment, they heard muffled movement within, and a fearful voice responded to the knock.

"Yes?"

"Jenna, my name is Tracer, and I'm . . ." She tried to think of the right words, to put herself in the other woman's shoes, and then decided just to tell the truth. "I'm a friend of your husband's."

A long moment stretched out, and Trace glanced back at Ezra, whose eyes were locked on her, a serious look on his face. She knew he had her back, no matter what this situation was, no matter how long it took.

"Brisby?" the voice said, the fear laced with sadness now.

"Yes," Trace responded. "And I'm here to help you. You and Rachel."

Almost immediately, the lock clicked and the door swung open. Trace found herself staring at Jenna Frost, whose eyes were puffy and red-rimmed from lack of sleep or crying, or both. Hiding behind the woman, a little girl peered out, her arms clasped around a pink plastic toy computer—which Trace recognized.

"I don't understand," Jenna said. "Where is he? I haven't heard anything from him in days." She seemed to suddenly notice Tracer's trench coat, the blood and bruises, and her eyes widened further in fear. "Wait. You're the woman Brisby mentioned. The one who works for the president . . ."

Jenna started to back up, clutching at her daughter, and Trace raised her hands. "I do . . . I *did* work for Bell . . . but I don't anymore."

She knew she needed to gain their trust and didn't want to take them out of there at gunpoint if she didn't have to. But she also knew that time was short. "And this is my friend Ezra. We know where Brisby is. And we want to bring you to him."

"*Where?*" Jenna demanded, her voice suddenly steely. Trace

admired the abrupt fire, but admiration didn't mitigate the increasing risk every second that went by.

"I'll explain on the way. I promise I'll get you to him, one way or another. But you need to get whatever you absolutely need, that you can carry on your person, and we need to get the hell out of PH City. *Now.*"

Trace could practically see Jenna's mind racing. After a moment, Rachel reached up and tapped her mother gently on the shoulder. Jenna leaned down, keeping her eyes locked on Tracer's. "What is it, honey?" she whispered.

"I remember Daddy talking about her," Rachel responded, her whisper ten times as loud as her mother's, and Trace fought back a sad smile. The little girl looked so much like her father. "She's on our side."

Jenna blinked as she considered her daughter's words, then nodded slightly and stood back up to her full height.

"We can be ready in two minutes."

Five minutes later, the four of them were huddled in the elevator, heading down to the second floor.

The pink computer clasped in her hands, Rachel kept looking up at Tracer, even though Jenna held her close. Trace wanted to tell them everything, but she knew there'd be time for that later. Right now, she had to keep her mind clear, keep the, at times, overwhelming pain at bay. Ezra was looking at her, too, but she ignored him as well.

The elevator shuddered to a halt, and Trace brushed past all of them once the doors opened, the SIG Pro clutched tightly in her fist. "Stay close," she ordered, not looking back. "And keep your mouths *shut.*"

She was greeted by silence behind her and was grateful for it. She thought about herself at Rachel's age—before she'd been traded over to the president—and how wild she'd been, how loud. She hadn't had half of the girl's poise, and she hoped she would have time to talk with Rachel—about her life, about her dad. But all of that would have to wait. They were one door away from getting the hell out of this city—this prison—but Trace knew in her gut they were far from being in the clear.

She thought about the last time she'd been in this hallway, which had also been the first, how Bell had talked her ear off. Trace realized she would never hear her adoptive mother's voice again, and part of her mourned that fact. It was ridiculous, and she silently berated herself, but it was there—a part of herself deep inside that loved the woman who had raised her, regardless of the woman's intentions and actions while doing so.

They reached the end of the long hallway, which was bathed in shadows, the single door hanging against the far wall like a waiting mouth. Trace took a deep breath and glanced behind her. The other three were close, just like she'd instructed, and they looked up at her with fearful, expectant eyes.

"Stay here," she said quietly. "I'll call for you if it's clear."

"Okay, Ms. Tracer," Rachel whispered back, and Jenna pulled her daughter even closer, her fingers trembling.

"We'll wait until you give us the signal," Ezra confirmed, and started to reach out but stopped himself. She had to keep from doing the same. There would be time for that later.

She hoped.

Trace entered the cavernous room, holding the gun out before her.

And found exactly who she was expecting.

30

"Lower your fucking weapon, Tracer," Gunnar hissed.

He was standing next to Goldie and had his gun aimed directly at her chest. It was the P226 MK, his favorite weapon, something he'd found during one of his first missions for President Bell. Trace preferred her SIG Pro but had seen how proficient Gunnar was with his gun, knew that she was already at a disadvantage here.

Tracer lowered her gun, holstered it, and raised her hands into the air.

"We can talk this out," she said, realizing the words sounded as hollow as they felt. She and Gunnar had never talked anything out, had barely ever communicated despite being raised together. All by design, she knew.

And he'd been adopted first, which meant he always looked down at her, considered her inferior—at least it seemed that way to Trace. And she was confident that he had always dreamed of finding himself in this exact position: pointing his gun directly at her.

He took a few slow steps forward, looking her over, focusing especially on the hole in the shoulder of her trench coat, the large blood stain there.

"What happened to you?" There was no concern in his voice—this was an interrogation. She knew because she had done the same thing hundreds of times before.

"It's a long story. Put your gun down, and I can explain everything."

"*No!*" he yelled, cocking his MK. "She told me to stay here, to guard Goldie, and that she'd call for me when the coast was clear."

Trace knew exactly who her adoptive brother was talking about. Potential lies raced through her mind: If she could convince him that she was here on a mission from Bell, that she'd been instructed to take Goldie again, then perhaps this could end without any further bloodshed.

But even though she'd been raised to hate Gunnar, to compete against him at all times, she knew he was smart. Knew that he followed his orders to the letter. If he'd been told to wait for instructions from the president, he wouldn't do anything else. There was no way she was getting out of this alive. She just hoped that Ezra, Jenna, and Rachel would know to run once they heard the gunshots. They could hole up in the Frosts' apartment for a long time—maybe figure out another way out of the city.

And since this was the end, Trace decided to tell the truth.

"President Bell . . . our mother . . . Gunnar, she's dead."

"*What?*" he asked in a harsh whisper, taking another step forward, aiming at Tracer's face now. "When? *How?*"

Trace once again fought against her better instincts and didn't lie.

"A little while ago. She tried to kill me. I defended myself. Choked her to death. I . . . I don't think I wanted to do it, Gunnar. But maybe I did. Maybe I always did."

"Why would she try to kill you?!" he screamed, eyes suddenly filled with water. Trace had never seen this kind of rage from him before and suspected she had made a grave error in judgment. His hand holding the gun was shaking, and she prepared herself to die. "You're lying!"

Trace took a step closer, the tip of the gun almost touching her forehead now. "Why would I lie about that, Gunnar? It would've been easier to tell you some elaborate lie—you and I have both done it a million times on missions, on her behalf—but I'm done lying. She's dead. I killed her. Before she could do it to me."

A tear rolled down his face, and he shook his head, clearly trying to process what he was hearing. "This makes no sense. She raised us. She's our mother."

"I know," Trace whispered, fighting back tears herself. Deep in her heart, she had always wanted this—a brother she could talk to openly, regardless of the consequences. She'd seen a flash of it the day Mackie died.

Now that Gunnar's walls were breaking down, Trace realized how overwhelming it was, how painful. She felt splayed open, vulnerable, and the part of her that had been trained to keep her emotions safe and guarded hated every second of this.

"She may have raised us, Gunnar," Trace said quietly. "Trained us . . . but she didn't love us. We were tools. Weapons. To be used when she needed. And as soon as I was an inconvenience, she tried to kill me." She took another hesitating half step closer, her voice beginning to waver. She wasn't sure if it was the fear of dying or the fear of revealing her emotions to someone she had been taught to compete against, to hate. "Did she ever say that she loved you, Gunnar?"

His eyes went wide as he considered the question, and she saw his finger tightening on the trigger. She kept her eyes open, didn't want to face death unseeing. She had known this day would come eventually, had always suspected it would be as a result of violence. And knew she deserved it.

"She . . . she's *really* dead?" Gunnar whispered, staring deep into his sister's eyes.

"Yes," was all Trace could manage, though there was more she wanted to say. But it was too late. Everything that mattered had been spoken.

Time seemed to freeze, and Trace thought about her entire life, about the little girl she'd been out in the garbage heaps, the young woman who had been trained by Mackie, the missions she'd carried out, and how her entire life had changed in the last several days. Thought about Brisby, and especially about Ezra. About that stupid smile she loved so much.

Gunnar suddenly lowered the gun, wrapped his arms around Tracer, and openly wept.

Shocked, Trace slowly raised her hands and hugged her brother back. The two of them stood there for a long moment, the room silent other than Gunnar's gentle sobs. Finally, they disengaged. Trace couldn't believe what was happening. She'd seen horrifying moments of violence from this man, open hatred directed her way for over a decade, and now he stood in front of her with a sheepish look in his wet eyes.

"I'm sorry I killed Mackie," he said.

Trace blinked at his words, emotion surging again, then put a hand on his shoulder. "You didn't kill him, Gunnar. *She* did."

His face contorted and then, after another moment, he nodded. "You're right," he said, clearing his throat and holstering his gun. "But I'm still sorry. I mean . . . about everything. Our entire lives. I always did whatever I had to do to make her happy. I thought she wanted me to hate you, so that's what I did."

"It's okay," Trace said. "She did the same to me. And we were just kids."

He wiped at his eyes, stood straighter, his face going smooth, and the old Gunnar reappeared. She had to stop herself from going for her gun, from reverting to deep-seated instincts.

"I assume you're here for Goldie," he said, his voice hard again. She tried to figure out how to respond and once again decided to be honest.

"Yeah. I need to go back to Apex City. Brisby is being held prisoner there. And I need to rescue him."

"Okay," Gunnar said, reaching into his pocket and withdrawing the car key. He held them out to her, a small smile appearing on his face—which also looked bizarre to Trace after decades of sneers and death stares. "Drive safe."

Trace gently took the key from him, then turned around, fighting every instinct when turning her back on Gunnar. She wanted to change, was determined to do so, but damn if it wasn't difficult.

"Ezra! Ladies!" she called out. "Time to go!"

After a moment, Ezra stepped through the doorway, followed closely by Jenna and Rachel. They all looked terrified but also confused when they saw Gunnar standing next to Trace.

"Let's get moving," she said, pointing to the car, which had been hastily patched up—the holes painted a slightly different golden color and the fourth tire having been replaced. The trio hesitated for a moment and then moved quickly past the siblings, though Ezra slowed for a moment, seemed about to say something.

"I'll explain later," Trace whispered, and he nodded and kept moving. He got into the passenger side, while the mother and daughter slid into the back seats, the two open doors slamming shut at almost the same time. Silence reasserted itself in the cavernous room. Trace stared at Gunnar.

"You should come with us," she said.

Gunnar laughed, a sound she had never heard from him

before, then shook his head. "That's tempting," he admitted. "I . . . wish I could get to know you a little better. But PH City is my home. It's all I've ever known. All I *want* to know, to be honest. And someone needs to clean up the mess you made, Trace."

"Fair," she said, then smiled at her brother. "And who knows? Maybe I'll be back someday."

"Maybe," he said quietly, then hugged her a final time and headed out the way she'd just entered. The door clicked shut quietly behind him. Trace stared at the door, disbelieving, wondering if it was all just some ruse, if he'd come bursting back through the door, gun blazing.

But no, he'd been a scared, abused child, too. Had been following orders his entire life, just like Trace had.

And now they were both free.

Trace turned around and headed to Goldie, got into the driver's side, and started her up. The engine roared to life, sounding even stronger than the last time she'd been in it.

"Guess she got a tune-up," Trace said appreciatively, and noticed that the gas tank had also been filled. She wondered absently how much plastic that had cost. Brisby would probably know just by looking at the gauge, before and after.

Brisby.

There was no time to lose.

She turned to Ezra, could tell he was still afraid, even though he was trying to act nonchalant. "You okay?" she asked. He nodded. Trace glanced back at Rachel and Jenna, who weren't trying to act nonchalant at all. The little girl was tight up against her mother, the toy computer in her lap, face streaked with tears. "You okay, too?" Trace asked, even though she knew they weren't, not really, but they nodded as well.

Tracer put Goldie into Drive and began heading down the ramp and toward the exit. It felt good to have her hands on the steering wheel again, to take a little bit of control back from a situation that had clearly lost it.

"So . . ." Ezra said, and Trace could hear the curiosity burning behind the single word. "What's next?"

"I have a plan," she replied after a moment, keeping her eyes locked on what was coming, on the garage door that was currently a pinprick in the distance.

"Oh yeah?" Ezra asked, turning slightly toward her. She could feel his eyes on her and loved the sensation. Wished they didn't have this final mission ahead of them, that they could go somewhere and just be together. But there was still one more thing to be accomplished. And she never left a job unfinished.

"Yeah," Trace said, reaching inside her trench coat and withdrawing the walkie-talkie that had been there since her night in Apex City. Ezra saw the item she was holding and cocked his head, clearly confused. She was enjoying his reaction and would explain everything during the drive. But for now, she thought about the steps they needed to take. Hoped her plan wasn't too crazy.

"We just need to make one stop first."

PART 6

THE ROAD

31

Trace leaned on the horn, the sound echoing out across the canyon.

This was her third time in Cajon Pass, and it was beginning to feel almost like a home away from home. She'd been here with Brisby, and then Ezra, and now she was here with three people, two of whom were trying to hide their looks of terror as they huddled in the back seat of the car.

Once they were clear of PH City, Jenna and Ezra traded seats, which gave the XN a chance to quietly explain what had happened to Brisby. The woman took the news better than Trace had expected, but perhaps she was just in shock. Still, she said she trusted whatever Trace thought was best, said that Brisby had spoken highly of her skills as a mercenary, and of her guarded kindness as well. Trace didn't know what to say to that, so she said nothing.

"You sure about this?" Ezra asked from the back, where he glanced nervously out his open window. He and Rachel had bonded during the drive, remarking on the world outside of the car—the first time Rachel had ever seen anything outside of

Puente Hills. Ezra even managed to make her laugh a few times, which seemed like a minor miracle to all the adults in the car.

"No," was all Trace said, then hit the horn one more time.

After a moment, a familiar figure appeared in the distance, stalking toward them with purpose. Trace got out of the car and waited. She wasn't at all sure about her plan. But she didn't feel she had any other choice.

Finally, Therese crossed the road, her semiautomatic cupped in her hand and leaning against her shoulder. She looked at Trace skeptically, confusion creasing the corners of her eyes.

"Not gonna lie," she said. "Didn't expect to see you again so soon." Therese glanced at the bloody hole in Tracer's shoulder. "What happened to you?"

"I got shot," Trace admitted.

"Hmm," Therese responded. "Well, I had to talk several people out of shooting you . . . again . . . just now. You can't just keep showing up here over and over again unannounced."

"That's totally fair," Trace said, "and it won't happen again. But I need a favor. Kind of a big one."

Therese considered her words, sniffed, and then nodded.

"Well, I kind of owe you a big favor. What is it?"

Trace glanced over at Ezra, Jenna, and Rachel, then back to Therese.

"It's a long story. And I need to sew up my shoulder, if possible. Would it be okay if you brought us . . . wherever it is that you live?"

Therese cocked her head at the request. Trace heard Ezra clear his throat behind her, so she looked back, and he immediately shook his head. Apparently, she was making some kind of mistake here, some kind of breach of Nomad protocol.

"No," Therese said in response to Ezra's silent warning. "It's fine. I mean, we've *never* let an outsider visit the Yard. Let alone four. But I'm the leader now, and I'm willing to make an exception. Under one condition."

"What's that?" Trace asked, turning back to the Nomad.

"Can you give me a ride? It's a few miles away."

The junkyard was sprawling.

The sheer number of broken down and smashed cars was mind-boggling, but Therese led them through the maze with the surety of someone who had made her way through it hundreds of times before.

The drive to the Nomads' hidden home had been without incident, Jenna slipping into the back seat with Ezra and Rachel while Therese got into the front. No one had spoken during the drive, which Trace deeply appreciated. Her mind was racing with what had happened that day, and what she still needed to do.

When they arrived outside of the junkyard city, Trace locked Goldie up and placed the key within the inner pocket of her trench coat, and then the four of them followed Therese into the wilderness of metal and glass. Trace had to keep herself from gaping at their surroundings, but Ezra and the Frosts had no such compunctions. The little girl's eyes were especially huge as she looked up at the towers of shattered vehicles.

Ten minutes later, they reached a large clearing at the center of the junkyard, and several shocked Nomads stood up at their arrival, reaching for weapons.

"Stand down!" Therese shouted, holding her own gun tight. "These four are my guests. Tracer is one of our former leaders, and she is therefore welcome here."

A few of the others grumbled but did as they were told. One

of the Nomads, a short bearded man, sprinted off into one of the many alleyways, no doubt to inform others of the newcomers.

"We'll be making our nightly fire soon," Therese said, turning toward Trace and the others. "In the meantime, I'll have our doctor summoned so she can look at your wound. And I'll have some food brought as well."

"I'm really hungry," Rachel suddenly said, stepping forward.

"Rachel!" Jenna said nervously, pulling her daughter back.

Therese laughed and stepped toward the little girl, squatting down so she could look her in the eyes. "Oh yeah? What kind of food do you like, young lady?"

"Umm . . ." Rachel muttered, suddenly shy.

"She isn't picky," Jenna volunteered, and Therese smiled, rubbing the little girl's already-messy hair, and stood up.

"We don't have many kids around here," the Nomad said to Trace, looking out at her companions, who were already back to work on their various tasks. "And the ones we *do* have grow up fast."

"Trust me, I get it," Trace replied darkly.

Therese looked into Tracer's eyes. "I'll bet you do." She readjusted the gun on her shoulder and looked around. "Okay. You four get as comfortable as you can. I have some things to take care of, and then we'll talk about that favor you need."

The fire roared, dwarfing the one Ezra had made only a night earlier.

They'd eaten their fill of roasted desert meat, Rachel shoving food in her face with a wild abandon that made everyone else laugh, and now the young girl was asleep in her mother's lap. Jenna's head was leaned back against a dented car, and her eyes were fluttering open and closed, a futile attempt to stay awake while the Nomads talked and shouted and moved in and out of the light thrown off by the blaze.

The doctor had sewn up Tracer's shoulder on both sides, and though she lacked Dr. Webb's experienced touch, Trace was deeply appreciative of the young woman's time and skill. And luckily she hadn't seen Korath or Finn. Maybe they'd heard about her arrival and didn't want to be in her presence again. Which was fine by her.

Ezra sat close to her by the fire, and she fought an urge to put a hand on his and instead just stared into the flames, her mind racing. Despite the energized pandemonium playing out around her, despite her growing respect for the Nomads' way of life, her final mission still loomed, huge and dangerous.

She wanted to get on with it.

As if reading her thoughts, Therese approached, her hair down and falling over her shoulders. Instead of holding her rifle, she now had a handgun tucked into the front of her pants. She nodded at Trace and Ezra as she approached.

"Okay," she said, "I think these savages can handle themselves for now. Did you want to talk about that favor?"

"Can we talk privately?" Trace asked, standing up. Ezra did the same.

"Of course. Follow me. There's a spot where we can keep an eye on everyone but also hear ourselves think."

They followed Therese to the edge of the clearing, out of the direct light from the fire, but still close enough that Trace could see the sleeping Frosts. She trusted the Nomads . . . to a point. There was no way anyone was going anywhere near Jenna and Rachel without her being aware of it.

"Talk to me," Therese said, leaning back against a column of smashed car parts.

"My friend is being held against his will in Apex City," Trace said, getting right to the point. "Jenna's husband. Rachel's dad. We're on a mission to rescue him. But even though Ezra knows the city—"

"Like the back of my hand," he interjected.

"Like the back of his hand," Trace confirmed, "we're still talking about going up against a major military presence. I need a way to get in and out without being detected."

"Hmm," Therese considered, staring out toward the raging fire but clearly lost in thought. "There's no love lost here for Apex. Probably every person here has had a relative killed by their guards. But we've been hesitant to fight back. We have plenty of weapons, but they have not one but two walls. Even just getting past the first one seems almost impossible."

"With what I'm planning, you won't need to have a direct confrontation," Trace said. "And I have no interest in putting the lives of your people at risk. What I really need is a distraction. Something big and loud that will allow me to slip in and out before they even realize what's happening."

"Your plan . . ." Therese said. "Will it hurt the assholes who kill my people?"

Trace thought about Chancellor Stewart, about the way he'd spoken to her. And thought about Captain Janus, too. The cold hatred in his eyes. The look on Brisby's face as he'd been dragged away.

"Yeah," she answered. "If everything goes right, I think it's gonna hurt them pretty bad."

A big smile appeared on the younger woman's face.

"I'm in." She pointed toward the other Nomads, who continued to shout and laugh and dance around the fire. "I just need to explain the situation to them. Even though they've accepted me as their leader, I still need to go through the proper protocols."

"I know we just got here," Trace continued, "and you've already been so generous. But how soon can we do this? I'm . . . worried about my friend."

Therese considered the question, then whistled to a nearby Nomad, who stood on the edge of the shadows, far enough away that he couldn't hear their conversation but not engaged with the rest of the revelers. He looked up at them, and Therese made a series of hand gestures at him. He nodded and headed out into the maze of junk.

"Who's that?" Trace asked.

"My cousin," the Nomad responded. "But I asked him to go get someone else. One of the older Nomads. Someone who has a knack for predicting the weather."

"The weather?" Trace said, not understanding where Therese was going with this.

"Yeah. You said you want something big and loud. Well, the last time I talked to her, she said there was a big storm heading our way. A day or two out. If you can sit tight until then . . . which will give us time to do this right . . . I'm betting we can ride that storm in and provide one hell of a distraction for you."

Trace looked at Ezra and was surprised to see that stupid, amazing grin on his face. Apparently, he liked the sound of Therese's plan. Then Tracer glanced over at the slumbering forms of Jenna and Rachel. They looked so peaceful, so different from how they'd appeared ever since Trace had met them earlier that day.

She knew they were as anxious as she was to rescue Brisby, but they had to take their next steps very carefully, even if it took longer than any of them wanted. They only had one shot at this.

Tracer looked back and locked eyes with the Nomad leader.

"Let's do it."

PART 7

APEX CITY

32

Timothy Janus stared out at the storm through the large window, the city twinkling below him, and took a long, satisfied breath.

Everything was fine now. At last. Their pyrolysis machine had been fixed. They had a permanent technician who would keep it in running order for the rest of his life, could teach the younger techs how to do the same. And everyone still thought Chancellor Stewart was in charge.

Just the way Janus wanted it.

He'd been working for years to put all the pieces together. But it hadn't been easy. He'd spent his childhood dreaming of walking these halls, staring up at the city's spiral with desire and envy in his eyes. His parents hadn't been poor, hadn't spent their days trudging through garbage, hands covered in muck while looking for tiny pieces of plastic, bartering for a credit here and a credit there. No, he'd grown up comfortable, the youngest of three—though his older siblings were lazy, a forgotten footnote in his adult life—while his parents had worked as guards on the walls. The outer wall at first, and then eventually the inner one—a symbol of status to be moved from one to the other.

He could have had the same life, probably would have even been able to start his career on the inner wall thanks to nepotism and stayed there. A coveted position. Could have taken a spouse, had children, lived a comfortable life. But simple comfort wasn't enough. Not for him.

When he was young and saw the way the city guards strutted, listened as they berated the wall guards—sometimes even his parents after an innocent mistake had been made—Janus hadn't reacted with fear or contempt. He felt admiration, saw the kind of man he wanted to be. And he determined at a young age that he would do anything necessary to work within the walls of Apex City.

And maybe even someday rule it.

He took another deep breath and watched a jagged line of lightning rip open the sky, followed a few seconds later by rumbling thunder. It didn't rain often in or around Apex, a fact that most of the citizens loved. But the rare storms calmed his nerves—he appreciated the discordant and unpredictable violence of the elements. It spoke to something deep inside of him.

His parents had been surprised when he applied to be a city guard, told him that only wall guards with years of experience were hired to work inside the city, directly for Chancellor Stewart. Even his siblings mocked him for his ridiculous aspirations when their parents were away at work—though the ridicule didn't last long after he silenced them with his fists despite being smaller than them. He had, after all, been lifting weights during every spare minute, his destiny crystalline in his mind. After that, his siblings kept their mouths shut when he argued with his parents about applying to be a city guard when he came of age.

They forbade him from doing so. But they also couldn't watch him every hour of every day. So as soon as he turned old enough, when they headed off for work, he left a few minutes later, turning toward the chancellor's administrative building.

The executives who oversaw job applications laughed when he told them why he was there. He argued, but they only laughed harder, seemed ready to throw him out on his ass. But one of them must have noticed the glint in his eye, seen something there, because the man pulled Janus aside and sat him down. Listened to what the young man had to say, his words spoken with quiet but determined passion. And he must have liked it because he left for a moment and returned with a thick sheaf of papers.

The test to be a city guard. The test that his own parents had been denied for years.

Janus didn't say another word, just went to work on it, which he'd secretly been studying for whenever he could sneak away. He would talk to any adult he could about it: friends of his parents, retired city guards drunk at local bars or public events, even street rats who trucked in rumor. Anyone.

It took him hours, but he finished the test, handed it over with confidence to that same man—whom he never saw again after that day. In the years that followed, he often wished he'd asked for his name, berated himself for not having done so. Now that he was in a position of immense power, he would reward that man handsomely if he could. For all Janus knew, however, he was long dead.

But it didn't really matter.

He had passed the test with flying colors, catching the attention of the captain of the city guard. The woman chuckled when she met him, when she heard that this was the man-child of a pair of married inner-wall guards. But her laughter faded when she pitted him against two of her officers in a "friendly" hand-to-hand combat exercise, and Janus literally wiped the floor with them.

From there, his ascent was rapid.

He moved out of his house within a week and moved in with the other city guards. His parents begged him to put in a positive word for them, but their previous words—how he wasn't good enough to work anywhere but the wall and never would be—rang in his ears. He wished them luck with their lives, told his older siblings to fuck off, and never looked back.

He kept his head low, did his job. Followed orders and hurt people when he was told to do so. The amount of plastic being brought into the city's coffers increased modestly at first, and then significantly once he was truly let loose. Even the chancellor took notice. Janus was promoted repeatedly within a few years. The city's oil production increased during that time, more and more buildings and businesses being built, and the lights of Apex City got brighter and brighter and brighter.

But it still wasn't enough for Timothy Janus.

The more time he spent with Stewart, the more Janus realized that the old man was weak. Complacent. Allowed people to walk all over him, allowed criminals to walk free when Janus believed they should be locked away. Or dispatched entirely.

Stewart also allowed people into the city, people who had no place in their society. Strangers, illegals. Murderers and rapists. It made Janus sick. But he kept his mouth shut, bided his time. He knew the current situation wouldn't last forever. Even if it sometimes felt like it.

When the captain who had tested him all those years earlier finally retired, Janus secretly lobbied for the job. He'd made many friends during his meteoric rise but just as many enemies. Bribes were made as needed, as were beatdowns in dark alleyways. Regardless of how it happened, Timothy Janus was appointed captain of the Apex City Watch. The youngest person to ever have the job. And something he had only dreamed of as a child.

And now, he stood in front of a giant window in Chancellor

Stewart's office—which would eventually be his, he reminded himself—staring out against a growing desert storm. He knew it was going to be a big one. Could feel the electricity in the air. And loved it.

The last few days had gone exactly how he'd hoped, had been the culmination of months of planning and execution. But as he went through the events in his mind, moment by moment, his mood suddenly turned sour. One person had almost fucked everything up. And even though she was gone—forever—it still bothered him. Her name echoed on the edges of his mind like a curse.

Tracer.

Even though he knew he'd never see her again, he wished he would. So he could show her, with his fists, what he really thought of her. That dumb bitch with her trench coat and her ridiculous ponytail and her sneering, never-smiling face. Just the thought of her made his heart rate increase with rage.

He walked across the room and poured himself a drink, getting control of his breathing. He was being ridiculous. He knew that. Everything had gone according to plan. The plan he had laid weeks and weeks earlier when Stewart had approached him, confided in him about their energy production. How he wanted to cut back on consumption, how they were going through oil too fast. It was unsustainable.

Janus had assured his boss that everything was fine, that the plastic was essentially never-ending. After all, people in the age before the Jar Flu hadn't cared about how much they used. The landfill in the ring around the city was miles and miles and miles long, and almost as deep—an exaggeration, perhaps, but it certainly seemed that way. They had nothing to worry about.

Stewart didn't agree. He ordered Janus to cut back on oil production, to instruct the businesses and the population about his new orders: Dim the lights of Apex as needed. Janus had agreed, verbally.

But in his mind?

Fuck. That.

He had already been taking control from Stewart for a long time, slowly but surely, and this ridiculous decree only justified what the city's captain had already been doing. He had a loyal crew who would follow whatever he instructed, so he methodically put together a plan, all while telling the chancellor that he was following orders—enacting the reduction of oil production.

All while ordering the city's pyro-techs to increase it.

His plan had worked, for a time. He was easily able to keep the aging leader in the dark, distracted with alcohol and men and rumors of increased trouble with Nomads. Meanwhile, he demanded more and more plastic from the plastic scavengers—inflicting pain and terror on them when they couldn't deliver.

Yes, the scavengers may have grown to hate him, but the plastic yield increased—all while Stewart believed they were becoming less and less dependent on oil.

The idiot.

Janus knew that plastic, and thus the city's energy, was boundless. And when he eventually took over as chancellor, he would double the production from the already all-time high. And then double it again.

Everything was going smoothly. Until the day he'd been called into a meeting with the pyro-techs. They were young. Exhausted. At the end of their proverbial ropes. They couldn't keep up with the new demands. One had even threatened to quit.

Janus hadn't meant to kill the tech on the spot. It had been impulsive, a rare moment of complete loss of control for him. But the kid had been mouthing off, using the word *impossible*, which Janus fucking hated. The moron wouldn't stop talking even when his coworkers told him to calm down. Said that the captain's orders were *unreasonable.* Janus had pulled his gun before he'd even realized what he was doing. Not a memory that made him proud. But it was the kid's own fault.

That left the operation with one less tech, and thus even less oil production than before. Which was an obvious problem.

That night, Janus considered his options. He could give in, go along with Stewart's decree, allow for the now-inevitable decrease in energy production. Or he could come up with his own plan. Could fucking *do* something about the situation, like he had always done.

So Timothy Janus headed over to Apex City's pyrolysis machine, in the dead of night, and sabotaged it.

The panic the next morning was delicious. The chancellor's eyes almost literally bugged out of his head when he saw the smoking contraption, pretending he understood how the fucking thing worked in the first place. The remaining pyro-techs looked at Janus, their eyes making it very clear they knew exactly what had happened, but none of them said a word. They were, after all, standing on top of the faded splotch of blood from their former coworker's ruptured skull.

Stewart went into full panic mode and convened multiple closed-door meetings. Janus very subtly guided his boss toward an inevitable conclusion: They needed help. And PH City wasn't that far away.

The two cities had only communicated a handful of times since larger society had collapsed. Suspicion and distrust were just too great after people had turned on each other with such unimaginable violence at the height of the Jar Flu and the depletion of fossil fuels.

No one trusted anyone else. The remaining cities on Earth

had been built on that simple tenet. But there was no choice. They were out of options. Just like Janus had planned.

Apparently, PH City was run with an iron fist by someone named President Bell. People in the streets and bars of Apex laughed at the rumors, how this other place was apparently more run-down, little more than a hovel, how the entire city was housed in a single slapdash structure.

But Janus ignored the mockery, focused on the details just under the surface. Like the rumors that the leader of Puente Hills was someone who knew how to wield her power, how to keep the masses in their place by any means necessary, and that PH City had multiple pyrolysis machines—not just one—and that their techs were far more advanced than Apex's own.

Janus was impressed by what President Bell had accomplished. Jealous.

And his next move was obvious.

He helped Chancellor Stewart craft a message to President Bell. A plea for help.

The leader of PH City replied quickly, assenting to sending help, but asked for something in return. A simple request. Laughable, really. Janus told Stewart it was a small price to pay, and the older man agreed. After all, who would miss a street rat? There were, after all, so many to choose from.

Everything was finally in place—all they needed to do was wait for the PH City pyro-tech and then make the trade. And they had. But not before Janus had been embarrassed in front of his own guards, and an entire bar full of people, by Tracer. Yes, they'd gotten what they wanted, even if Brisby Frost was being difficult. Janus would break the man's spirit eventually, and he would continue to build Apex into the perfect society that he envisioned—but the thought of Tracer getting the drop on him still rankled.

If only there was some way he could get revenge.

It was ridiculous, he knew that. But it reminded him of the way he had dealt with his siblings, who had bullied him for so long—until he had shown them the error of their ways. He just wished he could have the same kind of satisfaction with the PH City mercenary. But it wasn't going to happen. He needed to let go of his anger. Not one of his strong points, he admitted to himself.

His musings were abruptly interrupted by a knock at the door.

"Come in!" he shouted, half-annoyed at being disturbed when he'd given instructions to be left alone, but also half-relieved to be pulled out of his dark thoughts. Perhaps a visit to that same bar later that night would cure his melancholy. He'd find some new scavenger to beat into submission. The kind of drunken release that always improved his mood.

A young guard entered, the nervousness obvious on his face. Janus loved to see it—proof that people feared and respected him.

He had made it a point to memorize the name of every single officer in his command. It wasn't that he necessarily rated all of them, or really any of them, but he knew that when he made them feel like he cared about them, like he was invested in their banal lives, they would work twice as hard to make him happy. *Nick.* This one's name was Nick. A good, if unremarkable, officer.

"I'm very sorry to interrupt you," the young man said, voice trembling.

"That's fine, Nick," he said, letting a false smile slip across his face. He stepped up to the guard and stared down into his eyes, which seemed to be focused everywhere except on his commanding officer's. "But there must be something serious going on for you to disturb me when I explicitly requested the exact opposite."

Janus suspected it was something minor—a dispute between scavengers that had destroyed some more important citizen's property, or perhaps Brisby Frost was still being belligerent and an officer had hurt him. Yes, Janus had told his subordinates to keep their hands off the PH City pyro-tech, but Janus found the little man annoying, and would he really blame one of his soldiers if they'd popped the little whiner in the jaw? Janus almost laughed at the thought, waited while Nick struggled to get the words out.

"Spit it out!" the captain suddenly shouted, his own spittle ironically flying across the young guard's face.

"The Nomads, sir," Nick said, and before he could continue, Janus took another step forward, grabbed the guard's dress shirt, and pulled him closer.

"*What. About them?*" the Captain snarled, his patience having grown immediately thin. Janus had killed more than his fair share of Nomads during his time in the Apex military and often trained his officers out in the desert—teaching them how to track and kill the savages from a distance. It was good practice but also acted as a deterrent. The Nomads knew better than to come anywhere near his city.

Nick swallowed and then finally made eye contact with his superior officer.

"They're attacking."

33

Janus stormed down the hallway.

It made no sense. The Nomads had always been far too afraid of Apex's superior firepower to dare a frontal assault. Yes, they would sometimes attack a group of city workers on the rare occasion they'd venture out to map parts of what used to be Las Vegas that hadn't yet been cataloged. Janus thought the mapping was a waste of time—they had everything they needed within their walls—but Chancellor Stewart thought it was part of what he called the city's "adventuresome spirit."

In other words, *a waste of fucking time.*

But when the Nomads did make the mistake of assaulting a group of Apex citizens, Janus made the desert rats pay tenfold. And it wouldn't be like his occasional training exercises. No, this was personal. He would hunt them down with a vengeance and kill whoever he could find—whether or not they were the ones directly responsible for the attack.

Admittedly, it wasn't always easy to find them. They were shockingly adept at disappearing into the seemingly endless sand. But when he *did* get his hands on them after one of their brazen assaults, Janus got up close and personal. Got his pound of flesh. And then some.

Which made tonight's offensive all the more confusing. The Nomads had no hope of invading the actual city or hurting any of the guards—who had the higher ground, and thus the tactical advantage—and only risked their own lives in the attempt. Perhaps the uncharacteristically strong storm had emboldened them, made them feel they could hide within the deep shadows of night and cloud-covered sky.

But their reasoning didn't matter. Janus would ground them down into the sand they loved so much and then hunt the rest of the rats down the next day. It was about time that he exterminated them—once and for all.

Nick and another guard followed close behind, but all three of them halted abruptly when the elevator at the end of the hallway slid open and Chancellor Stewart stepped out, his face a furrow of anger and concern.

"Tim! What the *hell* is happening?"

Janus fought an impulse to plant his fist right in the middle of the older man's face. A vivid fantasy he had experienced many, many times before. He *hated* it when the older man called him Tim. Hated him in general, at this point.

"Chancellor," he forced through a gritted-teeth smile, "everything's fine. Just a small issue at the front gate. Nothing I can't handle. You should get back to bed."

"*Bed?!*" Stewart nearly screamed, and Janus could see the two guards squirming in his peripheral vision. "From what I'm told, we have Nomads attacking the front gate. *For the first time in the history of our city.* And you want me to go to bed? Who the *hell* do you think you are?"

The captain's vision went red, and before he knew what he was doing, he'd backed the tall leader of Apex against the wall next to the closed elevator doors. Nick and the other guard hung back. *A wise fucking choice*, Janus thought, staring up into Stewart's face. No one else needed to hear this.

"Who do I think I am?" he whispered harshly, and he saw the fear register immediately in his so-called boss's eyes. "I'm the one who runs this fucking city, Frank. And we both know it."

"I . . . I . . ." the chancellor stuttered, looking around as if someone there could help him. Janus glanced back. The guards kept their eyes on the ground.

"That's right," he said, turning back to Stewart. "You got nothing to say. So . . . go back to bed and stop pretending you have *any* idea what the fuck is going on around here."

The chancellor blinked rapidly, couldn't seem to get any words out. A long moment passed. The only sound was the rain pounding against the walls of the city. "Okay," Stewart finally said.

"Great!" Janus replied in his normal voice, smiling, reaching over to push the call button. The doors immediately opened. "You go and get some rest, and we'll handle this little inconvenience. You've got bigger things to think about, Chancellor."

Stewart nodded and practically slid along the wall, then entered the elevator.

"Good night," the captain said to the still-stunned leader, his eyes wide as the doors slid shut. The grin vanished from Janus's face. He turned to look at his guards and knew from the terror he saw in their eyes that they would keep their goddamn mouths shut. No one needed to know what had happened in this hallway.

"Let's go," he ordered, hitting the call button again. "It's time to kill some fucking Nomads."

The situation was worse than he'd expected.

The outer wall near the front gate was on fire in multiple places, despite the heavy downpour, and Nomads were running in and out of the shadows, hacking at the metal and wood that made up the first level of protection around Apex. The city guards were firing at the attackers, but in short, controlled bursts—just the way Janus had taught them. He felt a strange surge of emotion and realized it was pride. His job as the real leader of this city was to teach his subordinates how to protect the weak and the innocent—and to keep out the vile animals who would seek to harm them—and he saw that playing out directly in front of him.

Still, the Nomads' attack was more vicious and well thought-out than he would have expected. The storm complicated matters, with visibility significantly reduced and the rain getting in his soldiers' eyes, affecting their aim. The Nomads were used to living out in the elements. The city guards were decidedly not.

While Janus watched the chaos play out, he caught sight of one of his guards running along the wall nearby. The captain reached out and grabbed the young woman by the arm, pulled her close.

"Report!" he demanded. His mind went through its mental catalog. *Smith, Rebecca.*

The young woman blinked through the water, and then the realization of who she was talking to suddenly registered because she stood up straighter and saluted. He fought the urge to slap her hand down.

"The Nomads are attacking, sir!" she half-shouted, eyes flicking behind him and over the wall, where the attackers screamed from between the shadows. *No shit,* Janus thought, but allowed her to continue. His guards had never faced a situation like this before. "Several of them have almost made it over the wall, but we've managed to hold them back. We've hit a couple, I think, but I'm not sure if we've killed any."

"Yet," Janus added, looking deep into her eyes. She stood even straighter at attention.

"Yet," she confirmed.

"I'm going to walk the wall, Lieutenant Smith." He saw the slightest smile appear on her face at the fact that he knew her name. He would allow it. This once. "And when I get back, I want a full report and any suggestions you or your team might have on how we can keep these aggressors at bay—and then eradicate them from the face of the earth."

"Sir, yes, sir!" she yelled, saluting again, then hustled off toward her fellow soldiers, who looked at her with huge eyes.

It was unlikely Janus would take advice from her, from any of them, but he knew this was one of many ways to keep his lackeys motivated. Let them think they had a voice.

The same thing had worked for years with Chancellor Stewart.

Janus pulled his jacket a little closer around his neck as the rain increased. Blinking up into the dark sky, he wondered if he'd ever seen a storm this bad. Part of him appreciated the synergy between the elements and his mood. He'd once gotten his hands on something called a "Bible," a book that millions of people had apparently worshipped. Which was ridiculous, of course, but some of the stories in the first half had been fascinating—humans suffering at the whim of some unseen, capricious entity. With the storm of his lifetime raging overhead, he understood on some level why they had believed it—or had needed to believe it. That kind of belief was a powerful tool, and perhaps something he would begin to use in the coming days and weeks as he solidified his control of this city. Give the masses something to believe, something that would help them accept their lot in life, their miseries, and he could pretend to be one of the converted right along with them. They'd never know the difference.

At the sound of gunfire down along the wall and more screams below from the Nomads—which sounded more like rage than pain, unfortunately—Captain Janus continued his walk, hoping he'd personally get to kill at least one enemy before the sun came up.

As he strode forward, formulating the next steps in this battle, and in his larger plans for Apex, how he would implement them as brutally as possible, another one of his guards came rushing forward, panic etched into his face. The man, Lieutenant Jack Carlson, was slightly older than the other soldiers in the captain's employ, had more experience—which made the naked fear in his eyes all the more disappointing for Janus.

"*What?*" he said, already annoyed with the man's behavior.

"Sir, their attack is highly coordinated, very effective. They're using some kind of grappling hooks, and a few of them have almost managed to get over. They've even pulled down a few of the guards . . . though I think our people got away."

"You *think*," Janus echoed, feeling his anger rise again.

"Yes, sir," Carlson confirmed, nodding vigorously, apparently unaware of how angry his boss was becoming. "Your troops are ready and willing to follow your commands. Just say the word."

Janus fought back an urge to backhand this sniveling coward over the wall, let him plummet to the ground and then be put out of his misery by one of the rabid animals running around half-naked out in the desert. Instead, he gave his orders, speaking low and articulating every word so even a moron like Carlson could understand them.

"Radio the other stations on the wall. Tell them to head to us, immediately. We'll overwhelm these Nomads with sheer numbers, then hunt them down with strike squads, and make them regret ever coming *near* Apex City."

"S-sir?"

"Is there a problem, Lieutenant?" Janus barked.

"No, sir . . . but won't that leave the rest of the city vulnerable?" Carlson responded, his voice barely making it out of his mouth. The man was clearly at war with himself, trying to figure out what to say, how to say it.

Janus didn't care. He'd had enough. He grabbed his lieutenant by his uniform shirt and dragged the man to the edge of the wall. The drop to the ground, dozens of feet below, was dizzying. A terrified Carlson glanced at the attackers just below, then back at his boss, whose enraged gaze didn't waver as it bored into the younger man's eyes.

"No one has *ever* breached Apex City's inner walls since its inception. Do you want to be the one to let Chancellor Stewart know that we allowed that to happen?" Janus hissed, shaking the lieutenant, Carlson's feet slipping on the edge of the wall. "*Do you?!*"

"No, sir!" the man practically screamed, a primal utterance of absolute terror, and then Janus pulled him back onto solid ground and shoved the man farther along the wall.

"Call the fucking reinforcements," Janus ordered quietly. "*Now.*"

Without hesitating, Carlson grabbed the walkie-talkie from his belt and did as he'd been commanded. Janus brushed past him and continued along the wall until he found a spot with a better view of the chaos below. He removed his gun from its holster, took aim, and waited. After what felt like a very long time, he fired, and a Nomad went down in a wet puff of red.

Janus smiled. *The first of many.*

He watched as two Nomads appeared from the shadows and pulled their injured comrade into the distance. A half dozen more took the injured man's place, carrying rope and weapons. One of the Nomads, huge and fast, let loose with a spear, which sailed through the air and impaled one of the guards down the wall from where Janus stood. The man collapsed, and other Apex City guards mirrored the actions of the Nomads from only moments earlier, pulling their hurt—or possibly dead—friend out of further harm's way.

God damn it, Janus thought, wiping the rainwater out of his eyes. *I'm going to kill every single one of these motherfucking savages. Even if it takes me all night.*

"Get those reinforcements here!" he screamed at Carlson, moving back toward the lieutenant and wildly firing his gun at the oncoming Nomads. "And in the meantime, we need to hold the gate! Whatever it takes!"

Trace pulled Goldie along the southeastern side of Apex City's outer wall.

Even this far away, she could hear the distant conflict raging on the other side of the city. Their plan was working perfectly. So far.

While they waited for the storm to arrive, they had taken the time back at the Nomads' junkyard city to sleep and recuperate as much as possible. Everyone seemed relieved to get a bit of rest. She and Ezra had also been able to get some time alone, but Trace had a difficult time focusing on him, on their growing relationship. Like always, she found herself obsessing about the mission. And this was the most important one of her life.

Therese had offered for Jenna and Rachel to stay put during the attack on Apex City, but Trace had declined without even thinking twice about it. Therese would personally be leading the charge, after all, and although Trace appreciated all they had done for them, she wasn't about to take a risk and leave Brisby's wife and daughter in the hands of the nomadic tribe she had just met. Despite what they were doing to help.

Trace had also been skeptical about the older Nomad who had predicted an incoming storm. How the hell would she even know that? It seemed ridiculous. But as Trace stood outside Apex's southeastern wall under a merciless torrent of rain, she had to admit to herself that the woman had been more than accurate. The conditions were perfect for a Nomad-driven distraction and a very quiet break-in on the other side of the city.

The key had been how and where to break in. Which is where Tracer's gift from Darcy Jones had come in handy.

Once they were within range, Trace had made contact with the Apex City guard, who was surprised—and delighted—to hear from her new friend. But the delight dwindled once she heard what Trace was planning. There was a long moment of static-filled quiet after Trace made the request. Ezra and Jenna looked at the XN, worry etched deep on their faces. If Darcy wasn't who Trace thought she was, if the young guard took this opportunity to warn her superiors, their plan would be over before it even started. And Brisby would be trapped there for the rest of his life.

"I can't let you in, not even through the back gate," Darcy had finally said, whispering through the fuzzy connection. "I have too much to lose. I'm sorry. But I'll tell you exactly where to sneak in. It's a blind spot on the southeastern side that's never guarded."

And now Trace sat staring at the wall, Ezra sitting next to her in the front seat. She had used the natural landmarks that Darcy had mentioned to locate the blind spot, but she wasn't entirely sure she was in the exact right area. There was still a decent chance they would run into a dozen guards the minute they were over the walls.

"Okay," she said, looking at Ezra, Jenna, and Rachel. "I'm going in. You three stay here. Lock the doors. If I'm not back by the time the sun starts coming up, or if you see a single guard, take Goldie and go back to where we found the Nomads. They'll take care of you."

Jenna nodded. Trace looked at Ezra, who was biting his lower lip.

"I'm coming with you," he said quietly, his eyes on hers.

"What?" she responded, incredulous. "What are you talking about? That's not the plan."

"I know it's not," he countered. "I didn't want to get into it before, in front of Therese. I knew you'd argue . . . just like you're doing right now. But I'm going, too. I could literally navigate this city blindfolded, and we're going to have to be as fast as possible. Janus is a violent psychopath . . . and luckily for us, a hothead, which means the distraction is probably going to work. But he's also smart, so it won't work for long."

"Ezra, it's too dangerous. You're not trained to—"

"Trace!" he shouted, and she was shocked by the timbre of his voice. "I care about you. I want this mission to succeed. For both of us . . ." He glanced at Rachel and Jenna, then back at Tracer. "For *all* of us. And the most likely way for that to happen is if I'm with you."

A long charged moment passed while the rain pounded the roof of the car.

"He's right," Jenna said, leaning forward and gently placing her hand on Tracer's uninjured shoulder. "I know you're used to working alone. But you need him. And Brisby needs you."

Trace looked at the other woman and saw that tears had formed in her eyes. She realized they were probably around the same age, and she suddenly wanted to know everything about Jenna. Hoped she would someday be able to find out. She had never had a female friend, and she realized that Bell had actively made sure that nothing like that ever happened, and all the things she had lost or never even had in the first place broke her heart all over again. Trace let out the breath she hadn't even realized she was holding.

"Fine."

"Besides, you'll never get over the wall—either of them—without me showing you how. Especially in this weather," Ezra said, his usual charming and infuriating tone reasserting itself. Then he got out of the car and headed through the pounding rain toward the tall, dark structure without looking back.

"I like him," Jenna commented, nodding as she watched him through the water-shrouded window.

"Me too," Rachel added.

Tracer sighed. "Me too," she agreed, then got out of the car and followed Ezra to the wall, and whatever lay on the other side.

34

Tracer moved through the shadows, deeper into the heart of the city.

Ezra was just ahead of her, leading her toward the building that housed Apex's prisoners. Getting over the walls had been surprisingly easy once he'd shown her where to place her fingers in the small crevices between wooden beams and metal reinforcement. She watched in awe through the waves of rain as he made his way up the wall as if he were walking across a room, then struggled to replicate what he'd done—a frustrating task but one she had accomplished. Mackie had trained her how to climb difficult surfaces—but this was by far the most challenging she had ever traversed.

The in-between area was quiet, practically deserted—a result of the rain, Ezra explained. Normally, the scavengers would be out there day and night, but none of them were used to the rain, and they avoided it during the rare occurrences when it chanced to hit the city. A few brave souls still mucked about through the detritus, hoping to find bits of plastic despite the storm, but they were easy to avoid thanks to the thick rivulets of water that continued to pound down from the dark sky above.

They made their way through the in-between quickly, not saying anything to one another, but making frequent eye contact as they wended through and around the massive piles of garbage. They'd decided, for obvious reasons, to avoid any of the roads that led from the outer to the inner wall, but luckily Ezra knew the ins and outs of these human-made hills better than practically anyone in Apex City. Every time his eyes landed on her, Trace felt her stomach twist, and she knew it had nothing to do with the dangerous situation into which they were about to place themselves. She had never been so happy to be with someone in her entire life, even in the rain and out amid the seemingly endless refuse—and the realization both excited and terrified her.

Soon, they reached the inner wall, far away from either of the two gates that led inside, and Ezra once again pointed out the optimal locations and manner in which to scale this barrier as well. He made his way up, and Trace followed, finding it much easier this time. When she dropped down on the other side, they were standing close to each other, and he smiled, brushing an errant strand of hair out of her eyes.

"You're a natural," he whispered through the rain.

She wasn't able to stop herself and kissed him with an abandon that took them both by surprise. She wondered if this might be the last time their mouths would ever touch and suspected he might be thinking the same.

It was a short moment, and yet impossibly long, and when they finally separated, she looked around, got a sense of where they were: behind a large series of buildings and covered in deep shadow.

"Lead the way, street rat," she said, and he scowled at her playfully and then did exactly that.

And now they were approaching a dark, squat building from the back, no entrance on this side other than two rows of windows on top of each other, like some kind of sick smile daring them to go through with their plan.

Ezra pulled Trace closer, and she blinked through the rain at him.

"I can't guarantee he's in here," he whispered, wiping water off his face, though it was pointless. "But this is where they keep 'enemies of the state,' as Janus likes to put it. My guess is that they don't want Brisby to get too comfortable, at least not yet. Based on what you and Jenna and Rachel have said about him, I'm guessing he's being difficult. Janus will want to break him. And this is the place the lovely captain puts people when he wants them broken."

"Okay," Trace said, her mind clicking into battle mode, eyes taking in the building. There was no question that these windows would be shut and locked tight, particularly because it was nighttime and especially because of the storm. And she didn't want to knock on the front door. She noticed some piping along the upper half of the structure, above the second row of windows, and did a quick mental calculation.

"Stay here," she instructed. "I'll be right back."

This time, she didn't give Ezra time to argue, and apparently he agreed with her decision on some level because he didn't follow. Trace reached up and grasped one of the lower-level windowsills, heaved herself up, and then repeated the maneuver with a second-floor window. She took a deep breath and made sure her footing was secure—or as secure as it could be on a three-inch sill in the rain—and then stretched her right arm up as much as possible. At first, she thought she had miscalculated, and cursed herself for it, but then her fingers connected with a thin stretch of piping and she wrapped them around the metal, hoping it would be anchored enough to hold her weight.

Trace got her other hand on the pipe and felt the dull ache from the recently stitched shoulder wound but ignored it. Then she slowly raised herself up as if doing a pull-up during training and felt her feet leave the windowsill below. She held her breath.

The pipe held.

Emboldened by her success, Trace continued her way up the back of the short building, using the pipes as a makeshift ladder, and soon found herself standing on the roof. The clouds were extremely thick, the rain continuing to fall in sheets, so it took her a moment to fully take in the details of where she was standing.

And then she saw what she'd been looking for. A small curved metal structure jutted up from a corner of the roof. Some kind of cooling unit. She approached it quickly and saw that entry into the vent was prohibited by a slatted grate. Squatting, she noticed that it was held in place by multiple screws—it wouldn't just pop off. She cursed. Didn't have time for this.

Trace gently placed her fingers in between two of the slats and pulled. There was a bit of give, which was encouraging. This wasn't a brand-new unit, which probably meant the screws weren't new either. But ripping the cover off wouldn't exactly be quiet. And while the distraction the Nomads had created was clearly working, based on the lack of guards anywhere in sight, there was no guarantee that this building didn't have additional security. According to Ezra, this was a prison after all.

Trace racked her brain, was about to chance it, when the answer presented itself. A flash of lightning lit up the sky momentarily, and Trace tensed as a result, tightening her fingers around the metal slats. When the thunder followed a few seconds later, she pulled with all her strength—and just hoped she didn't pop a stitch.

The grate came off with a grinding complaint, and Trace silently thanked the thunder. The resistant metal had been even louder than she'd expected, and she just hoped that no one in the building below her had heard it. She waited a moment while the last of the thunder died away and then slid feet first into the vent.

Just hope I don't get stuck, she thought grimly, and then wiggled her way in.

Brisby Frost pulled his knees up even closer to his chest.

His new room was adequate—there weren't bars on the windows, and he had plenty of food and water and even a few old, musty books—but this was still a prison.

He missed his wife and his daughter desperately. Couldn't believe that he hadn't had a chance to say goodbye, and wondered if he would ever see them again. He cursed President Bell, and not for the first time. If she had simply asked, he would have been willing to move to Apex City and work on their damn machine—as long as his family could come with him. Instead, they had traded him in return for some kind of mail-order husband. A slave for a slave.

He was sitting on the floor in a corner, cold and uncomfortable, but he felt guilty lying in that foreign bed, pulling strange-smelling blankets up to his chin while Jenna and Rachel were miles and miles away, probably scared out of their minds.

During the last couple of days working on the pyrolysis machine for Stewart and Janus, he'd done his best to take stock of the buildings and the city itself, which he glimpsed during his trips to and from his duties. And based on what he saw, the sheer number of guards in this city, and its size in general, there was no way he was ever getting out of there. He was stuck. For the rest of his life.

He sighed and closed his eyes, resting his head back against the concrete wall. Decided he would just do the best he could, keep their machine running smoothly, help out these younger techs—teach them. Maybe if one of them got good enough, the chancellor would let Brisby go home.

Don't delude yourself, a part of his mind chimed in.

Fighting a wave of anxiety, Brisby worked hard to clear his mind and sat like that for a long time until merciful sleep finally began to claim him.

A loud banging noise from outside his door jarred him back to consciousness.

As the sound grew louder—were those grunts and shouts of pain?—Brisby pushed himself up along the wall until he was standing and quietly crossed to the door. Unsure if it was the wisest thing to do, he placed his ear against the wood.

All was quiet. He waited for a full minute. Had he imagined all of that? He hadn't been getting much sleep, was barely eating. But was he losing his mind now, too?

"Brisby? You in there?"

It took him a moment to place the voice, and then a huge smile crossed his face.

"*Tracer?*"

The door handle jiggled, and Trace's voice came again, muted by the barrier between them. "Can you open it?"

"No," he responded. "They lock me in at night. Maybe you can find a key?"

He heard what sounded like laughter, and then Trace simply said, "Step back."

Brisby complied, scrambling backward, knowing firsthand that Trace wasn't the most patient or subtle person on the planet when action was required.

And sure enough, about five seconds later, the door crashed open, and Trace's figure was outlined in the doorway, lowering her boot to the ground. She stepped in, and he noticed right away the additional bruises on her face and neck, the blood on her trench coat.

"You look terrible," he said, his smile even bigger.

"So do you," she responded, stepping up to him, taking in his appearance. "Are you hurt? Can you move?"

"No, not really—and yes, absolutely."

"Okay," she said, starting to turn away. "Stay close, and make sure you—"

Brisby gently grabbed her shoulder—the one without the new blood stain. She spun to look him in the eye, and he saw the desperation there. Wished he could hug her—knew that he might get punched in the jaw for even trying, or shot—maybe just in the leg.

"Jenna . . . Rachel . . . are they okay?"

A small smile rippled across Tracer's face, and Frost felt a huge weight lift off his shoulders. "They're outside the city, in Goldie. They're safe. But we need to move, *fast*, if we want to keep them that way."

"Then what are we waiting for?" he responded, then let go, and took a final look back at the room. He'd only been there a few days, but in his mind, it would have been his home for the rest of his life—and part of him had been resigned to that, had begun memorizing every inch of it, thinking about ways to personalize it. And now he would never see it again.

"Good fucking riddance," he murmured, and then raced after Tracer.

Entering the hallway, he saw three guards sprawled in various uncomfortable-looking positions, all unconscious with blood running from mouths or noses or both.

"Looks like they fell asleep on the job," Brisby observed as he caught up to Trace.

"More like they fell onto my fists," she replied, not looking back.

"Was that . . . ?" he said, mouth dropping open slightly. "Was that a *joke*, Trace?"

She still didn't glance back, but he thought he heard the smile in her voice when she replied, "Maybe. Guess you'll never know."

He laughed quietly as they took a turn down another corridor, speeding up as they went. Whatever had happened to her since last they saw each other, Brisby suspected she was no longer the exact same person he'd known for the past few years.

They made their way deeper into the building, and Frost quickly realized that Trace had no idea where she was going. Pushing his out-of-shape lungs even harder, he caught up and then passed her.

"Follow me. There are some stairs over here. No one ever uses them, from what I've been able to tell. They prefer the elevator."

He pushed through a door at the end of the hallway and hurried down the steps, not hearing Trace behind him but knowing she was there. He was impressed by her ability to stay silent—he could hear his own feet slapping the concrete stairs and worried that everyone else in the building would be able to hear it, too.

When he finally reached the bottom floor, he burst through the door just as Trace hissed behind him, "Brisby, wait!"

But it was too late. He found himself staring at the front door of the prison and the city guard who was standing next to it, a shocked look on his face and a large handgun on his hip. The man's reaction time was impressive because, before Frost could even think of something to do, the guard had his hand on the gun and was withdrawing it. There was a blur of motion in Brisby's peripheral vision, and then Trace slammed into the man, hard, against the floor-to-ceiling window next to the door. The glass spider-webbed as the breath exploded out of the guard's lungs and his gun clattered to the floor.

This front vestibule was partially lit by a single overhead bulb, but it cut out when Trace grabbed the man's shirt and slammed him into another wall, apparently hitting a light switch at the same time. There was the sound of a vicious blow, a pained grunt, a thumping sound, and then all was silent and still. Brisby blinked against the darkness but couldn't see anything. He took a step forward, then stopped. Had no idea what had happened, who was still standing.

The light suddenly blinked back on, and Trace stared at him, her arms held out in a mock-frustrated way, like she'd been waiting for him for hours. The guard was unconscious at her feet.

"You coming or what?" she asked.

"*That* . . . that was definitely a joke," he said, but she just smiled, turned the lock on the door, and headed out into the night. Brisby shook his head, made ready to follow her, then noticed something on the floor.

A moment later, he left the building, his prison, hopefully for the last time ever.

35

Trace made her way around the prison building, heard Brisby stomping along right behind her.

Could he be any louder? she wondered, but deep down, she was overjoyed to hear him clumsily following after her. Seeing him standing there in his prison cell, somehow even skinnier with huge bags under his eyes, had filled her with emotion. She wasn't sure how to be a friend, wanted desperately to know how, but wondered if she would ever act, or feel, like a normal person. People like Brisby Frost made her feel like maybe she had a chance.

She reached the back of the building, where she'd left Ezra, and stopped. Brisby clearly wasn't paying attention because he crashed right into her, nearly causing her to stumble as well. "Sorry," he mumbled. She shook her head. She'd been overjoyed, yes, but he still annoyed her at times. She helped him to his feet, and then the two stood, waiting, as the rain continued to fall on them, seeming like it would never end.

"Ezra!" Trace called out in a harsh whisper.

"Ezra . . . ?" Frost said, confused, but quickly realized she was talking about the man he'd been swapped for. He'd heard about him when he was first told that he wouldn't be leaving Apex City and had only seen him in passing the day the actual swap had taken place. What the hell was he doing here? Brisby looked into Trace's eyes, and her look said, *Not now*, so he didn't say another word.

After a moment, Ezra stepped out of the shadows and approached them. Brisby noticed Trace physically relax at the sight of the worried-looking man.

Interesting, he thought.

"I'm Ezra," the man said, holding out a hand. Brisby shook it.

"Nice to officially meet you," he said, and meant it.

"You two can bond later," Trace said, starting to move away, farther into the shadows. "We need to get the fuck out of here."

The two men watched her go for a second.

"She's so pushy, isn't she?" Ezra joked.

Brisby laughed; then they both headed after Tracer. "You and I are going to get along just fine," he said, darkness swallowing the trio as they ran.

The rain had slowed slightly by the time they reached the inner wall.

"Um . . ." Brisby said, looking around, then up at the imposing structure. "Is there a door or something?"

"No," Trace responded, all business now. "We're climbing. Ezra and I can help you."

"It's a piece of cake, Doc," Ezra said, patting Frost on the back.

"I'm not a doctor," Frost replied, taking off his glasses and wiping the water from them, but the other man was already moving forward, feeling the wall, finding holes that were otherwise hidden by the continued darkness of the thick clouds hovering above them.

"Okay," Ezra explained, "I'm going to go first. Watch closely where my hands and feet go. Trace will stay beneath you, and she can support you if you slip. The key is to take your time."

"We don't *have* time," Tracer snapped, looking around. "I can deal with a few guards here and there, but if the entire city figures out we're here, this is all for nothing."

Ezra nodded, then started clambering up. Trace turned her eyes to Brisby, saw the terror on his face.

"You can do this," she said quietly.

"I . . . I can't, Trace. Literally. Even if it wasn't raining, I'm simply . . . not strong enough, and I'm terrified of heights. I suffer from severe vertigo. I will *literally* pass out halfway up. I'm so sorry. You two should just go without me."

She stepped closer to him, stared at him through the falling water. "Are you kidding me? You're the whole reason I'm here. You are my *friend*, Brisby. And I'm not leaving you. We'll figure something else out."

A slight smile played on his face, despite the circumstances.

"Are you two coming or what?" came a harsh whisper from above.

"Change of plans," Trace replied, blinking up at Ezra. "We're going out the back gate."

Ezra came scrambling down, faster than seemed possible. He landed on the ground and stared up at Tracer, pushing the wet hair out of his eyes.

"The back gate. The one that's most likely guarded by a bunch of people holding guns and hoping to shoot us."

"Yep, that one," Trace said, and then started moving toward it, leaving them behind again.

Ezra and Brisby stared after Tracer, both shaking their heads.

"Is she always like this?" the Apex City thief asked, looking at the other man.

"No. And that might be the most amazing thing about this whole night. Now . . . shall we get the hell out of here?"

"After you, Brisby Frost," Ezra responded, holding out his arm as if escorting a new friend to a night out on the town.

The pyro-tech hurried after Trace, and the smile faded from Ezra's face as he glanced behind him at the still-quiet prison building. Despite the jokes, he knew they were in serious danger. If they had climbed the wall and were heading across the in-between at that very moment, he would've placed their odds at escaping safely at fifty-fifty. Now, with this change of plan, the three of them heading to probably the second-heaviest guarded site in the city, that percentage was very, very different.

Ezra sprinted after them, trying to shove those thoughts out of his mind.

Trace watched the back gate from her hiding place, painfully aware that the rain had almost entirely stopped.

The end of the storm meant the possibility that the clouds would begin to thin and that moonlight might slip through, making their mission all the more difficult.

Based on what Ezra had told them during the planning phase with the Nomads, there would normally be at least a half-dozen guards positioned in and around the back gate. But now, with the diversion hopefully still happening out front, she only saw three. But unlike the trio of guards she had taken out in the prison hallway, these three looked alert and held their automatic weapons like they absolutely knew how to use them.

"Shit," she whispered, pulling back deeper into the shadows

of one of Apex City's many buildings. Ezra had informed them that this was a store, with no lodging on the second floor, so no one would be inside.

"I'm sorry," Brisby whispered. "You two should have gone over the wall while you still could."

"Stop," Trace snapped, and she saw his eyes go wide. She was still slipping into her soldier mode at times, treating people too roughly, and it was something she desperately wanted to stop doing. *Get them to safety first*, a part of her mind ordered. *And then be nice.* "Sorry," she said to Frost despite her mind's instructions. "But we're getting you back to your family. End of conversation."

Brisby nodded, and Trace turned back to the problem at hand. She was an expert markswoman, could most likely take one of them out from here using her SIG Pro, despite it not being intended as a long-range weapon. But then the other two would open up on her position, and then they'd be running for their lives. In other words, not a real plan.

"What's the matter?" Ezra asked, sidling up to her. His warmth felt so good against her body, especially after the cold rain. The pain still radiated like a constant background noise across her entire body. She wished she could pull him into her arms, pretend none of this was happening. But it was.

"I've been on more missions than I can remember, and can usually figure my way out of anything," she admitted, "but I'm not sure I can get us through that gate."

"Maybe this will help?" Brisby said haltingly from behind them.

Looking back, Trace saw that the pyro-tech was holding up a gun—the one that the prison guard had dropped when she slammed into him.

"Why you crafty little bastard," she said, laughing slightly.

"I guess you're rubbing off on me a little," he said, handing it to Tracer.

"This definitely helps," she said. "But we still need a plan."

"I have an idea," Ezra said after a moment, reaching down and grabbing some mud off the ground, wiping it on his face. "Trace, give me your coat."

"What?" she said, completely confused. "What the hell are you doing?"

Ezra ignored her and turned toward Brisby. "Put your glasses in your pocket."

"*What?*" Frost asked. "Why? I'll practically be blind."

"Perfect."

The two drunks came stumbling out of the shadows.

They were yelling and singing, soaking wet from the storm that was just ending. Two of the three guards—Tompkins and Faulkner—moved forward, raising their guns up as the stumbling men approached. One was dressed in typical street-rat clothes, and the other wore a long black trench coat that looked far too big for the man's wiry body. While they'd been instructed by Captain Janus to be on the lookout, that warning had specifically been regarding Nomads—not a pair of common Apex City drunks. The kind that both Tompkins and Faulkner had handled many times before—separately and together. They both enjoyed smacking around inebriated street rats now and then. A good way to burn off a little steam after a long shift.

"Hey!" Tompkins shouted. "What the fuck are you doing? You know you're not supposed to be anywhere near the gates this late at night!"

"Officer Faulkner! Officer Tompkins!" one of them shouted,

slurring, spreading his arms as if greeting long-lost friends. "I was just helping Johnny here get home, and I guess we took a wrong turn. These streets are a goddamn maze, am I right?"

"*Back. Up*," Faulkner barked, pointing his semiautomatic right at the speaker's midsection.

"How do you know our names?" Tompkins asked, tilting his head slightly. There was something very familiar about this street rat. His hair was sticking in every direction, and his face was caked with mud. But the eyes . . . there was something about the eyes. Tompkins knew him from *somewhere*.

"Everyone knows you two!" the man said, staggering forward, nearly running directly into Faulkner's gun. The guard took a step back, moved the barrel up, and pointed it right in the drunk's face.

"I will blow your brains all over the ground if you don't step back. *Right now!*"

The other man, the one with the trench coat, grabbed his friend, pulled him back. There was very obvious terror in his eyes.

"Come on . . . *man*. Maybe we should just go."

That guy doesn't sound even vaguely drunk, Tompkins thought, his mind racing, nerves on edge because of the assault by the Nomads. He glanced back at the first man, who was still talking, making some kind of dumb joke, and it suddenly clicked into place.

Ezra fucking Jenkins. The guy who had just been traded to that other city across the desert. Tompkins hadn't been part of the detail that had handled the transfer, but he'd had a particularly nasty incident with this street rat, and some of his criminal friends, a few years earlier.

Tompkins opened his mouth to scream a warning to Faulkner when a loud popping sound punctured the darkness and blood exploded out of his left leg, followed by a crippling blast of pain. Screaming, he fell to the ground, losing his grip on the semiautomatic and grabbing at his shattered thigh.

Blinking into the distance, he saw a woman in a black T-shirt approaching, a gun in each of her hands, a look of cold determination on her face. Tompkins was losing consciousness, wasn't sure if what he was seeing was real, but she looked like some kind of avenging angel in his dimming vision, like a spirit that had descended upon the world and judged them unworthy.

36

Trace fired both guns, eyes vacillating between the two people who were standing between her and the exit.

Despite people yelling and rain falling again, all sound fell away. She found herself reverting to that other version of herself, a version she now hated, but it was the Tracer needed in the moment.

She shot the remaining two guards at the same time, and they collapsed with pained grunts to the ground in a spray of crimson. She wasn't sure if she'd killed them or not, hoped on some level that she hadn't—and on another level that she had. She watched them, ready to fire again. Two of the three were unconscious, bleeding but breathing, but the third was awake, staring up at her with terror in his eyes.

"Puh . . . please . . ." he said, holding up a bloody hand. "I have a kid."

Trace pointed the SIG Pro directly at his face while gesturing toward Brisby with the other gun. "So does he. But you were still going to keep him locked up here, away from her, for the rest of his life."

"I had nothing to do with that!" he screamed, tears running down his face.

The fact that he knew exactly what she was talking about made Trace believe otherwise. She took a deep breath, knew that time was short and they couldn't have this guy alerting others. She was about to act when she felt someone's hand wrapping around her forearm. The one holding the SIG Pro. She glanced over. Ezra. In her state of mind, she barely recognized him, and hated herself for it.

"Trace," he said quietly. "Don't kill him."

Wresting her hand free, she brought the gun down and slammed it across the guard's face, knocking him unconscious instantly. Which was exactly what she had planned to do.

"I wasn't going to," she snarled at him, angry at his assumption but angrier about how many people she had killed in her life, and how many more she might have to kill before they got the fuck out of Apex City.

As if in response to her thoughts, bullets sounded and the ground exploded around them. She shoved Ezra forward with her shoulder, her bad one—pain erupting along her arm—then raced forward and shoved Brisby, too.

"Go!" she screamed. "I'll cover you and catch up!"

The two men didn't need to be told twice. Ezra grabbed the nearly blind Brisby by the arm, and they bolted toward the gate without looking back as incoming fire continued to blister the ground all around them. As Trace turned and began firing at the shadowy figures that were rapidly approaching, a bullet nicked her cheek, and she swore, rolling along the ground and then coming up firing both weapons with one knee planted in the mud beneath her.

The rain was growing heavy again, which worked to her advantage. She was wearing all black while her attackers had those stupid white stripes on their shoulders, which practically glowed in the dark.

Fucking Janus. She had no doubt in her mind that he'd been the one to add that ridiculous touch to their uniforms.

She tried to make out the exact number of attackers in the misty gloom and calculated there were at least four.

Three, she thought as she tagged one in the midsection, and the man collapsed like a puppet whose strings had been cut. She could feel the blood running down her face but ignored it. It was the least of her problems. She needed cover.

Continuing to fire with both guns, more to scare the shit out of them for the next few seconds than to actually connect, she bolted for a nearby structure—probably some kind of office for whoever was working the gate, checking papers or whatever the fuck they did in this obnoxious city. One of the guns, the one that Brisby had grabbed, clicked empty, so she dropped it and rolled again as more bullets chewed up the earth around her. Trace fought back a scream as she felt at least one of the stitches on her left shoulder pop. The pain was almost unbearable, but she bit down, slowed her breathing, just like she'd been taught.

By Mackie. She thought of him strapped to that chair, then thought of Joe in the same situation years later.

Focus, Trace berated herself, leaning around the side of the structure and taking out another of the advancing guards. She pulled back as scalding hot metal tore at the wood, tiny fragments further cutting up her face. She spat blood that had dripped into her mouth and leaned against what was left of the structure. She wanted desperately to check her ammo but didn't have time—that was the kind of delay that could cost her everything. She heard the guards coming closer, knew she had to do something.

"Fuck it," she muttered, then stood up and began firing, exposing herself slightly but taking the guards by surprise. It was obvious when she saw their faces, almost on top of her, that they hadn't expected their pinned-down enemy to suddenly appear right in front of them.

She took out two of the shocked guards with direct shots to their chests and then sprang forward and crashed into the final guard, both of them tumbling to the ground in a tangle. The man, panicking, fired his weapon, which made her ears feel like they were rupturing yet again, but the shots were wild, nowhere near her. Using his weight against him, she allowed herself to be flipped—let him think he had the advantage—and then ended up on top of him, the SIG Pro positioned directly under his chin.

"You fucking bitch," he growled.

"So I hear," she responded. "Now drop your weapon or I'll introduce the back of your skull to the rest of the city."

He didn't hear her—hell, she could barely hear herself—or didn't care because he began bringing his own weapon up to bear, so she gritted her teeth and pulled the trigger.

There was nothing except another clicking sound, though it was distant in her ears, as if heard from a far distance. *Ironic*, she thought, remembering President Bell's face when her own weapon proved to be out of bullets.

The guard smashed Trace in the nose with his weapon, and she toppled over, fresh blood bursting forth.

He got on top of her in a strange mirror to how she'd just been straddling him, placing his gun under her chin. She blinked against the pain that radiated from her nose and the still-bleeding slash on her cheek and all the other small cuts from the exploding wood. His leering face was only inches above hers.

"I'm gonna do this nice and slow. And I'm gonna enjoy every second of it."

Keeping the gun under her chin, he began to reach down with his other hand toward her body when a shot rang out and a hole appeared in the side of the man's head.

"Oh," he said, a small sound, and then toppled soundlessly off Tracer. She scrambled to her feet, pointed her now-useless weapon as she turned in a circle, wondering who had saved her and if she might be next.

Darcy stepped out of the shadows, smoke trailing from the barrel of her gun, tears running down her face.

"I've never killed anyone before," she said, looking down at the man's corpse, a surprised look in his wide-open eyes. Trace stepped toward her and wrapped her arms around the younger guard for a moment.

"I'm sorry," she whispered. "But thank you. *Again.*"

Darcy stepped back, looked like she wanted to say something, but then let out a long breath and wiped her eyes with the back of her hand.

"I heard on the radio that something was going down back here," she said. "Figured it was you. And got here as fast I could." She glanced down at the dead body again. "But not fast enough."

"No," Trace said, pushing her palm against the cut on her face. "You saved me. You were just in time."

Darcy nodded, glanced behind her back. "Get out of here, Tracer," she said. "They won't know I was ever even here. But they know someone is inside the city now. And they're going to be coming after you. *All* of them."

"Okay," Trace said, holstering the empty SIG Pro and grabbing the semiautomatic from the dead guard on the ground next to her.

"See you later," Darcy said, holding up her free hand in a small wave.

"For both our sakes," Trace responded, "I hope not."

Then she sprinted off after Ezra and Brisby.

She caught up with them halfway through the in-between.

Brisby had his glasses back on and handed Trace her trench coat. She looked at it for a moment, then threw it onto a nearby pile.

"I don't need it anymore," she said, and the two men didn't say anything, just nodded solemnly in understanding.

They quickly made their way along the edge of the garbage mounds, with the paved road on their left. If needed, they could slip into the mountains of trash if anyone caught up with them. Not optimal but better than being cut down by enemy fire. They were all out of breath, Trace fighting against a significant amount of pain, but they moved as fast as possible. None of the other guards had figured out they were back here, not yet, but Trace knew it was just a matter of time.

As they continued moving forward, their speed ebbing with every step as pain and exhaustion overwhelmed them, Trace began to notice movement out amid the piles of refuse. As the storm finally began to subside, the scavengers were coming out of hiding, once again on the hunt for precious plastic, the lifeblood of Apex and the other cities left around the world. As Trace caught a glimpse of one of the Dwellers' faces, she marveled at how similar he looked to the man she had considered her father for the first years of her life. It wasn't him, she knew that, but the resemblance made her heart ache. The man looked hollowed out, his eyes huge black sockets, wisps of wet hair clinging to his large pale skull.

They made eye contact, and the man stared at her with what looked like compassion. She had to force herself to keep moving forward—despite desperately wanting to stop and talk to him, find out his name. But she knew she would never see him again, just like she would never see her real parents again. They were possibly still rooting through trash hundreds of miles away, hoping to get enough plastic to make it from one day to the next.

Despite herself, she took a final look back at the man and saw that not only was he still staring at her but now he was pointing at her, and his mouth was open wide as if shouting. As if *warning* her.

Realization hitting her, she ducked, tumbling to the ground, and heard a popping sound and felt something whizz directly overhead. If she hadn't moved, she realized, the bullet would have hit her in the back. Maybe directly in the head. The scavenger had saved her.

Getting to her feet, confused, she found herself staring at the approaching Captain Janus, his pistol trained directly on her.

"Drop your fucking weapon!" he yelled.

Trace quickly looked around. They were close to the gate but not close enough. There was no way they could make a run for it without getting shot. Ezra and Brisby looked exhausted and terrified. They knew it was over. They had failed.

Glancing back at Janus, Trace figured she *might* be able to raise her gun up in time but knew in her heart it was a long shot. The way Janus held his weapon—hell, the way he held himself—this was a guy who knew how to shoot, how to fight.

How to kill.

She was out of options. She had lost. And gotten Ezra killed, too. Brisby would probably be thrown back in prison, forced to work on their goddamn pyrolysis machine for the rest of his life.

And Jenna and Rachel would be sitting out in that car. Would eventually make their way back to the Nomads—if they weren't caught. And would never know what had happened to their husband and father.

The thought almost broke Tracer.

She dropped the gun. Then slowly unholstered the empty SIG

Pro and dropped it into the mud, too. She was bleeding from more places than she could count, was having trouble feeling her arm again, and her entire face was pounding with agony. It was over.

As she readied herself for the end, she suddenly noticed more and more eyes out amid the hills of garbage. The scavengers. Here for the show. At least there would be a crowd for her execution.

"Just get it over with," she said, locking eyes with Janus.

He took a few steps closer and laughed, looking her over.

"*Tracer*," he mocked. "You think you're so tough. So exceptional. Running around in your stupid little car, mocking people. *Shooting* them. Coldcocking people when they aren't ready for it."

Something clicked in her mind as she watched the captain's eyes while he spoke. Realization dawned.

He had shown up alone—probably racing ahead of his subordinates—like the overconfident bastard he was. And he could have shot her by now, but there was something else he wanted. He had tried to shoot her from behind—maybe to injure her or maybe to kill her—and had almost succeeded, but now that they were standing, face-to-face . . . ? Something had happened. Something had changed.

He wants closure, she realized. *Or revenge.*

He took another step closer. She could practically reach out and snatch the gun out of his hand, but it was still too risky. She could see the indecision on his face. Had to keep him talking.

"You mean, when I beat the shit out of you and your two buddies the other night?" she said, forcing a smile onto her face.

She got the exact reaction she was hoping for. *Men in power and their pride.*

"What the fuck did you just say to me?" he whispered, eyebrows beetling over enraged eyes.

"When I beat. The shit. Out of you. Come on, *Captain Janus*, did I hit you so hard in your big dumb face that you already forgot? There were three of you. Against me. And I wiped the fucking floor with you. Is any of this ringing a bell?"

"You sucker punched me!" he screamed, sounding like an angry adolescent. "You got lucky. That would never happen again." The man's voice had softened as he continued to speak, but still trembled with barely contained rage. "*Never.*"

"Prove it," Tracer said, extending her arms out slightly, fingers extended.

A challenge. An invitation.

And one that he accepted, holstering his weapon. Rolling up his sleeves.

"Let's go, you little *bitch.*"

Trace was about to say something, keep him talking while she figured out a plan, but Janus threw a punch incredibly fast, and she barely had time to throw her head back, his knuckles coming within millimeters of connecting with her face. He followed up with a left hook to her ribs, and this one connected, but luckily it was his weaker arm.

It still hurt like a motherfucker though.

She lashed out with a boot and caught him in the left knee, and he went down into the mud, screaming in pain. But her advantage was short-lived as he countered with an uppercut—stealing her signature move—landing it directly in her stomach. The breath exploded out of her lungs, and she saw stars, fought to stay on her feet.

Staggering back, seeing that he was standing now, too, Trace circled him, and he matched her movement, a sick smile appearing on his face.

"What . . . you thought you were just gonna waltz out of here with your two boyfriends?" he hissed, fists up as he eyed her. She did the same, both of them clearly schooled at reading an opponent's slightest movement. "Do you know how much work I had to do to get that pyro-tech here? How much time and planning that took? Do you know what you have *cost* me?"

"I don't care," she yelled, lashing out with a punch on her last word, but she was hurting, wasn't as fast as usual, and Janus slapped her fist down and staggered her with a rabbit punch to her already fucked-up nose. It wasn't a devastating blow, but the pain was enormous, and she went flailing back, did everything she could to stay upright.

She was losing this fight, and she knew it. She was too injured, too exhausted. And Janus was mostly untouched, other than a slight limp from when she'd kicked him. Maybe in her prime, she could have taken him. But she was far from it right now—both physically and emotionally. On top of her injuries, she was too invested in the safety of Ezra and Brisby. Her feelings for them made her weak. She didn't regret it, not anymore, but it was just another in a series of vulnerabilities when she couldn't afford to have a single one.

Janus rushed forward and tackled her, the two of them tumbling into the mud, Trace landing a powerful blow to his face—blood exploding from his mouth—but he was too strong, and he continued to hit her, smaller punches that nonetheless increased her pain and exhaustion.

He managed to roll on top of her, but before he could get his fingers around her throat, which still ached from her encounter with Korath, she used all the energy she had left to spring up, smashing his nose with her forehead. There was a horrifying cracking noise, and his nose exploded with blood, and Trace laughed, thinking back to Jevon Nix in that dingy little apartment—a million years earlier.

She kicked Janus off her, and the two both got to their feet yet again, slowly, staring at one another through mud-caked faces.

"I can't wait to fucking *bury* you," he growled.

"I was thinking the same damn thing," she responded.

They raced at each other and collided with an audible smack, both attempting to gain a tactical advantage. Her strength fading, head spinning, Trace let everything fall away, thought back to her training, how Mackie had pushed her to the brink over and over and over again, just in case. Just in case, someday, she was in a situation where it was over. Where she lost.

But it's never over, Mackie had said. *Never. Not while you have breath left in your body.*

She screamed and attacked Janus savagely, his eyes widening in surprise. *He thought he'd already won*, she realized. She somehow managed to grab him by the shoulders, placing a leg behind his, and shoved him as hard as she could. One of Mackie's favorite moves, one that he had made her do every time they trained, even after she had more than mastered it. As she finished the maneuver, another two or three stitches popped. Trace nearly lost consciousness at the blast of pain but fought against it, somehow staying on her feet.

Janus went flying backward, landing on his back. He fought to catch his breath, to get to his feet, as Trace limped toward him.

"Stay down," she ordered. "It's over."

"Fuck you!" he screamed, rage filling his face. He reached for his gun, clearly determined to put an end to this despite his earlier words. When his fingers grasped the empty holster, he glanced down, anger replaced with confusion, then back up at Tracer.

She held his gun and pointed it directly at his face. He hadn't even noticed when she stole it while they'd grappled. The throw was only part of Mackie's signature move—a distraction for the attacker's real goal.

"Like I said," she uttered as she took a few more unsteady steps in his direction. "It's over."

He stared at her, and she wondered if the man would beg for his life. But no—he was too prideful, too used to getting his own way.

"Do it!" he screamed, leaning forward in the mud.

Tracer cocked the gun. It would be so easy. She could snuff him out like he'd never existed, then make her way out of this city, once and for all, with Ezra and Brisby. Figure out a place where they could live in peace.

After a long moment, Tracer lowered the gun.

"No. No more death. No more killing."

And she walked away, toward Ezra and Brisby and freedom.

"It doesn't matter where you go!" Janus shouted after her as she limped away. "Once we deal with the Nomads, we'll come after you! I will scour the entire planet until I find you! And then I'll kill you . . . *all* of you . . . so slowly. You'll wish you *had* killed me."

Trace didn't look back, suspected he wouldn't charge at her while she still held the gun. She was probably making a mistake leaving him alive, but it was a mistake that felt better than any she had ever made in her entire life. She didn't want any more blood on her hands.

"Don't walk away from me, Tracer! Come back and fight! I'm not done with—"

His voice suddenly cut off, and the captain of Apex City let out a strange gurgling sound. Despite fearing it might be some kind of trick, Trace stopped and turned around, raising the gun. But then lowered it when she saw what was happening.

Two large scavengers had taken hold of Janus and were trying to pull him toward the mounds of garbage. The captain fought one of them off, landing a powerful blow to the smaller man's face, but Trace watched as more and more of them materialized out of the deep shadows, all approaching Janus. None of them in a rush.

"Get *off* me!" Janus screamed, punching wildly at the growing horde, landing several blows, but more and more scavengers were appearing—grabbing at him and pulling him toward the heaps. "Don't you know who I am?!"

If they did, they didn't say so, and soon he was almost completely covered by a mass of humanity, pulling his screaming form inexorably toward the mounds of garbage, which twinkled in the growing moonlight. It was almost beautiful. Except for the shouts of terror.

Trace watched. Part of her felt like she should save him, but then she remembered what Darcy had told her. About the glee Janus had taken in hurting the scavengers, abusing them with his soldiers for fun. And maybe what she was witnessing was justice, and maybe it wasn't, but as the captain of Apex City vanished into the wasteland, a single sob punctuating the night, Tracer turned and walked away.

"Tracer!"

Ezra came running up to the gate as Trace limped through, nearly falling as he wrapped his arms around her, keeping her from collapsing. And then Brisby was there, too, and the two of them held her, spoke to her, but she couldn't understand the words, not right away. She nodded and whispered, "Yes" and "Thank you" and "Let's please get the fuck out of here right now."

They made their way along the wall, its shadow hiding them from the suddenly very bright moonlight. She could feel Ezra's eyes on her, smiled sadly at him as he took off his own shirt and pressed the cloth against her reinjured shoulder, which was bleeding badly now. She wasn't sure if she'd survive the walk to the car. Didn't care. She was with her friend, Brisby.

And Ezra.

Looking over at him, she thought back to that night on the rooftop, deep inside the city they had just escaped. On some level, she had known, even then, who he was and what he would eventually mean to her.

She stumbled, but he held her up, kept her moving.

"I'm sorry we didn't have more time," she whispered, but he just shook his head at her.

"I don't want to hear that," he responded. "We're almost to the car."

After a couple more minutes of walking, all of them silent as they focused on keeping Trace on her feet, the car came into view. Two figures exited the vehicle and sprinted toward them. The smaller one held a rectangular pink object in her arms.

"Daddy!" she screamed.

"Go!" Ezra said to Brisby, excited for his new friend. "I got her."

Frost didn't argue, gently let Tracer go and raced forward, nearly collapsing into his wife and daughter, tears streaming down his face.

"Oh my god," he said. "Oh my god."

Jenna kissed his face, nearly knocking his glasses off, while Rachel hugged her father's legs, all three of them crying now.

Brisby kneeled down and looked at his daughter, at what she was holding. "You got my present, huh, baby?"

"I love it, Daddy." Rachel sniffled. "It's my favorite thing in the whole world. Thank you."

Trace looked over at the wall, realized they were still in a serious amount of danger. Janus might be gone, but that wasn't any guarantee.

Trace opened her mouth to order everyone into the car, but darkness abruptly introduced itself to her senses, and she felt herself falling, an endless descent into blackness. She welcomed it, all the pain and exhaustion falling away.

EPILOGUE

NOW

I blink and after a moment realize I'm lying on top of Goldie's hood, and Brisby is standing over me, a grim smile playing on his face.

"What happened?" I ask, confused, smiling back. It's nice to see him.

"You passed out," Ezra explains, appearing next to Frost. "Brisby and I got you into the back of Goldie—"

"Barely," the pyro-tech adds.

"Barely," Ezra confirms. "We're nowhere near as strong as you."

He holds out his hand, and I take it, and he helps me to my feet. "Where are we?" I ask. My mind is swimming, but I fight through it, force myself closer to clarity. Looking around, I see that we're out in the middle of the desert somewhere, and the sun is just beginning to redden the sky in the east.

"Brizz drove for a little while," Ezra says. "Just far enough that we felt safe, and then we got you out here onto Goldie so Brisby could stitch up your shoulder."

I glance at the pyro-tech, who looks at me sheepishly. "Let me get this straight," I say, poking a finger into his chest. "You sewed me up?"

"I owed you one," he admits.

"Damn straight you did," I say, smiling at him, rolling my shoulder, and testing the new stitches. He did a good job for his first time. I quickly take stock of the rest of my body—my nose hurts like hell and the various cuts and bruises throb in time with my heartbeat. But I'll be okay. I'll survive.

"Let's get out of here," I say, then glance at Brisby. "I'll drive."

"You sure?" the pyro-tech asks, concern on his face. "You're still pretty banged up."

"Yeah, I'm sure," I respond. "You spend some time with your ladies. You've earned it."

He doesn't argue, and the five of us get back into Goldie.

"Where to?" I ask. Ezra looks at me from the passenger seat while Brisby and Jenna and Rachel snuggle close in the back seat. I've known Frost for years and have never seen him as happy as he is right now.

"It doesn't matter," Brisby says, pulling his wife and daughter closer. "As long as we're together."

"You're so corny, Dad," Rachel says, rolling her eyes, but she leans into him, resting her head in the crook of his arm.

"Definitely corny," I agree, winking at Rachel in the rearview mirror. "But not wrong."

"Shall we?" Ezra says, putting his hand on mine.

I smile again—surprised how much easier it is than ever before in my life—then lean over and kiss him, gently. I try to think of what to say to this man I'm falling in love with, how to express the depth of emotion I feel for him, and then realize I don't need to say anything. He already knows.

I turn and look out into the desert. There are so many places in the world I've never been, and I have no idea what might be out there.

I'm more than ready to find out.

"Let's do it," I reply and pull out into the beginnings of daylight.

I speed down the empty highway, gaining speed, heading east, a cloud of dust churning up in my wake and then settling slowly to the earth, until all is quiet and still.

AUTHOR'S NOTE & ACKNOWLEDGMENTS

I have been very, very lucky to have had six novels published. *Tracer* is my third original book but the first one in seven years. And I started writing it over ten years ago.

I didn't expect to get caught up writing other people's intellectual property, but shortly before my second original novel, *The Chrysalis*, was published, I had written a picture book entitled *Night Night, Groot*, which came out a month before the movie *Guardians of the Galaxy, Volume 2* (introducing Baby Groot). To my pleasant surprise, the picture book (illustrated by the great Cale Atkinson) became a runaway hit, spawning not one but three sequels, which were published three years in a row.

At some point during that Groot-a-palooza, I had a meeting with an editor at Titan, who read the first chapter of *The Chrysalis* and pretty much instantly offered me an opportunity to write a Morbius novel.

I grew up loving science fiction and horror and comic books, so the idea of writing a novel starring one of Spider-Man's coolest villains was a mind-blowing opportunity. The catch was that I had to write the novel (an original story of my own creation set within the boundaries of the Marvel Universe) in *two months*—a ridiculously short amount of time—to coincide with the *Morbius* movie.

Around this same time, I also somehow managed to sell a Green Arrow middle-grade graphic novel pitch to DC Comics—a total dream come true, and a character I have loved for decades.

This all took place in 2019 before COVID changed everything.

Despite writing *Morbius: Blood Ties* in two months, the movie (and thus the book) would be delayed for two years. A cruel irony, perhaps, but during those many months spent stuck at home, I dabbled with fan fiction, something I had always dismissed but that I now found to be very fulfilling. I wrote a new *Alpha Flight* #29 (a deep nerd cut), a new *Grendel* comic book starring Anson Spar (an even deeper nerd cut), and a treatment for *Alien 3*—the version of the story I wish had been made, rather than David Fincher's controversial debut film.

At some point during this fan fiction haze, I got an email out of the blue from a separate editor at Titan. I had written multiple *Rocket and Groot* picture books and a *Morbius* novel—would I be interested in writing a *Guardians of the Galaxy* novel, where I would get a chance to rewrite/reinterpret the origin of the team?

I believe my answer was something like: *Hell yes, I would.*

The catch, once again, was that I had to write it in two months in order to get the book out in time for the third *GOTG* movie. I hit my deadline and was finally ready to get back to writing my own original novel, *Tracer*, which I had started in 2014 but kept on getting distracted away from by shiny Marvel and DC properties. But it was finally time to get back to a world where plastic was gold.

And then I got an email from my original editor at Titan.

He had finally, after eighteen months of it sitting in his inbox, read my *Alien 3* reimagining concept—and *loved* it.

But . . . there was another catch. They didn't want *Alien 3*, didn't want another story about what "really" happens to Ripley, Newt, Hicks, and Bishop. They liked my plot—but asked if I would be open to rewriting it with a completely new cast of characters set in the larger *Alien* universe.

I believe my answer was something like: *Hell yes, I would.*

Writing an *Alien* novel was a dream come true, but it once again pushed *Tracer* to the back burner. After I wrote several drafts of *Uncivil War* in a fairly short amount of time (not two months this time, thank God), including notes from three different publishing entities, I was pretty burnt out. I couldn't write another word for months.

And then, finally, I turned myself back to *Tracer*, a book I hadn't touched in ten years. I reread the opening seventy-five pages and was reminded of why I liked this story so much in the first place. And while writing books starring some of my favorite characters owned by other companies is fun, nothing compares to writing your own novels with characters you have created from the depths of your own imagination.

The idea for *Tracer* emerged one night over a decade ago when I was cleaning my kitchen—which was just as glamorous as it sounds.

Whether it actually matters or not on a larger scale, I am a recycling fanatic. I hate throwing anything away that *might* be able to be recycled, so I study plastic waste with the eye of a surgeon, looking for that telltale triangle that indicates it can be put into the blue bin. On this occasion, the plastic item I was holding didn't have that triangle, and I swore under my breath as I threw it into the garbage.

That got me wondering—how much plastic is thrown away

every day? (And I'm fully aware that a lot of "recycled" plastic ends up in the dump as well—as much as it pains and annoys me to admit that fact.) I imagined tons and tons of plastic scattered throughout garbage heaps around the world.

This got me wondering further—plastic is made out of oil, which means that if you were able to turn this "garbage" back into its core constituent, it would be worth a lot. I did some research and discovered that this exact kind of machine was actually in development, though in its earliest stages. After a little more research, I found out there are six major landfills on Earth—seven, if you include the Patch, a floating garbage "island" in the middle of the Pacific Ocean.

My author brain took this to the next logical step: If oil ran out, and the "pyrolysis" technology was perfected, discarded plastic would suddenly become the most valuable thing on Earth.

I threw in a global plague that wiped out most of humanity (this was six years before COVID) and a mercenary with a bad attitude, and *Tracer* was born.

I just hope everyone enjoys this novel as much as I enjoyed writing it. And honestly? I'm glad I was diverted away from this book for a decade while I got to write about all these other amazing characters. Those books made me a better writer, and thus made *Tracer* a better novel.

Despite all of this, no artistic endeavor ever happens in a vacuum. There were key people throughout the entire process.

One of the first people I ever pitched this concept to was one of my absolute best friends, Marty Zito. Not only did he love the pitch, he kept asking me about it every time I saw or spoke to him. His excitement for this plastic-driven world kept me excited about it as the years ticked by with me focused on other writing endeavors.

The first professional response I got regarding the material was from Dan Ehrenhaft, who's an editor at Blackstone Publishing. I was a little worried about having him read the pages—they were, after all, a decade old, but I shared them anyway. To my surprise, he got back to me quickly, saying he loved the concept and the characters, and offered to publish the book. I asked him if he could wait until I finished writing *Guardians of the Galaxy*, and he said yes. Then I asked him if he could wait until I finished writing *Alien*, and he said yes. His patience, fantastic editing acumen, and general awesomeness have made this entire process a pleasure.

There are so many people at Blackstone that I need to thank, and that includes: Josh Stanton, Anthony Goff, Anne Fonteneau, Greg Boguslawski, John Lawton, Stephanie Stanton, Jesse Bickford, and Joe Garcia—and especially Caitlin Vander Meulen (for amazing copy edits), Sarah Riedlinger (for that killer cover), and Bri Jones and Sarah Bonamino (for telling the world about the book). I appreciate all of you more than I can properly express.

One of the best parts of being an author is hearing your book read by a professional narrator. It can often make it seem like you're listening to a story written by someone else, which sometimes feels like nothing short of a miracle. I would like to thank Candace Fitzgerald for bringing the world of *Tracer* alive in a way that I, alone, could never have accomplished.

Every time I write a novel or graphic novel, I listen to one album. In the case of *Tracer*, however, I listened to one band. The band, as you may have guessed from the quote at the start of the book, was Silversun Pickups. I discovered SSPU (as they're called by hardcore fans) right around the same time that I started writing this novel, and the song "There's No Secrets This Year," in particular, makes me think about Tracer and her love story with Ezra ("You better make sure you're looking closely before you fall into your swoon"). I've seen the band live eight times(!) since I started writing this book, which I realize may be a bit obsessive. Regardless, maybe I'll be able to hand them a copy of this book during my ninth show.

In a similar vein, I also (finally) developed a taste for bourbon right around the time that I discovered Silversun Pickups and was first writing *Tracer*. My first bourbon love was Buffalo Trace, and I'm not saying the title for this novel (and the name of the main character) came from that particular brand of alcohol, but I'm not *not* saying that either. Regardless, thanks to Buffalo Trace (and all the other brands of bourbon that I've branched out to in the past ten-plus years) for making the writing smoother. "Write drunk, edit sober"—as *someone* once said.

Penultimately, I would like to thank my wife, Kim. She's been reading my fiction since 1994, and she was the one who helped shape the original concept for *The Ninth Circle*, my first published novel and the book that got my entire author career rolling. I am constantly telling her about my ideas, and she always listens with good humor and pushes back when she thinks one of my ideas needs work or doesn't work at all. She is, simply put, my muse.

Finally, I would like to thank anyone reading this. Whether it's the sixth novel of mine that you've read, or the first, I appreciate the support.

And hold on to that plastic! You never know what it might be worth.